UNDER THE GUN

The  granny Series

UNDER THE GUN

Kelsey Browning and Nancy Naigle

Crossroads Publishing House

www.CrossroadsPublishingHouse.com

Under The Gun

Copyright © 2016, Kelsey Browning & Nancy Naigle
Trade Paperback ISBN: 978-0-9911272-9-0
Large Print ISBN: 978- 0-9964884-0-2

Cover Art Design by Keith Sarna
Digital release, May 2016
Trade Paperback release, May 2016

Crossroads Publishing House
P.O. Box 55
Pfafftown, NC 27040

We dedicate this book to the folks who've taken care of loved ones with cancer. For all the times you've been patient and selfless. For all the times you've been strong, hidden your tears, and put aside your own fears. For all the times you've offered strength and hope.

You are the world's true heroes.

UNDER THE GUN

BOOK FOUR
The Granny Series

KELSEY BROWNING AND NANCY NAIGLE

CHAPTER 1

The six-shooter was pointed right at Sera, momentarily jolting her out of her sorrow.

Thank goodness it wasn't a real gun, but a float-size wreath in the shape of a revolver, which might've looked right at home had she been back in California for the Rose Parade, rather than in Georgia with Lil and Maggie.

As Sera and her friends walked closer to the massive building looming in front of them, Holy Innocence Mausoleum looked anything but innocent today. A crowd was growing in the area surrounding the cannon-size handgun wreath. So lowbrow. Besides, hadn't these people been taught never to point a gun? Even one made of flowers.

Sera lifted a handkerchief graced with tiny, hand-stitched hummingbirds on one corner to dab at a tear beneath her Miu Miu sunglasses. "I still can't believe she's gone."

"I hate that these terrible circumstances brought you back to us." Maggie grabbed Sera's hand. "But it's good to see you."

Lil tugged at the peplum of her yellow suit jacket. "Look at all these people. I've never seen so many Western hats in one place. She was obviously loved by many. Bless her heart."

"My goodness. Would you look at that wreath over there?" Maggie pointed toward a spray of all-white carnations with a fringed cowboy boot in the center. "Wish Abby Ruth was here to see this. She'd have loved it."

Sera sniffed back a tear. "Only Abby Ruth would have expected that boot to be blazing red."

Lil and Maggie both nodded, the tender thought lightening the heavy mood.

"It's odd not to have her here," Sera said. Standing tall and strong, Abby Ruth was always the one anchoring their foursome. Instead, Sera's husband, Marcus, made up the fourth today. Well, he would be once he parked the car and caught up to them.

More floral arrangements stood nearly eight-feet deep along each side of the mausoleum's entrance, giving the otherwise cold, harsh facade an inappropriately festive look.

"I know folks are trying to show their love

and appreciation." The words caught in Sera's throat. "But she'd have hated the waste of all of these flowers. The money could've been spent on something that would help others."

"Even if they were cheap sunflowers and alstroemeria, with so many, the money adds up quickly," Maggie agreed.

"More than Summer Shoals raised at the last High on the Hog event," Lil said with a quick *tsk*.

"Easily, and they'll all be wilting and dying before sunrise," Sera said. One more dreary sign of death, which seemed to be the subtitle in every direction.

The tiny pillbox hat balancing atop Lil's freshly dyed blue-blond curls—a combo not too many people could pull off—gave the matriarch of Summer Shoals a look of royalty. A thin man with a bad highlight job darted out in front of them and snapped pictures, clearly focused on Lil, who looked like a Hollywood A-lister today.

"No pictures," Sera said, waving the skinny guy away, a habit she fell back into so easily. "How are we supposed to mourn with these vultures all over the place? What was her family thinking with all this fanfare?" If she had to guess, they'd probably tipped off the paparazzi themselves.

Once the photographer moved on to another victim, Maggie said, "Everyone shows their love in a different way. Can't really judge that, can we?"

Sera, Lil, and Maggie walked in lockstep. Three styles. Three sizes. But three women equally affected by today's sad affair for their own reasons.

True friends.

Sera was thankful that Lil and the other girls hadn't pitched a hissy fit and thrown her out on her fanny when they'd found out the truth about her life in California. During the time she lived with them here in Georgia, she'd omitted the tidbit that she was the wife of Marcus Johanneson, one of the most influential men in the Hollywood film industry. A triple threat, Marcus had been an actor first, then he began directing and producing his own movies. Only a few people had a résumé as impressive as his. He had the magic touch when it came to selecting blockbuster movies, and everyone who was anyone wanted to be considered for one of his projects.

"There are so many people here." Lil's head swiveled right and left. "I think I saw Michael Douglas over there. Sera, tell me you've met him. Or even better, his daddy."

"We've met." Although Sera had told herself she'd never keep anything from her friends again, elaborating on the fact that Michael and Kirk were much more than business acquaintances didn't feel appropriate.

Lil touched her heart. "I do love those men. I swear, I think they could wake up my last working hormone."

Maggie nudged her best friend. "Lil, we're not *that* old."

Lil's eyebrows danced. "That might be true, because I do believe that I'd be tempted to rise from the dead if all these folks showed up at my funeral."

Sera would've never expected anything less than a standing-room-only, Hollywood-style full house for Jessie Wyatt. Even in death. Jessie might've been one of the most famous movie stars of her time, but to Sera, she'd been a dear friend. Since the day they'd met on one of Marcus's movie sets, Jessie had been Sera's lifeline and advisor during the tumultuous tides of her marriage.

Sera wished Finn, could've made it for the funeral. She would've simply said, "Lil, Maggie, Abby Ruth, please meet my son." Then they would've been so taken with his good looks and charm that they would've easily forgiven her. And it would've kept her from having to explain yet one more thing that she'd hidden from her friends.

She shook back her long hair, chasing away the nostalgia and past mistakes to focus on today.

Although the interment would be inside the mausoleum, the family had opted to have the service outside. Probably a good decision with this many people in attendance, and the May weather was perfect for it. The crowd of thousands mingled close to the building. The mourners' muted wardrobes were occasionally punctuated by a bright spot of white and fringe. One that couldn't be ignored, because an entire group of women were dressed up like Jessie, in all-white cowgirl costumes.

"Mrs. Johanneson, excuse me."

Sera turned to face another reporter with a cameraman hovering behind him. "Jessie starred in several of your husband's films. Someone said that you two were very close. Could you comment?"

She sucked in a breath. "Jessie Wyatt was one of the most genuine people I've ever met. She was not only a friend but also a mentor. I'll miss her terribly." She lowered her head after her statement. Once, she and Jessie had spent three weeks together when Marcus was shooting in the wilds of Zimbabwe. If anything could bring two women from different generations close together, it was sharing toiletries in the jungle. And Jessie had been generous with not only hard-to-attain supplies but also advice and encouragement. A gift that had changed Sera's life in so many ways.

The excited reporter closed in on her again. "Wasn't Jessie from Macon? Why did they decide to bury her here in Myrtle Knolls?"

"Someone in her family can answer that. We're here to honor the woman, not the location. No more questions, please. This is a difficult day for us all." Sera raised her hand politely, and the reporter backed off. Automatically, she scanned the crowd for security. She'd learned to be sure she knew where help was in case the reporters got out of control. Happened all the time with Marcus.

Off to the far side of the funeral area, Teague Castro stood tall, wearing his Bartell County Sheriff uniform. His dark good looks and muscular build fit right in with this attractive Hollywood crowd. Myrtle Knolls wasn't his jurisdiction, but that was the cool thing about small towns. The attitude of the residents was one of community and goodwill. Teague and his men were here to help keep things under control because it was the neighborly thing to do, something that would never happen in Hollywood.

Lil's fingers dug into Sera's hand. "Is that Luke Bryan?"

The reporter who'd still been hovering around must have heard Lil because he took off in Luke's direction, waving over his shoulder for the cameraman to follow.

Whoomp-whoomp-whoomp. One look at the helicopter circling overheard told Sera the bottom-feeders who couldn't score a press pass to the funeral weren't letting that stop them. Paparazzi. Those fools would crash any event if they thought it would tantalize the public. The funeral location should've been kept under wraps, but with this many attendees and Jessie's family's propensity to blab, that had probably been unrealistic.

Sera and her little group finally made it close enough to get a glimpse of Jessie's casket through the throng of family, fans, and A-listers, where a young preacher stood holding a leather folio.

"The deceased has often been described as a force of nature," he said, his gentle but strong voice calming the crowd to an eerie silence. "She will be sorely missed by many, including the NRA, which she supported generously throughout her lifetime."

A smile touched the corner of Sera's lips. She should've thought to introduce Abby Ruth and Jessie. Those two would've gotten along like a house on fire. Then again, together they might've set the house on fire.

On her left, Lil squeezed closer to her. The older woman looked like a tiny Vienna sausage among a tall package of frankfurters.

Sera tapped the huge man in front of Lil on the shoulder. "Mr. Hogan, would you mind giving us a bit more room?"

He pulled his massive arms into his body and smiled down at Lil, his bushy blond mustache twitching to one side. "You want to climb up on my shoulders?"

"Lord have mercy," she breathed, that little hat hanging on by a bobby pin. "No, thank you."

"Let me know if you change your mind."

Lil gave him a vague, star-struck nod.

The huge tan man turned to the side and ushered all three of them in front of him. A front-row view.

"If you'll bow your heads and join me in blessing Jessie Wyatt's soul so she may pass peacefully to the other side," the preacher said. At the end of his prayer, multiple words rippled through the gathering.

"Amen."

"Blessed Be."

"Namaste."

Finally, the crowd pulled back, and Lil and Maggie worked their way closer to the casket.

Before Sera could move to join them, a warm hand brushed the small of her back. Marcus. There was a time when he'd led her into a crowded room with that gesture and she'd felt as if she was the most special woman in the world. Today, she wasn't sure what his touch made her feel.

Still, she smiled up at her husband—as handsome as ever with his lean build and million-dollar smile. He'd aged gracefully with sexy silver lacing his hairline now. Had she caused those grays? He'd have worried about her even though he'd left her alone to find her way. He was like that.

"Did you get the car parked okay?" she asked him, her nerves insisting that she make small talk with her own husband. Her mind needed the break from the overwhelming sadness if only for a moment. "I thought you'd missed the service."

"Sorry it took me so long. Ran into Sylvester Stallone on the way back from the lot and stood by him while the preacher was talking."

Of course he had, because Marcus

Johanneson was a magnet for Hollywood types, and a slew of them had shown up today.

"It was a beautiful ceremony." He wrapped his arm around her. "How are you doing?"

She rested her head against his shoulder, needing his strength today. "It was lovely, made more so by how pretty it is here in Georgia."

"But nothing can compare to you," he said, dropping a kiss into her hair.

Sera reached for his hand and gave it a squeeze. Returning to her adopted state for Jessie's funeral had been hard, but being back a few days, Sera knew this was where she belonged. Marcus seemed to want their marriage to return to the way it had been when they were newlyweds, before Finn came along, when she'd always been the one to mold to Marcus's career, his life. Yet she yearned for her days back here in Summer Shoals, where she was simply Sera. No reputation. No money. No expectations.

Only Marcus wasn't a part of that life, and she didn't know if she could live here in the place she loved without the man she loved.

"Georgia, and Summer Shoals in particular, has become one of my favorite places in the world," she said with complete honesty. Saying the words aloud seemed to give them wings but left her shaky. She needed to be away from Marcus for a moment to get her head together. "I'm going to go pay Jessie my respects."

"Then let's—"

"Alone, please."

He dropped her hand. She regretted hurting him. But she needed a little more time and space to work out how she planned to go forward with her life. And her relationship with Marcus was still a work in progress. Jessie's death made it even clearer that a person's time on this earth was limited. Each day needed to be cherished.

A crush of people had quickly separated Sera from Maggie and Lil. So Sera tried to slowly edge her way around and was captivated by the elaborate casket spray. The blanket of the tiniest perfect bluebonnets, with Indian paintbrush tickling stalks of red clover, resembled a Texas sunset. Jessie hadn't ever lived in the Lone Star state, but most people considered her the perfect Texas cowgirl. Funny how a fictional role could change the whole world's perception of a woman.

Not only had someone spent a fortune on the out-of-season Texas wildflowers, but they'd also integrated Jessie Wyatt's signature Wild West outfit of white leather into the flowers. And right on top were her famous deerskin gauntlets with fringe of gold and stones that had once been rumored to be genuine sapphires, rubies, and diamonds.

"Are they going to entomb her costume?" a woman next to Sera asked.

"Sure looks that way," someone else whispered.

"But it's a collector's item—a representation of an important Hollywood icon. Seems like it would be better served in a museum somewhere."

Sera couldn't agree more. Especially the gauntlets, because although Jessie had owned several skirts and vests, only one pair of authentic gauntlets existed. One night over sangria at an after-party, Jessie had shared a secret with Sera. Those gauntlets were insanely valuable, given to Jessie by her husband as an anniversary present. Not that anyone else knew that. Rumors had been bandied about for a few years, but with some well-executed PR by Jessie's agent, the gossip had eventually been written off as Hollywood lore.

The helicopter took another spin above, and camera lenses shimmered in the bright sunlight. Then more flashes and clicks came from beyond a private family mausoleum less than fifty feet away, just outside the funeral's security perimeter. Entertainment rag reporters were wily and persistent.

Apparently, she wasn't the only one to spot the intruders, because several Bartell County deputies raced off toward the culprits.

One of Teague's guys hollered, "Y'all need to get on out of here. This is a private event."

"Dude, this is a free country," a so-called reporter yelled back. "Maybe I'm here visiting my grandma."

"With that camera equipment? What? Were you planning to take family portraits?"

Sera tried to suppress a smile, because truthfully, those country boys weren't prepared for the likes of ruthless paparazzi. They had no remorse and no manners. And if a story put them in the position to make a buck, they didn't care one bit who they hurt.

CHAPTER 2

*H*and in hand, Lil and Maggie worked their way through the crowd of chattering people, including locals and some of the biggest movie and television stars in the industry. A strange mix, to say the least. Darrell Holloway was standing next to Sam Elliott, whom Lil still preferred over Sylvester Stallone any day of the week.

The entire situation was throwing her off balance. Then again, her equilibrium had been helter-skelter since Sera and her husband showed up at Summer Haven dressed like the Kennedys and driving a foreign car Lil was sure Summer Shoals had never seen the likes of.

A few months ago, just when Lil had begun to become accustomed to the Summer Haven sisterhood, Sera had returned to her real life back in California with her husband. Lil had missed her. It seemed like only yesterday that Teague had threatened to arrest Serendipity Johnson for boondocking at the Walmart. But then his caretaking side emerged, and he brought her over to Summer Haven. Lil had had a good feeling about her that day.

And although their hippie-type friend hadn't shared everything about herself, Lil felt certain they knew parts of the real Sera. And all the secrets in the world wouldn't erase the friendship they'd formed. But now, there was definitely a void at Summer Haven where Sera used to shine.

Thank goodness Lil and Maggie still had each other, would always have each other.

"Can you believe we're this close to Jessie Wyatt?" Maggie said, awe in her low tone. "I mean even if she's dead, this is still kind of mind-boggling."

"She's a legend." What an amazing life Jessie had led. The money. The glamour. The legacy. "I swear I might be one of her biggest fans. I can recite all her movie lines."

Maggie's brows rose behind her bangs. "Remember that scene when she shot—"

"—Johnny Hatcher because she found out

he was the one who'd murdered the sheriff so he could rob the bank on the other side of the jail wall."

"And she was so in love with Johnny Hatcher. Well, the man he was pretending to be. The ultimate betrayal." Maggie gulped. "I love that movie."

"Me too." Lil leaned closer to the casket, trailed her fingers over the famous cowgirl skirt and vest. "She wore this very outfit. And the gloves. Those gems glittered when she pulled the trigger." She shifted one of the gauntlets to the left so it was perfectly aligned with the other. "That fringed glove is heavy."

"There used to be a rumor that the stones and gold were real." Maggie's eyes danced beneath her dark bangs.

"Hollywood hype. I remember all the hubbub about it, though. But for fake movie props, they sure look fancy up close." Then she whispered, "On anyone else it would've come off as too much. But not Jessie Wyatt. Can you imagine being that bold and strong? Shedding all those expectations placed on a Southern lady? Only for a little while, of course. What woman wouldn't want to wear that much gold and sparkles and fringe?"

"Lil, I don't see you as the fringe type."

Lil laughed. "You might be surprised."

"I know what you mean. Years ago, George and I went to a masquerade party, and I dressed up as Jessie Wyatt. Boy, did that cowgirl look turn George on. He didn't look half bad as an Indian chief either." The reminiscent smile on Maggie's lips made Lil think of their sorority-hosted parties back at William and Mary.

"Those are the memories that keep us old girls going, aren't they?" Maggie's husband, George, had passed away a year earlier than Lil's Harlan.

"You know that's true."

Maggie pulled her black jacket across her thinning midsection. Beads in the shapes of flowers and leaves shimmered on the lapel. A tiny gold-and-black bumblebee pin was tucked in the center of the flower above her still ample bosom.

Lil smiled. Maggie was right. The flashy cowgirl outfit was much more Maggie's style, and with the weight she'd lost recently, she'd look pretty darn good in it. "Speaking of things being out of character. I can't get used to seeing Sera all dressed to the nines."

"And with no bells on her ankles," Maggie said. "It's like aliens abducted our old Sera."

"That outfit she has on is a Donna Karan. I bet it cost every bit of three thousand dollars."

"How do you know?"

Lil wasn't about to admit she'd taken a peek at the label when Sera came down asking for Lil's steamer. "I have an eye for fashion."

"Three thousand? But that dress couldn't be more than two yards of material," Maggie said, unconvinced.

"I knew there was more to her from the first time I laid eyes on her. She has real style."

Maggie smiled. "I feel awful for judging Serendipity when she first arrived at Summer Haven. Looks can be deceiving."

"Yep. Still hard to get my head wrapped around all the changes each of us has been through." Lil tried to take a step back from the casket, but the crowd had pressed in.

People walked by, laying more flowers on top of the lush blanket of bluebonnets. A beautiful outpouring of respect and love for the joy this Hollywood star had given the world.

As onlookers paid their last respects, folks started to wander away from the mausoleum.

Lil's shoulder brushed Maggie's. "Looks like most people don't plan to stick around and watch the actual interment. But I've never seen one and I'm curious. Aren't you?"

"Oh, yeah. Plus, we're talking Jessie Wyatt. Let's go inside so we can get a good place."

The funeral director and his team wheeled the cart carrying Jessie's casket toward a pair of open double doors. As they pushed the casket inside the building, a white rose fell to the ground.

Lil stooped down to pick up the abandoned flower and followed behind. Inside, the mausoleum was a stark expanse of gray granite crypt facings interspersed with small urns of flowers, many of them artificial. Of course, Lil preferred to decorate her loved ones' resting places with the real thing, even if Harlan only rated carnations most weeks. The huge expanses of stained glass were an attempt to make the mausoleum look more colorful, but the high ceilings seemed to suck away the cheer.

She twisted the rose in her fingers as two workers in blue coveralls prepared for the interment, moving through their duties as if there was no one else around.

"It's like casket condos. Kind of freaks me out." Maggie craned her neck, looking around the cold space.

Slowly arranging for the interment, the two

workers unscrewed the four rosettes holding the shiny marker in place, and together they lowered it to the ground and laid it aside. Lil rose on tiptoe to get a look inside the crypt. "Apparently, Jessie's condo already has one resident, probably her husband."

One of the workers, the scrawny one, climbed a ladder and crawled into the danged hole to push the other coffin farther into the crypt.

Maggie covered her mouth with her hand and took a baby step backward. "Now that's even more unsettling."

The fellow scooted back to the crypt's edge and retrieved his caulk gun. With a couple of quick clicks of the handle, a goopy drip hung from the tip.

"That's a regular old caulk gun," Maggie said, nudging Lil and pointing. "I have one just like it."

"We could get you a part-time job here."

"Real funny," Maggie shot back. "I'm not crawling in one of those. No, ma'am. Plus, the outfits they're wearing aren't very flattering."

Lil whispered, "Does seem like the mausoleum could dress them nicer during a service. Those are plain old coveralls, like a mechanic wears to change your oil. Just doesn't seem appropriate."

The skinny guy grabbed what looked like a square piece of hard plastic and went headfirst back into the hole while the well-fed worker wheeled a portable forklift toward the casket.

"Now what's he doing?"

"Sealing her husband in. I guess to keep them separate? Why, in heaven's name, I have no idea."

"It seems cold and harsh." Lil's gaze wandered across the gigantic stained-glass windows and concrete slabs as big as Stonehenge. No, when her time came, she'd take a grassy spot under a tree, thank you very much. "Give me Gabriel Acres in Summer Shoals any day, even with those new flashy angel-wing gates."

"Before today, I didn't know they built places like this."

The smaller guy emerged and shimmied down the ladder. "Out of caulk," he said to the other worker, then disappeared down the aisle. A quick minute later, he returned with a new tube and climbed back in. He finished up and then tossed what looked like beads into the hole.

"What in the world?" Maggie asked.

Lil shrugged.

The forklift whirred as it raised the casket to the precise level of the crypt opening, and as they began to slide the copper-trimmed mahogany casket into the vault, someone screamed like a banshee from across the way, "Whoa! Stop. Stop right there."

Lil and Maggie spun around. A tall redheaded woman, her face the color of her hair, bounced up and down like someone had dumped fire ants in her pants. "Stop, I said!"

Maggie stumbled back, but Lil stood frozen. What the heck was going on?

"It's gone!" the woman screamed.

"Ma'am, can I help you?" A Pitts County sheriff's deputy gently pulled the woman to the side, and someone from the mausoleum stepped forward with a box of tissues.

A small crowd gathered, and those still remaining outside rushed in to see what all the commotion was about.

The woman shook off the deputy's grip. "Unhand me. I am Jessie's cousin." She batted the tissue box right out of the mausoleum employee's hand, sending it flying across the room like a drunken dove. "I do not need your consoling, you nitwit. Can't you see someone has stolen Jessie's priceless gauntlets right off the casket!"

A collective gasp rippled through the crowd. "But we were all standing right here," a woman said.

All eyes were on the half-interred casket, but the maintenance guys kept right on working, totally ignoring the kerfuffle around them.

"People probably flip out during this part all the time," Maggie whispered to Lil. "It is a bit strange to see your loved one shoved into what's basically a big safe deposit box."

Sam Elliott's voice thrummed through the crowd. "Maybe the gauntlets went inside the vault already."

"They aren't there!" The cousin raced across the room to the casket. "Look!"

Sure enough, the skirt was draped on the blanket of bluebonnets across the casket, but those sparkly gauntlets were nowhere to be seen.

"The gloves are missing?" someone echoed.

"They were worth a fortune."

"They are not. That was an old Hollywood legend. Get real."

Snippets of comments speared the air.

"...solid gold fringe."

"Probably fake...what's the big deal?"

"...diamonds...rubies..."

"Americana..."

The deputy spoke into his radio then announced, "No one is to leave the building. Everyone, please stay where you are."

Maggie leaned into Lil. "I didn't notice anyone near the casket. Did you?"

Lil shook her head.

The workers continued to maneuver the casket until the deputy approached them. "My orders apply to you too."

Caulk seeped from the end of the smaller guy's gun. He'd just outlined the hole with a healthy stream of the goop.

"Look inside there!" Jessie's cousin demanded.

The worker held out a protective hand. "Careful. You'll get caulk on you. This stuff won't come off."

"I don't care. Do you have any idea what that outfit is worth? Maybe you've heard of Dorothy's ruby slippers? Well, I can promise you Jessie's outfit would bring way more than whatever Leo DiCaprio paid for those nasty old shoes. Who wants to wear another woman's shoes, anyway?" The woman scanned the people nearest her, and her attention landed on Lil like a bad spin on a Game of Life board. "You! You were closest to it. What happened?"

Lil felt as her heart had leaped right into her throat, almost suffocating her. A prison lesson popped into her mind: *Never say anything. Innocent or not. Zip it.* So she simply stood there.

The deputy stepped between the redheaded cousin and Lil. "We'll handle this, ma'am. Be patient and let us secure the area."

A group of deputies hustled inside, and one peeled off toward Lil and Maggie and pointed at them. "I need everyone in here to line up behind these ladies." Once everyone was in a single file line, another deputy walked behind the group, herding them into one of the chapels.

Lil and Maggie took seats and waited. In short bursts, more people were ushered into the room.

Then, a dozen women—dressed in white leather skirts and vests so blinged out that the reflection almost blinded Lil—were brought in and placed in the separate family pews, and a security guard was stationed in front of them.

"Now those gals know how to dress for a funeral," Maggie said.

Lil sniffed. "This isn't like a midnight showing of *The Rocky Horror Picture Show.*

Costumes at a funeral aren't appropriate, not even if those women think they're honoring Jessie by dressing up like her."

The deputy gathered together the mausoleum director and his workers. Although he scooted them toward a corner, Lil could hear their hushed conversation.

"I didn't notice if the gloves were there when we slid the casket in." The stout guy nodded in Lil's direction. "But outside, I did see that woman touch them."

Unfortunately, Lil didn't seem to be the only one who was eavesdropping because Jessie's cousin screeched at her. "Is that true?"

"No, I was only—"

"Officer, someone needs to question that woman now! She stole Jessie Wyatt's precious gauntlets. They were priceless."

Priceless? So the rumors had all been true. Now Lil wanted to deny being anywhere near them, seeing as she could end up in jail again for lifting a fifty-cent pack of gum. But she was unable to get words of denial past her suddenly dry throat. Just when she was starting to get her post-prison life back on track, the last thing she needed was to be a crime suspect.

Lord knows, at her age, she couldn't

survive another vacation in the slammer.

CHAPTER 3

$\mathcal{L}$il spotted Sera among the last batch of people ushered into the chapel. "This feels a lot like prison right now," Lil said, grabbing Maggie's arm and weaving through the crowd.

"What's going on?" Sera said.

"Apparently someone stole Jessie's gauntlets."

"Who would do such a thing?" Sera's gaze swept the room and landed on the group of Jessie Wyatt lookalikes. Then she glanced at the Pitts County deputy and back to Teague. "Come with me," she said to Lil. "Maggie, you run interference for us."

"Run interference for wh—"

"Roll with me, Lil."

"Got it." Maggie assumed an at-ease

military stance.

Lil strolled across the room at Sera's side. "First I'm going to shake every hand, looking for any clue one of those women is wearing the real gauntlets," Sera said. "Then..."

Lil waited, but Sera didn't continue. "Then?"

"I'll bunt."

Bunt? That didn't seem like a particularly well-thought-out plan.

Sera wiggled her way into the group of Jessie lookalikes. "Hey, girls. I'm Marcus Johannesson's wife. Jessie and I were dear friends. We met on the set of *A Love To Last*. I wanted you to know that she would've loved you honoring her this way. You all look wonderful."

Sera braided herself through the group of women, chatting and smiling, and shaking each hand. She inclined her head in Lil's direction.

Lil stepped behind a particularly chunky lookalike. Could she possibly be packing those gauntlets rather than a few extra pounds? Lord, how to frisk a stranger without her realizing she was being frisked? Only one thing to do. Lil meandered over and pretended to stumble into the woman, wrapping her arms around her midsection.

"Pardon me!" she said, making sure to pat the woman down. Hmm...nothing but love handles. Lil shook her head at Sera.

Sera whispered something to another of the Jessie lookalikes, who immediately squealed. The others spun in their direction, and once Sera had everyone's attention, she lowered her voice and cut her eyes toward Lil. "We don't want this to get out, but this is Jessie's sister."

Lil pushed her breasts forward and leaned her weight on her right leg, doing her best to emulate Jessie Wyatt's posture and mannerisms.

A rustle of excitement rose from the group, and Sera put her finger to her lips. "Shh. She wanted to hear your stories about her dear sister. Do you mind sharing?"

The Jessie lookalikes clamored around Lil, and she improvised. "Which of my sister's movies did you like best?"

The women nearly climbed over one another to share their favorites, while Sera maintained eye contact with Lil as she poked into a short Jessie lookalike's fringed hobo bag, but came up empty.

The sound of footsteps thudding against

the chapel's short carpet caught Lil's and Sera's attention, a clear warning of the Pitts County deputy approaching them. Sera grabbed Lil's arm. "I'm not feeling well all of a sudden," she said, placing her hand on her forehead. "Will you take me to get some water?"

"Of course, dear." Lil whispered, "Panic attacks" to the women, who all nodded in understanding. Lil smiled and scooted Sera back into the crowd.

Before they could return to Maggie, Teague came striding toward Lil and Sera like a man used to people heeding his authority. And sure enough, all those celebrities and gawkers stepped to the side. He called out, "Okay, everyone, we apologize that it's warm in here, but we're trying to move as quickly as possible."

Then in a lowered voice, he said to Lil, "Come with me."

At the familiar sight of her local sheriff, the tight feeling directly behind her breastbone eased slightly, but she was still having a hard time catching her breath.

"I demand you arrest that woman." Jessie's cousin pointed a long-nailed finger at Lil as if she wanted to stab her with the ruby-red dagger.

Teague stopped in front of her and put his hands on his hips, his fingers brushing his gun. "Ma'am, I'd take it very kindly if you allowed the trained law enforcement professionals to handle this situation."

"But...but..."

Sera smiled at Jessie's cousin, but Lil could tell the expression was fake. Still, Sera took the other woman's arm and said, "This has all been so traumatic today. Why don't we find a quiet place and—"

"And who are you?"

"Marcus Johanneson's wife."

That shut Jessie's cousin up right quick, and she flashed a simpering smile toward Sera. "It's *so* nice to meet you."

As Sera led the woman away, Teague said to the Pitts County deputy, "Why don't you take the group of costumed folks while I'll work through this group?"

The deputy tugged on his hat and headed for the group of sparkling fringe-wearing women.

When Teague turned to Lil, his face was grim, but his eyes sparkled with mischief. "Ma'am, if you'll peaceably come with me, I'd like to ask you a few questions."

Maggie came rushing up. "You know she didn't do a darn thing—"

Lil grabbed hold of Maggie's arm to stop the tide of words coming from her mouth. She had a feeling Teague didn't want anyone around them catch on to the fact that they all knew one another. "Let's do as the officer requested."

Maggie's mouth tightened like a mule being pulled over the side of a canyon, but she gave a sharp nod.

With a gentle hand, Teague took Lil's elbow and led her through the crowd with Maggie a step behind. His face was an expressionless mask. Boy, he was good at this playacting thing. Maybe he *should* be on one of those cop reality shows.

Leaving the throng of people yelling over one another behind them, Teague steered them out the chapel door.

"We left Sera back there," Lil told him.

"She'll be fine. Don't say another word, Miss Lillian. We don't want anything to be overheard or recorded by those hyena reporters."

"Oh." Goodness, this being famous thing was fraught with complications, wasn't it?

Teague inclined his head toward the

security guard as they passed the building's entry. "Can you direct me to a private area?"

The security guard was preoccupied, ogling one of the starlets who'd already been questioned. Never making eye contact with Teague, the guy said, "Every place around here is pretty quiet, but if you're looking to be alone, you might want to try the break room on the basement level."

"Appreciate it."

Always the gentleman, Teague directed Lil toward an elevator.

"Teague," Maggie said. "I want to know what in the world you think—"

"Hush, Mags," Lil warned. "I trust Teague and you should too."

"Fine," she huffed, crossing her arms under her bust.

Once they were on the bottom level, Teague didn't hesitate, just stepped off the elevator and hooked a right.

"Do you know where we're going?"

"Doesn't matter," he said. "What matters is that you always *look* like you know where you're going and what you're doing."

Yes, that piece of wisdom had helped Lil bluster her way through a few situations in prison camp. They found the break room behind the second door to their left, and it was mercifully empty. Teague handed Lil into a chair. "Would you like some water?"

"Oh, goodness, yes." If her nerves sucking every last bit of moisture out of her mouth wasn't bad enough, the lingering smell of reheated leftovers in the microwave overlaid with pine-scented floor cleaner was making her stomach spin.

Teague went to the water cooler and poured cups for both Maggie and her. Once they were all situated at the small café table, Teague leaned back in his chair. "Want to tell me what that was all about out there?"

"I...I don't completely know. One minute, Maggie and I were watching those boys squirt caulk on panels and crawl around in the crypt, and the next, that woman was screaming."

"She said you were handling the gauntlets."

"No. I wasn't. Well, not in there. I did touch them while we were outside."

"Why?"

"Because they're lovely." And now she knew why. Because they were worth a fortune. She should've known it from the get-go because paste never had the luster of the real thing. "I was straightening them. It's not like I put them on or something."

He sighed and leaned forward. "Miss Lillian, you don't need to be in the middle of a big scandal, you know that, right?"

She shot him a disgruntled schoolteacher look. "I am not a ninny. I'm more than aware that I need to stay away from any sort of misdeed. It wasn't as if I went courting trouble."

His eyebrows rose, and one side of his mouth quirked up. "Strangely enough, I do believe trouble is courting you."

Lordy, she hoped not. "You don't think I actually stole those fancy gloves, do you?"

"You *were* just saying how much you liked that outfit." Maggie chuckled and patted the table in time with her hilarity.

"With friends like you, Margaret Rawls, a body doesn't need enemies."

Leaning over, Maggie gave her a one-armed hug. "You know I'm joshing you."

"I wouldn't joke like that in earshot of anyone," Teague warned her.

"I did not take those gauntlets." Lil leaped to her feet and twisted at the waist. "There's nowhere to hide those things. I simply scooched the one that was all cockadoodled to line it up with the other, and I could feel how heavy it was." She opened her small satin clutch. "If you don't believe me, check my bag. Frisk me. Do a strip search."

Teague clamped his eyes shut. "That will *not* be necessary." He blew out a slow breath and reopened his eyes. "Now, did either of you happen to see anything that looked out of place?"

"This mausoleum is crawling with people who look out of place in our neck of the woods. Hollywood types, reporters, photographers, those Jessie Wyatt lookalikes. Who would know?" Lil said.

Maggie's forehead wrinkled. "Lil's right. Nothing in particular caught my attention."

"Did you notice if the gloves were on the casket spray when they rolled it inside?"

"No. This is terrible," Lil said. "No doubt the disappearance will get some big airtime if this isn't resolved quickly."

Teague's expression softened. "We'll figure it out. I'll be working closely with the Pitts County boys on this, and there's a team pulling the casket back out now. And believe me, deputies from both sheriff's departments are out there questioning everyone."

"I promise I didn't take them, Teague."

"Of all the things I could imagine you stealing, Miss Lillian, a sexy cowgirl outfit is the last thing on my list."

Well, sake's alive, she should probably be offended by his assessment. "I'll have you know I made a very attractive flapper that year the Junior League hosted a '20s speakeasy night."

Teague just shook his head.

"Sure wish I'd seen something," she grumbled and slid back into her chair. "I would've taken that perp down with one flying leap."

"Perp?" Maggie's eyes went wide, and then she smiled. "Lil, you're getting the lingo."

Lil sat taller. That comment made her feel more like one of the gang. It was no fun being the last one to the party after Maggie, Sera, and Abby Ruth had spent a year playing private detective without her.

"Listen, you two, I want you to promise to stay out of this whole thing. Nothing good can come of you sticking your nose in a situation the Pitts County Sheriff's Department will head up. Do you hear me?"

"Of course we do, dear." After all, Lil wasn't in need of a hearing aid. "If you don't mind, I think Maggie and I will rest a spell right here. You know, calm down from all the excitement."

Pushing back his chair and standing, he looked down at them. "I mean what I said."

"We understand perfectly."

As soon as he cleared the door and turned the corner, Maggie leaned on the table. "We have no intention of keeping our noses out of this, do we?"

"Absolutely none."

CHAPTER 4

*A*fter everyone was released from the mausoleum, Lil and Maggie slid into the fancy backseat of Marcus's rented Maserati with him at the wheel and Sera riding shotgun.

"We've been invited to a private gathering in Jessie's honor with friends from Hollywood," Sera said. "Most of the folks headed straight over after the service. It's probably in full swing now. Would you like to join us?"

"I'm beat," Lil said. All she wanted after the missing gauntlet fiasco was to go home and crawl in bed.

Sera turned and sat up on her knees in the passenger seat to face Maggie and Lil. "It'll be fun. Come on." She mouthed, *Please. I need you.*

Lil wondered if Sera was always this uptight when she was with Marcus or if her behavior was a result of the stress of the funeral and the loss of her friend. She hadn't been her old self since she and Marcus had arrived in Summer Shoals. Maybe she needed Lil and Maggie to provide a social buffer.

Besides, skipping the party might make Lil look as if she had something to hide. Because what small-town person would pass up the chance to go to a Hollywood gathering?

"Thank you for inviting us. You're sure we're not intruding?" Lil asked Sera, who smiled a thank-you.

Marcus chimed in, "Of course not. We'd love you to come."

And so she and Maggie did. They partied with the rich and famous. Sipped Krug, Jessie's favorite champagne. Chatted with people they'd only seen on movie screens. Lil even danced with Mr. Hogan, who was much lighter on his feet than he appeared.

It was evening by the time they returned home, and Lil was worn to the bone. But the excitement of talking to the likes of Sam Elliott and Sylvester Stallone as if they were old friends had been worth it. Such sweet men.

She collapsed into one of the six rocking chairs on Summer Haven's broad front porch. Lord have mercy, she'd thought prison was exhausting, but a party filled with those Hollywood types was almost more than she could handle.

Now, her worry about the missing Jessie Wyatt gear was making her darn near sick to her stomach. How could those fancy fringy gauntlets have disappeared when she and Maggie were standing right there? And why the heck had she felt the need to adjust the dad-burned things?

"What's wrong, Lil?" Maggie asked.

"I can't stop thinking about those gauntlets. Why would someone take them? Grab them in plain sight?"

"It *was* a bold move."

"We have to find them." Weary tears welled behind Lil's eyes. "We need a plan. I can't go back to prison camp."

"You didn't do anything and you won't go back." Maggie came to Lil's side and leaned over to hug her. "Don't worry."

"A lot of women in prison swore they were innocent."

"Well, you really are. If the Pitts County boys don't get a quick lead, we'll jump right on the case," Maggie reassured her. "After all, we're getting dang good at solving crimes."

"But it seems like it's just the two of us now, what with Abby Ruth off somewhere and Sera...well, I don't rightly know what Sera's status is." Sera and her husband had still been chatting it up when Lil and Maggie accepted Sam Elliott's offer to have his limo driver bring them home. "I still can't picture Sera in that glitzy environment, even after seeing her among them tonight. Her face looks like our Sera's, but her clothes look like someone famous body-snatched her."

"We knew all along she was from California."

"Well, there's California and then there's Hollywood."

Maggie slumped against the front porch column, and her mouth mimicked the movement. "Do you think she'll leave Summer Shoals for good? It is slightly less glamorous."

"Slightly?" Lil scanned the property she'd lived on all her life. In her mind, it was still as grand as it had been when her momma and daddy were still alive. But even with her waning eyesight, she could see that Summer Haven needed a fresh coat of white paint, and it seemed like every other week the old

Georgian-style house needed some attention. And attention cost money. "I looked Sera's husband up on Wikipedia."

"And?"

"You're telling me you haven't checked him out?"

"I didn't want to intrude."

Although no one was around, Lil hunched forward and whispered, "The man is worth in the neighborhood of $900 million. Do you know how close that is to a billion dollars?"

Maggie snorted a laugh. "About a hundred million."

"Still, what reason would Sera have to stay here when she has all that to go home to?"

Maggie reached over and grasped her hand. "Maybe because *this* is where she really feels at home. We've become her family."

"A woman's husband is her family first and foremost."

"Did you forget Marcus filed for divorce?"

"And did you see the way he looked at her during the funeral? That man is still in love with her." And who could blame him? Sera was the best looking fifty-something woman Lil had ever set eyes on. Yoga kept her in tiptop physical shape, and apparently all that clean eating she went on and on about had merit if it kept her buns that tight.

Lil yearned for the days of her youth—heck, her middle age—again. Getting old was hell. Everything creaking and aching. "Her van sitting next to the creek has started to look like part of the scenery these days. I guess if she decides to stay with Marcus, she'll take that too."

"Probably. It's been kind of comforting that she'd left it behind. Like she might actually come back."

"I wish she'd stay, but I doubt there's much chance of that." Lil sighed and rocked, wondering if this was how an empty-nester felt when her kids left for good.

"I think we could both use some cheering up." Maggie hauled herself up from her chair and headed for the front door. "Maggie's special tea coming up in two shakes of a lamb's tail."

She had no sooner closed the door behind her than a Waltz Blue 1940s sedan came rumbling up Summer Haven's driveway. And only one person in Summer Shoals drove the car that had once been Lil's daddy's.

Angelina Broussard.

Lord, Lil would need a handful of ibuprofen on top of the bourbon Maggie generously mixed into her tea. Still, she raised her hand in a polite wave when Angelina climbed out of the Tucker and marched toward her dressed, as usual, in a pair of sparkly jeans, a shiny silk blouse, and boots with heels as tall as the Baptist church's steeple.

"Good evening, Angelina."

She stomped up the front steps with so much force Lil was surprised her heels didn't leave dents in the wood planks. "Do you have any idea how long it took me to drive over here?" With a dramatic sigh, she flung herself into the rocking chair next to Lil's.

Since Lil was certain Angelina meant that as a rhetorical question, she simply smiled and cocked her head in a halfway curious motion.

"Thirty-five. Three. Five. You would not believe what Main Street looks like. Cars lined up nose to tail, one after another. And not your run-of-the-mill rental cars. Limousines, Lamborghinis, and some other Italian ones."

Hmm. Lil would've expected Angelina to be completely up-to-date on every make and model of fancy car ever manufactured. But by her awed tone, this was the first time she'd laid eyes on some of them. "You don't say."

"You probably can't see them all from here." With a sweep of her silk-covered arm,

Angelina gestured toward the trees that partially concealed Summer Haven's view of Main Street.

A wicked temptation came over Lil. She set a demure and innocent half-smile on her face, then rolled her comment on out like a hand grenade. "Actually, I spotted a few of them in the parking lot earlier."

Angelina's smug rocking came to an abrupt halt. She leaned forward, her eyes narrowing. "What parking lot?"

"Why the one over at Holy Innocence Mausoleum, of course. And the gathering afterward. More a party if you ask me. Jessie's family went Hollywood instead of hometown on this funeral."

"Party?" Angelina's voice hit a note Lil thought only opera singers could reach.

"Well, certainly no fine lady from Georgia would've wanted that kind of shindig. But then that's my opinion."

Angelina's mouth dropped as wide as that hole they'd shoved Jessie's casket into. "You crashed Jessie Wyatt's burial?"

"We certainly did not."

"You were pulling my leg. I should've known."

"No. I'm saying Maggie and I were invited."

"You have got to be kidding me." Angelina's grip was so tight on the rocking chair arms that her fingers were ghostly white.

Lil's momma had always instilled Southern manners in her only daughter, but darned if Lil didn't want to say something a tad snarky to Angelina about now. Lil might've privately received her comeuppance for past crimes, but the Summers *were* the founding family of this town. Why wouldn't she be invited to such a big event? "I'm afraid not, dear."

Angelina's lips pursed up like a llama ready to spit.

"You know," Lil said casually as she spotted Maggie coming out the front door carrying a tray holding a pitcher and two glasses, "On screen, that Sam Elliott is a handsome man, but in person, he's...what would you call him, Mags?"

"A hottie."

Angelina's eyes widened.

"Oh, yes. He most certainly made me want to fan myself." Lil hid her small smile behind a fluttery wave.

"Angelina," Maggie said, "I didn't realize we were expecting you."

What went unsaid is that they never expected Angelina, but when she showed up, she inevitably brought along trouble.

Angelina glanced up at Maggie and immediately reached for one of the tea glasses on the tray. "Oh, thank goodness. I can't tell you how stressful it was to drive through all that traffic on the way here. I'm parched." Without a thank-you, Angelina lifted her glass and drained half of it. When she pulled it away from her mouth, she was wheezing. "Wha...what's in that?"

Maggie's eyebrows lifted until they were hidden by her dark bangs. "Excellent quality loose leaf tea, well water, and ice. What else?" With a wink at Lil, Maggie passed her the second glass and whispered, "Figure you need this more than I do now."

Angelina took a more careful sip of her drink this time. "You may be wondering why I'm here."

Out of Angelina's line of sight, Maggie rolled her eyes, but Lil said, "Oh, you mean this isn't just a neighborly visit?" Of course it wasn't. Angelina had more agendas than a corporate board meeting.

"I'm sure it won't surprise you to hear that Broussard B&B has been in high demand with all these actresses and actors. I hear those Hollywood folks are staying all over four counties, but, of course, I was booked up not two hours after they announced where Jessie Wyatt's funeral would be held."

"Congratulations?" Lil said. If Angelina had a full house, a body would think she'd be there seeing to her guests instead of sitting on Summer Haven's porch getting snockered on Maggie's tea.

"But Summer Shoals being the friendly small town it is, I knew my neighbors would want to pitch in at a busy time like this."

So help her, if Angelina asked her to come over and help clean up after her guests, Lil might have to contemplate a felony offense. Her first job at Walter Stiles Federal Prison Camp had been bathroom duty, and if she never saw a soiled commode and toilet brush again in her life, it would be three days too soon.

"A guest of mine needs a room for two nights. Normally, I don't have a problem accommodating him at the last minute, but this time..." She trailed off and shot a hopeful smile at Lil.

"Well, that's too bad."

"He's a regular, and I hate to disappoint him."

Yes, Lil was certain Angelina's regular

customer probably paid regular prices for his room at the B&B whereas she was probably charging the Hollywood people several times that. "Maybe you could bump one of your other bookings."

Angelina, currently mid-sip, gasped and choked. She coughed, and although she politely covered her mouth with her hand, a trickle of Maggie's tea escaped from the corner of her lips. "That would be...be..."

The headache that had sprouted in Lil's head when the ruckus was raised about Jessie's missing outfit now bloomed fully. And with it, her patience vanished. "Let's cut to the chase. What is it you want from me?" *Oh yeah, you'll have to grovel for this, Angelina.*

"My normal rates are two hundred dollars a night." She lifted her chin toward the front porch columns, currently rotting from the bottom. Lil cringed inside that others could so plainly see that Summer Haven's glory days were in the past. "And I thought you, of all people, might need an influx of cash. Of course, you couldn't charge him full price to stay here." With a manicured hand, she reached into her purse and pulled out a wad of twenties. "But I have three hundred right here. He only needs a place for two nights."

Oh, no. She would not open her house up to a stranger. Who did Angelina think she was? "Summer Haven is not a hotel."

"Charlie Millet is good customer. And he's no trouble. It's only two nights, Lillian." She dug back down into her purse. "Fine. I'll give you three hundred and sixty dollars."

Maggie bumped Lil's chair with her hip. "We have an empty room. What would it hurt?"

"Think about it," Angelina said, waggling that stack of bills.

"But the only empty room in the house is Abby Ruth's." While Lil had still been in prison camp, she hadn't been too thrilled to discover Abby Ruth Cady, an abrasive Texan, was squatting in the Sweet Vidalia Room with no plans to leave.

But since Lil's return to Summer Haven, she and Abby Ruth had finally stopped circling each other like a couple of junkyard dogs. Then, a few days ago, Abby Ruth had taken off on a mysterious trip, and Lil strangely missed the woman's big and bold personality.

Maggie grabbed the arm of Lil's rocking chair and swung her around to exclude Angelina from the conversation. "Why are you so against this, Lil?"

"Summer Haven is a genteel family home, not some fly-by-night boarding house that opens its doors for any stranger off the street."

"I can understand you're a little hypersensitive after I took in Abby Ruth. And now Sera's husband is here. But, Lil, we've begged and begged you to let us pay rent."

"Out of the question."

"Exactly. Which is why saying yes to Angelina's request is a good idea. You don't have to feel guilty taking money from a stranger."

"It's not guilt. It's...it's..." What was her issue with accepting money? Maybe she had a hard time because until the past few years she'd never wanted for anything. But then Harlan had squandered her inheritance on lottery tickets.

Or maybe it was because her momma had always said ladies should never sully their hands with business concerns.

Then again, Momma wasn't living in the twenty-first century. God rest her soul.

Lil sighed. "I don't know, Mags."

"You're right," Maggie said briskly. "We shouldn't consider it. After all, it wouldn't be polite to let a stranger invade Abby Ruth's space. This *is* her home."

Abby Ruth's home? Abby Ruth might be growing on Lil little by little, but she did not have more of a claim on the Summer family home than Lil did. No, sir. Not now, not ever.

She turned to Angelina and gave her a sharp nod. "We'll do it. But the Sweet Vidalia Room is as nice as any of the rooms at your B&B. And from the looks of that stack, you have the full amount." Lil held out her palm. "So you can hand over four hundred. After all, that would be the neighborly thing to do. Don't you agree, Maggie?"

"You bet."

Angelina huffed and slapped the cash into Lil's hand with more force than was strictly necessary. Still, the weight in Lil's palm felt right nice. "He'll expect breakfast as well. So don't y'all go thinking you can shortchange him."

"We wouldn't dream of it."

When Angelina stood, she tottered slightly on those high heels, but quickly steadied herself. "It's all settled then."

Unfortunately, Lil couldn't imagine the day when things between her and Angelina Broussard would ever be completely settled.

CHAPTER 5

Sera cleared her mind, trying to concentrate on the yoga and Maggie's breathing beside her. But it was a challenge with Marcus watching from a rocking chair on Summer Haven's front porch. When she woke this morning, he wasn't in bed beside her, and his car was gone. But he'd returned a half-hour ago, whistling an off-key tune and answering with a vague "out and about" when she asked him where he'd been.

"He looks at you like he can't believe he's lucky enough to have you," Maggie said, as she moved into the warrior pose. "George used to look at me like that."

Sera was proud of Maggie. She'd obviously kept up her yoga practice while Sera had been away. Maggie had slimmed and toned and was moving with the ease of someone who'd practiced for years.

Sera spoke quietly as they changed positions in unison. "There's something I probably should explain to you about Marcus. Have you ever wondered why I left California in the first place?"

"Several times, but I figured if you wanted to talk about it, you would." Maggie laid her hand on Sera's arm. "It doesn't change who you are to me. To any of us here."

"Thank you." Hearing that lifted her spirits. These ladies knew what real friendship was. But they still deserved, more than deserved, an explanation. "When my dad died a few years ago, I had a hard time. He wasn't rich when it came to material possessions, but he was so prosperous when it came to friendship and love. He didn't leave much behind, but one thing he treasured was—"

"That van." Maggie smiled gently. "Understandable."

"After he died, I took a long look at my life, and I wasn't very happy with what I saw. I'd allowed myself to become an accessory."

"What do you mean?"

Sera slid into another pose, unsure how to explain how trivial she often felt around

Marcus. So instead, she blurted out, "We have a grown son."

Maggie glanced away. "I could say I didn't know, but that wouldn't be true. You taught me some pretty good computer skills. When Lil and I found out your boy Finn was a musician, I went right out to iTunes and downloaded all his band's songs. He's talented. Obviously takes after his mom."

"Do you hate me for not telling you everything?"

"Of course not. You had your reasons."

"Life is so complicated." Tears blurred Sera's vision. "But when I lived at Summer Haven, it was simple. All made sense, and I was truly happy."

"It wasn't always simple. What about running down those baddies? And the time you fell through the ceiling?"

"Yeah, that was one wild ride." Sera laughed. "Maybe not simple, but it was fun and spontaneous. Genuine. I always felt like I was making things better. And I liked who I was when I was here." She took in a breath. "I don't always like who I am when I'm with Marcus."

"What do you mean? It's more than obvious he loves you. And I can't imagine you being anything but the gracious and kind woman we know."

"Marcus also loves his work. Maybe more than is healthy. At least more than is healthy for me. By the time Finn was born, I was tired of following Marcus from location to location. Our entire marriage, we were apart more than we were together. That's no way to build a relationship, a family. He wasn't about to give up his movie career for me, and in all honesty, I didn't ask him to."

"So things have been strained for a long time?"

"Well, after Finn left home, Marcus retired, at least unofficially, which gave us more time together. Then someone came to him with a project he was so excited about, luring him back in. He just couldn't say no to it. And he didn't. He'd been on location for about two months when my dad died. Not long after, I told him I was going to take some time to myself."

"And you landed in Summer Shoals."

"Yes, after a trek across the country, I found my way here." Sera tried to breathe away the tight feeling inside her. "Marcus is a good man, full of creative brilliance, but that brilliance comes with a cost. He's passionate, but that passion is often channeled with a very single-minded focus. He forgets life goes on, with or without him."

"You make it sound like he never paid attention to you."

Oh, when Marcus had been focused on her, it was like the sun after a long, hard winter. And that made it even tougher when his attention shifted away, because his movie always became his mistress. "One time, when he was between projects, he rented a hot air balloon for an entire week. He took me on a sunset ride over Santa Monica and Malibu. Then the crew moved the balloon and we soared over Napa and Sonoma. Did the same with San Francisco and the Sierra Nevada foothills."

"That sounds so romantic."

"It was. Champagne and laughter and making love every night." She sighed, remembering. The closeness and love she and Marcus had shared was indescribable. Still, sometimes she'd longed for a normal marriage, one where they lived together day-to-day, did normal things like shopping for groceries and going to the movies instead of hosting catered parties and making movies.

She and Maggie went through the final

moves, ending stretched out in the savasana pose. Three deep breaths, and Marcus knew her routine well enough after all this time to notice she was done. His nervous energy was thrumming—practically waving its way from the porch across the yard to her. But she was determined not let his go-go-go attitude ruin the peace inside her.

"You've promised to show me around town ever since we got here," he called to her. "Can I get a date with my best girl?"

She sat up. Maggie gave her a hug of support and headed back inside the house.

"It's a beautiful day for a ride." Marcus leaned forward, his forearms on his knees. "Come on. It'll be fun."

Her memories of their past—both bitter and sweet—still occupied her mind, and right now...she was exhausted. "It's still crowded in Summer Shoals. Lots of people stayed after Jessie's funeral. Traffic will be crazy. Why don't we wait until—"

"Traffic? Have you forgotten we live in Los Angeles? I doubt Summer Shoals's main drag can compare with the 101 at rush hour."

True, but every time he asked, all Sera could think was that she didn't want to share Summer Shoals with him. It was hers. But

Marcus was a man used to getting what he asked for, so he wouldn't let this drop. "What do you want to see?"

"I'm not sure, but I have a feeling about this place." He breathed deep, making a show of taking in the fresh country air, and he sauntered across the yard toward her. "Something unique. Special."

Oh, no. When Marcus said he had a feeling about something, it always meant he had a feeling about making a movie. Might as well give him the penny tour. Maybe she could throw him off the Summer Shoals scent.

"You're right." She pulled her legs underneath her and stood, glancing down at her spandex tights and tie-dyed tunic top. It had made her happy and lighthearted to shed the slick outfit she'd worn to Jessie Wyatt's funeral yesterday and change back into her Summer Shoals clothes. "It is a great day for a drive."

Marcus rewarded her with a smile, the one that still gave her goose bumps. He reached for her hand and she let him take it, allowing the prickles of awareness to sweep over her.

He headed for the Maserati he'd rented.

"No, sir," she said. "If I'm leading this tour, we do it my way." She veered off toward Dad's

VW van. Technically it was hers now, but it would always be his in her heart. She'd missed it while she'd been in California. "Come on. Ride with me."

"I'm not driving that thing," he said.

"Didn't say I'd let you." She skipped around to the driver's side, happy to be back in the down-to-earth comfort of the van. It was more than simply a memory of her dad now. She'd grown to love this old ride. And it had been a dependable and good one all the way across the country.

He reluctantly climbed in then leaped in the air as if a crab had pinched his butt. "For God's sake!"

"What's the matter?"

"There's a spring coming through this seat. Why are you still driving this clunker? And if you're so hell-bent on keeping it, you could've at least put it in the shop for restoration." He swiped his hand across his butt. "Snagged a hole in my favorite Tom Ford pants." With a muffled *damn* under his breath, he balanced on the edge of the worn seat.

"Sit back, you can't ride all day like that. Besides, you've got five more pair exactly like those."

Chuckling, he picked up a newspaper from

the floor and slid it under his rump, then he plopped down on the seat. "This is the only pair I packed."

"You won't need slacks in Summer Shoals anyway. Please tell me you brought blue jeans." There'd been a time when she'd have packed his things for him, but their relationship had been different since she'd gone back to California to try to make things work with him. Careful not to fall back into the role that she'd run from before, she no longer doted him. She loved him. After all, he was a huge part of her past, the father of her child.

But she missed being just Serendipity Johnson. Yoga instructor. Not a worry in the world. Well, except for the social security fraud, the online dating scandal, the art fraud...okay, different worries.

By the time she'd pulled out to Main Street, Marcus finally relaxed into the seat. She cruised through Summer Shoals, pointing out the landmarks, and with each one she recalled special moments she'd had there...but she kept some of those memories to herself.

She turned at the city municipal building and then showed him around the town square. "Holloway's has any kind of hardware you could ever need. And all the other basics are right here too."

"What about an art supply or music shop?"

"You mean like the type of place where we used to buy Finn his drums and keyboards?"

"Yeah."

What a strange question. "I think the local kids get their band instruments somewhere closer to Atlanta." She pointed toward a trio of neat brick buildings. "But there's the flower shop and the bakery, which has the best eclairs in the whole world, and the salon-slash-bookstore is on the square too."

"Eclairs? You telling me you were eating pastries?"

"I've tried them," she admitted. But her friends had tried her way of eating too. It all worked. A good balance somehow.

"You led a different life here."

She smiled to herself. A good life.

"Where do you buy your Mike & Ike's? Don't tell me you didn't sneak those while you were here."

She laughed. "You know me too well. I wasn't that different here. I still had my stash. And I was able to get them right down the road at the Piggly Wiggly, but trust me, if I couldn't find them, I'd have shipped them in."

"Now that's my Sera," he said, reaching

across the open center to rest his arm on the back of her seat. "My sweet Sera. But I admit, I like this other side of you too."

She drove by the library and took him out to the far edge of town, past the landfill. Boy, those stakeouts there had been interesting. She couldn't share those memories, though. Marcus would have a fit if he knew she'd been following bad guys and breaking and entering. That certainly wasn't a hobby he'd want the press to get wind of. But more than that, Sera simply wanted something of her own, and all the escapades she and the Summer Haven girls had experienced were hers.

Marcus pointed out a renovated old cotton gin. "What's that?"

"The Gypsy Cotton Art Gallery."

"Looks empty."

Which broke Sera's heart. The high-ceilinged space was so airy and welcoming, and the people of Summer Shoals had been so proud to have a cultural touchstone in town. No more. "Let's just say the owner had other, more pressing, commitments. So she had to walk away from the gallery."

"Someone should do something with the space. It's too architecturally interesting to stand empty."

Maybe Sera should mention it to Jenny, since she taught art part-time at the high school. Then again, it would take a lot of time and effort to get a gallery up and running again. But it was also a perfect spot for community get-togethers. Not only art showings, but potlucks, parties, fundraising events.

Oh goodness, it would be great for yoga classes on days when it was too cold or rainy to host them on Summer Haven's lawn. If only her life would allow her to spearhead something like that.

She looked away from the abandoned building because it hurt too much to think of things she wasn't free to do. "And up here are the schools. There are some beautiful old farms on this side of town, and the sheriff lives out this way."

"Summer Shoals is perfect for my next movie." He hummed as she cruised down Main Street. "A romantic comedy. I think the Southern twist could make it more engaging. Can you imagine a couple walking down this street? In the rain! Yes."

Was it her imagination, or was Marcus tapping out the tune of AC/DC's "Back in Black" on the door panel? Finn's band had included that cover song on their last album. But when she glanced over, Marcus was gazing out the window, clearly in his own world dreaming up another award-winning scene. She let him immerse himself in his own world because, although his work-work-work tendencies sometimes made her feel like an outsider, there was something to be said for a couple being so comfortable that they didn't need to fill every space with conversation.

She let him hum, drum, and daydream as she tooled around town and then went back to the town square. She pulled the van into a parking spot and got out. Marcus piled out of the passenger seat, still talking to himself about his next movie.

Sera took a minute to draw in the Georgia spring air, which was beginning to turn thick and damp. In the time she was back in California, she'd had to laugh when some of her old-life friends had complained about the "horrible humidity." People in Los Angeles had no idea what *real* humidity was.

But her normal pleasure at the balmy weather was suppressed because of Marcus's persistent chatter about this quaint Southern town.

It was like he'd already put Jessie's funeral

out of his mind. It wouldn't be that easy for Sera. Jessie had as much influence on her life as her dad, and losing another special mentor was heartbreaking. It made her feel vulnerable and panicked. Made her wonder if she was living up to their expectations. If she was truly living her best life.

"Without a doubt, the American public is ready for another Southern-set romantic comedy. Think *Sweet Home Alabama*, but set in Georgia. The economy is just depressed enough that people need something happy and lighthearted in their lives." He began humming "Für Elise." That was more like the Marcus she knew. That habit had been absolutely adorable when they first met, but now it was a sign not to bother to say anything important because his wheels were turning.

"But there are plenty of other locations you could scout."

"You have to admit Summer Shoals is terminally charming, though. And it's obvious the town could use an influx of money." He held out his arms and turned in a circle as if bestowing his blessing on the town.

"That's more than a little condescending."

"Wasn't meant to be. Just thought it would be nice to help a place you had ties to, and who doesn't want their town to be in a movie?"

Plenty of people. *Me for one.* The last thing in the world she wanted was for her Hollywood life to invade her Summer Shoals life, the one she considered the more real of the two.

"Shooting a movie here could change this town forever," he said.

And not in a good way. "My point exactly."

"How do you think Lil would feel about Summer Haven being used as a movie location?"

Sera's insides swirled like the water down a drain. She gaped at her husband. "Excuse me?"

He held out his hands in a goalpost gesture as though he were looking through the viewfinder of a video camera. "It could be like a modern-day Tara. Now, there's an idea, a romantic comedy remake of *Gone with the Wind.*"

How in the world he could translate a movie set in the Civil War into modern day and make it a romantic comedy, Sera had no idea. But if anyone could, it was him. After all, he'd built his entire career and reputation from trying outrageous projects that no one else would touch. He'd once made a feature film about the Tamil Tigers' impact on Sri Lanka and terrorism in that region. Only Marcus could've made that both a critical and commercial success. "You realize there are antebellum houses all over the state, all over the Southeast. Why Summer Shoals?"

He paused in his hungry study of the quaint streets. "Because you obviously love it. And anything you love, I love too."

How true had that been back when all she'd wanted was a normal family life and he was flitting off to Sri Lanka to shoot that movie? That had been the initial breaking point for her.

Had she been a total fool to think things would be different now?

Marcus wasn't a bad man. He was simply passionate, and when he was passionate about something, it consumed him completely.

He wrapped his arms around her and pulled her close to his chest. And although his ocean-fresh scent reminded her of good times, happy times, the steel in his arms made her feel trapped and claustrophobic. Something inside her resented the fact that he was falling in love with Summer Shoals.

This was her place. Hers.

That I-need-some-space feeling took over

again, and she eased away.

She approached the window of Holloway House & Home Realty and spotted a sign in the lower right corner that robbed her of breath. "No."

"What's wrong?" Marcus came to her side and put his hand on her lower back.

She hadn't realized she'd uttered the word aloud. "The Gypsy Cotton Gallery is for sale."

"We drove by that. Over near the school."

"Yes."

"I wouldn't think a town this size has much of an art culture."

She stared at the For Sale flyer detailing the old warehouse's square footage and amenities. "You'd be surprised. You've heard of the sculptor Colton Ellerbee?"

"Ellerbee? Yeah. He makes reclaimed artifacts into sculptures, right?"

Reclaimed artifacts? Junk was more like it, but whatever. "His studio isn't far from here. This gallery sold some of his pieces and was actually doing well there for a while. Then some unfortunate things happened, but I'd hoped the gallery would rebound."

"Doesn't look like it."

"No." She pushed her hair behind her ear. "It's such a disappointment." It never occurred to her that the gallery would be in jeopardy of closing permanently because of the bad press it had suffered last year. Very short-sighted of her.

He tugged on her arm until she turned to face him. "It's clear how much you love this community. I think you might rather be here than California."

If she admitted that aloud, they'd both know their marriage was over. After all, Marcus would never leave Los Angeles. "The people here are good," she said. *Real.*

He leaned over and peered closer at the flyer in the window.

Someone from the other side of Main called out, "Gonna buy a place around here, Marcus?"

He raised a hand to a man across the street. "Hey there, Jimmy. I haven't forgotten about that lip-sync challenge. I'll have my people get with your people."

Jimmy grinned. "You're on."

Marcus lip-syncing? Since when? And it was a bit surreal to have her husband waving and talking to people in Summer Shoals like he belonged here. It was as if he'd picked up all of Hollywood and plopped it down in Georgia. She'd be glad when all these people climbed on an airplane and went back home.

If this town wasn't careful, its quaint streets, hometown shops, and cute town square would be glitter-fied. Someone would probably put up a big white SUMMER SHOALS sign on the hill near the landfill.

Before she could ask Marcus why he was urging her down the sidewalk, he greeted some others. "Ellen, great to see you. Love that short haircut, as always. And Steve, I'm working to get a team together for *Celebrity Family Feud*."

There wasn't a single fan trailing any of the three TV personalities. Surely the townspeople knew who they all were, but it was refreshing to see they were being respectful and giving the stars space and privacy. That had to feel like complete heaven. Probably why so many of them were still hanging around.

Sera triple-stepped to keep up with the speed Marcus was guiding her along. "Where are we going?"

"Right inside here." With a dramatic flourish, he swung open the door to the Realty office. He flashed his most charming smile at the receptionist and leaned on the countertop separating them. "Hello there, sweetheart. I'd like to see Daisy Holloway. Does she happen to be in?"

The receptionist blinked as if trying to decide why she was so entranced with a man who was almost old enough to be her grandfather. Marcus affected all women that way. Eight minutes to eighty years old, there wasn't a one of them he couldn't charm senseless. In fact, he and Teague reminded her of each other in that way. "She's...uh...I think..."

A professionally dressed woman in a blazer with Holloway House & Home Realty embroidered on the lapel came through a doorway. "Did I hear someone ask for me?"

Marcus swung his charm superpower in her direction. "I understand the local art gallery is for sale."

The Realtor's eyes flashed with interest, and she thrust a hand in his direction. "I'm Daisy. Why don't you join me in my office and I'll pull the file on it?"

As had happened so often in the past, the woman barely glanced at Sera as she waved Marcus through the doorway. Sera trailed the pair. How many times had she looked at Marcus's back while she followed him somewhere? Realtor's office, parties, Hollywood premieres. Heck, she'd probably seen her husband's backside more than she'd seen his front side.

Although she had to admit his backside was still plenty fine.

"The gallery space is newly renovated," the Realtor said. "Such a shame what happened with the owner, but her misfortune will definitely be someone else's boon. I don't think I'm talking out of turn by telling you her husband is a very motivated seller."

Rather than sitting in the blue leather chair next to her husband, Sera wandered around the office until she came to the window. Within three minutes, she spotted Tom Hanks, Emma Stone, and Ryan Reynolds.

It was disorienting to have her small-town streets being strolled by the rich and famous, as if her old life had invaded her new one, and she could feel the muscles in her shoulders slowly coil into knots. She reminded herself what she preached to her friends here all the time. Relax. Align your chakras. Breathe in and out. Slowly. Cleanse your mind. Only her advice didn't seem to be working today.

In fact, tears were stinging the backs of her eyes.

"How much is he asking?" Marcus asked the Realtor. He'd never been a patient man.

Daisy shook her curls and grinned. "Only $280,000. A bargain, I'm telling you. Almost giving it away."

Marcus finally turned his attention toward Sera. "Did you hear that, darling? Only $280,000."

Sera had never met Daisy, but she'd heard Darrell mention that his sister was an excellent businesswoman. The word he'd used was ruthless. The gallery was probably marked at $100,000 to anyone without a California zip code. "That's still a lot of money around here, which means it'll be a long time before someone buys the space, if ever." She tried to swallow the sadness welling up in her, but when she spoke, her words were thick.

"Sera, are you okay?"

She swiped at her eyes. "I'll be fine."

Marcus quickly reached inside the breast pocket of his sport coat and dropped his card on the Realtor's desk. "Please keep me posted on this property, Ms. Holloway."

Then he ushered Sera out onto the sidewalk and around the corner so they weren't in view of everyone walking down Main. "I didn't mean to upset you."

"It's not you. I just..." She held up her hands then let them drop helplessly against her sides.

"You miss Jessie, don't you?"

"So much." Oh, goodness, Sera's waterworks went haywire. "I wish I'd stayed in closer contact with her. I've barely seen her in the past few years, but…"

Slowly, gently, giving her plenty of time to pull away, Marcus drew her into his arms. "But she was incredibly important to you. In the past few years, you've lost some of the people you love most in the world."

"I'm in my fifties, which means it's going to happen. I can't avoid death, no matter what Hollywood wants us to believe."

"No, but you know I'm here for you. Here to listen, here to hold you, or here to talk with you about Jessie."

"Thank you." Although Sera drew away from his embrace, she slipped her hand in his and glanced back at the real estate office. "Marcus, what would you do with an art gallery?"

When he flashed Sera the smile that had won her heart all those years ago, she felt something give inside her chest. "I don't know yet," he said. "But there's something there. It'll come to me."

And she was certain it would, because that

was how Marcus was. He had an instinct that led him in all the right decisions. Why couldn't she have that same clarity about her own life?

CHAPTER 6

*L*il had been nervous about renting out a room to a stranger, but to her delight Charlie Millet was a delight, even commenting on the quality of the towels and the way she'd folded them. *Take that, Angelina.*

So on her paying guest's first morning at Summer Haven, Lil got up early and cooked peaches and cream French toast, since Charlie had mentioned he was a fan of breakfast breads.

He was obviously a discerning man who appreciated small touches, which made Lil happier than she could've imagined. Why had she balked at the idea of having a paying guest? Maybe overnighters were exactly what this old house needed to keep things interesting.

From the moment he'd cruised up in his big blue SUV with tinted windows, Charlie had been nothing but fun to fuss over.

This morning, she'd hoped the smell of breakfast and fresh coffee would lure him out of his room, but he hadn't made his way downstairs yet.

Since she hated for food to go to waste, Lil took the stairs to the second floor. Sera and Marcus were sleeping in too, although Lil had no idea how Sera could sleep through that man's snoring. In fact, she'd worried Charlie might complain about it, but he hadn't.

Before Charlie arrived, Lil had half-teased Sera, saying perhaps she and Marcus might want to camp in the van down by the creek for old time's sake. But Marcus had given both Lil and Sera the stink-eye. "You were sleeping outside? In the van?"

"Not because Lil made me. It was my choice," Sera said, looking a bit frazzled about admitting to Marcus how different her life here had been.

Afterward, Lil felt bad about the slip.

Needless to say, they'd remained in the room where Abby Ruth's daughter, Jenny, had stayed for a while. But Lil wasn't a hundred percent certain that Sera wasn't sneaking outside and sleeping under the stars once Marcus set to snoring each night. And she couldn't blame her a single bit.

Lil rapped the back of her knuckles on her guest's door. "Excuse me, Charlie. Breakfast is ready." She pressed her hand against the door, leaning in to take a listen.

The old oak planks creaked under the weight of Charlie's feet. He swung the door open with a smile, his phone against his ear. His dark hair sparkled with water droplets and his mustache was neatly combed. Now this was a young man who knew something about proper grooming. "I'm on a call."

"I'm sorry. I didn't mean to interrupt, but I wanted to let you know I made French toast and bacon. Everything's hot."

"Just a sec." He held up a finger, turned his back to her, and spoke quietly into his phone. He murmured a few words Lil couldn't make out then shoved the phone into his back pocket and turned to face her again. "You've been so accommodating. I can't tell you how much I appreciate you opening your home to me."

Lil's heart did a mini cha-cha. If she and Harlan had ever been blessed with a son, hopefully he would've been like Charlie. He was probably the type to visit often and handy enough to come by and help out from time to time.

"You're welcome to stay here any time. Just give me a call. I usually have a spare room in this big house."

"Thank you, Ms. Fairview," Charlie said.

"Lillian." She wagged a finger at him. "How many times do I have to tell you?"

"Thank you, Miss Lillian. Being here is more like fancy couch-surfing with friends rather than renting a room in a stuffy, fussy place like Angelina's."

Couch surfing? That was a new term for Lil, but it sounded pleasant enough.

As they descended the stairs together, Charlie said, "I noticed this month's *Guns & Ammo* magazine in the bedside table last night. Somehow that doesn't strike me as your kind of entertainment."

Lil laughed and took the elbow he offered, steering them both toward the dining room. She'd already set the table with the one small collection of Haviland she hadn't had the heart to pawn. "No, I'm much more a *House Beautiful* kind of woman. But a friend of mine normally stays in that room, and she's what I'd call a gun nut. Then again, what do you expect from a Texan?"

"I hope my visit didn't put her out."

"She's on a little vacation right now, so the timing was perfect. Besides, if she was around, you'd know it. Her personality is probably the reason for the saying that everything is bigger in Texas." The words tumbled out before Lil could keep her Southern lady behavior in check.

"Sounds like a pistol."

"She has enough of them." Lil chuckled at her own joke, then she hurried to the sideboard to fill a plate for her guest. "Do you like butter and syrup with your French toast?"

"Yes, ma'am."

Although it didn't seem completely proper, at Charlie's request she sat with him and sipped a cup of coffee while he ate. After he'd tucked away three helpings, he finally wiped his mouth. "Miss Lillian, that was the best breakfast I've ever eaten."

"Surely, Angelina—"

"I think she buys day-old donuts from the grocery store."

Oh, my. "Well, then, your mother must—"

"Momma's not much of a breakfast cook. Your French toast outdoes her half-cooked pancakes any day. But she can stir up a good pot of Brunswick stew."

A better cook than his own momma? Lil glowed from one of the best compliments a woman could hope for. She cleared his plate and freshened his coffee. With a pat on his hand, she said, "You're a nice young man. Your momma raised you right regardless of her cooking skills."

As she took the dishes into the kitchen, she had a flash of brilliance.

Perhaps the way to let Summer Haven sustain its own upkeep had been right in front of her all along. Young businessmen like Charlie could stop and stay for a much lower price than the two hundred bucks Angelina was charging, and Lil could still turn a pretty profit.

It was high time she figured out a way to make enough money to keep this place in good running order, since she'd never charge her friends rent. That wouldn't be right, but this was different. Definitely worth looking into.

Big Martha, her roomie at Walter Stiles, had always talked about how easy it was to set up a business online. Maybe couchsurfing.com was the answer to Lil's financial constraints. Plus she could meet some nice people. Look how well it worked out with Sera. And now Charlie. And...well, she was still deciding about Abby Ruth.

Being the matriarch of Summer Shoals had long been what made Lil happy. But now that her reputation was tarnished—if only among the few folks who knew where she'd actually been while she claimed to be on vacation—things were different. Time in the big house changed a gal, and not in a good way. If she wanted to make ends meet, she needed to keep her possibilities open.

But the most important thing she'd learned in prison was that she never wanted to go back. She couldn't sit around and wait for the law to clear her name. Lil needed to find Jessie Wyatt's darned gauntlets herself.

JENNY, Teague, and Grayson had spent the better part of Sunday out at the baseball field. Teague coaching, Grayson playing, and Jenny cheering, so she was glad they'd been invited to dinner at Summer Haven tonight.

Not having to cook was always a plus, but Jenny'd had her doubts that Grayson would eat Lil's chicken mull, because what ten-year-old liked stew? But he surprised her and gulped it down like Popeye with spinach. *Guess I'll be learning to make this white chicken stuff.*

"Miss Lillian, I can honestly say I've never had better chicken mull." Teague sat back from the twelve-person fruitwood table in Summer Haven's formal dining room and patted his flat stomach. He flashed a grin at the others in the room—Maggie, Sera, Sera's husband, and Grayson—before aiming its full wattage in Jenny's direction.

Just to needle him, she poked him in the side. "You better watch your waistline. Otherwise your wedding tuxedo won't fit." Which was a big bunch of baloney because she'd seen the six-pack he was sporting under his shirt. It would take a lot more than Lil's delicious dinner to make the man she loved flabby.

"Until our friend Charlie stayed for a visit, I'd honestly forgotten how much I enjoy cooking for a man," Lil said.

Teague slid a sideways look Jenny's way. "Sure wish Jenny felt the same."

"It's called modern family life, Castro." This time, she threw a halfhearted punch toward his shoulder, but he caught her fist and pulled her into his lap. "I work, you work. I cook, you cook."

Grayson piped up from the other end of the table. "I like it best when Teague cooks pizza."

Jenny laughed. "It's interesting how he cooks pizza and it always ends up in a Pizza Pie in the Sky box."

Teague's arms tightened around her. "I know my limitations."

Jenny pressed a slow kiss to his cheek, letting him know that in her mind, he had no limitations. Then she started to rise. "Lil, let me help y'all with the dishes."

"No, you young people enjoy sitting still for a few minutes. Maggie, Sera, and I've got it."

A few minutes later, the three women returned with coffee for the adults and a mug of hot chocolate for Grayson.

"Teague," Lil said. "Anything new on the Jessie Wyatt case?"

"No," he said. "Only dead ends so far. It's like those gem-stoned gauntlets vanished."

"Please tell me you found out they're not actually worth anything except for the sentimental value," Lil said hopefully.

"No. Jessie's family has confirmed that the gauntlets were actually worth quite a bit. They'd had them appraised."

"That makes this a lot more serious crime,"

Lil said.

"After questioning everyone who was inside during the interment, it seems that the gauntlets had to be taken before the casket was ever rolled into the mausoleum."

"I feel like they were still on the casket inside." Lil slowly shook her head. "I wish I could be certain."

"We'll get it figured out," Teague assured her.

Lil turned her attention to Jenny. "Have you heard from your mom? We're getting worried because she hasn't called."

"Not even a text," Maggie added.

"Y'all know Mom. If God himself told her the ocean was full of fish, she'd figure out a way to argue they were dinosaurs. She's just flexing her independence muscles. When she was on that around-the-country road trip before she landed here in Summer Shoals, sometimes I wouldn't hear from her for more than two weeks at a time."

"Weren't you concerned?" Lil asked.

"Absolutely not. If I got anxious every time Mom went her own way, I'd need a pharmacy full of Prozac," she said with a laugh.

Sera shifted in her chair to look directly at her. "For some reason, I have a bad feeling about this vacation of hers. I think we need to get in touch with her."

"Do you know something we don't?" Maggie said.

"No, it's just one of my feelings."

Jenny wasn't normally one to put a lot of stock in woo-woo stuff, but when Sera had a feeling, she listened. "What do you mean?"

"Her aura seemed grayish months ago, before I went to California. Maybe she was just tired and needed this holiday as much as she claimed."

"What color is Mom's aura normally?"

"You have to ask?" Sera said.

"Turquoise?" Maggie asked.

Teague tapped his fingers against his coffee cup. "I bet it's amber, like a shot of quality whiskey."

"Oh, no," Sera said. "She's fire red all the way."

Everyone at the table laughed because that was totally Abby Ruth Cady. But Jenny quickly sobered. She and her mother were developing a closer relationship now that they both lived in Summer Shoals. But they were private people and wore shells of self-protection that would do an armadillo proud. So if Sera and the others were concerned, Jenny should be too. She reached into her purse and pulled out her cell. "I'll put her on speaker phone."

Sera's quick smile broadcast her appreciation.

With one tap on her favorites, Jenny's phone was dialing her mom's number. And with every ring, her stomach tightened more. Why wasn't voicemail picking up? More importantly, why wasn't her mom picking up?

Finally, the ringing stopped. "Hello?"

Relief rushed through Jenny even as she realized her mom's tone of voice sounded different. Distracted. Beat down. "Mom, where are you?"

"Well, hello to you too, Miss Nosy. I could ask you the same thing."

"I'm at Summer Haven having a family dinner. We missed you tonight."

"That's why you sound like you're at the bottom of the well. You have me on speaker phone, don't you?"

"Everyone wanted to say hi."

"Hi, Mimi," Grayson hollered, grinning through his marshmallow mustache. "What are you gonna bring me from your vacation?"

"Grayson!" Jenny scolded.

"Well, I'm debating between a gun that shoots pieces of potato or a catapult. You have a preference?"

"Both," he said.

On the other end, she chuckled, but the sound was missing something, some of its edge. "We'll see."

"So." Jenny tried to sound casual. "Where are you now?"

"Do I have to remind you this is a grownup vacation and that not everyone sitting at that table is of age?"

"Things aren't the same without you around," Maggie chimed in. "Are you having a good time?"

"If by *good time* you mean Bill, Bob, and Billy Bob, then yes, I'm having a fine time."

"Grayson, I think it's time for you to go play with your Legos," Jenny said quickly.

Teague was shaking his head in a way that said he wanted to cup his palms over his own ears. "C'mon, Gray. Let's go make that castle we were talking about earlier."

"Bye, Mimi," Grayson yelled. "I can't wait to see what you buy me!"

"Sorry, Mom," Jenny said when the two men in her life were in the other room. "Apparently, he's being raised in a barn."

"Nothing wrong with a man who wants to expand his arsenal."

Lil blew on her coffee and took a dainty sip. "You never did tell us exactly where you are, dear."

"Somewhere between here and there," Abby Ruth replied.

"Are you worried we're planning to come crash your date with Billy Bob?" Maggie asked, laughter clear in her voice.

"No. I'm wondering why you feel the need to check up on a grown woman who's been running her own damn life for a lot of years now."

Jenny reeled back at the bite in her mom's words. True, Abby Ruth Cady was not fond of people getting up in her business, but that was uncalled for. "Mom, these are your friends. And in case you've forgotten, I'm your daughter. You're *only* daughter. We care about you, so please don't snap off our heads."

"I didn't ask any of you to care about me."

Lord, the chest punches just kept coming. Her mom could be a ring-tailed tooter, but this...this...attack from her felt like the reaction of a Rottweiler put in one too many dog fights. Something had her mom backed into a corner. "If you don't want to tell us where you are, that's absolutely your right. Forget we ever called and—"

"Fine, I'm in New Orleans," she barked.

"Louisiana!" Sera bounced in her seat. "Oh, I love jambalaya. And jazz. And Jackson Square."

"Have you visited Café du Monde?" Maggie leaned in toward the phone. "I swear I gain five pounds just thinking about all the powdered sugar on those beignets."

"The Audubon Aquarium is definitely worth a visit," Lil added.

"I'll take your suggestions under advisement," her mom said, but Jenny knew that meant she had no intention of doing anything they'd mentioned. What in the world had put her in this mood?

"Do you know when you'll be home?" she asked her mom.

"You'll know that about the time I get there." And she hung up.

The sudden silence on the other end of Jenny's phone seemed as dark as her mom's out-of-whack aura.

CHAPTER 7

*L*il's heart was hurting for Jenny after the conversation that prompted her to punch at her phone's end button until they were all certain the call had been disconnected.

From the other end of the table, Marcus cleared his throat. "I feel as if I was privy to something personal, something I shouldn't have been listening to. If you'll all excuse me, I'll head upstairs."

Sera shot everyone at the table an apologetic smile and followed her husband.

"I'm so sorry about that," Jenny said. "I don't know why Mom was so testy."

"Maybe she simply had a bad day." Lil tried to infuse her words with surprise, but the truth was Abby Ruth seemed to be moody pretty often. She had a short fuse, that one.

Jenny sighed. "I'd like to say it's just Mom in one of her moods, but something feels off."

"Lil?" Maggie tilted her head, as if she were looking at a particularly suspicious crack in a house's foundation. "You and Abby Ruth didn't by chance have an argument before she left, did you?"

Everyone fell silent, and Lil's mouth dropped wide. She set her coffee cup down and folded her arms. "Absolutely not!"

"Well, don't act like it's a farfetched an idea. You two have had a scuffle or two."

Jenny picked up her cup and stared into it. "She did leave in a hurry. Mom's always been a bit of a tumbleweed, but this trip came out of nowhere. She missed Grayson's talent show, which she'd been looking forward to."

"She didn't leave because of me. I miss her as much as y'all do." Okay, so maybe she and Abby Ruth didn't always see eye to eye, but she had not left because of Lil. She raised her right hand, ready to swear on the Summer family Bible. "I promise."

Maggie gave her a smile. "I'm sorry, but I had to ask. Sometimes you can be a bit bossy. And when you two lock horns, I never know who to put my money on. But since Summer Haven is your home, I knew all along if someone had to leave, it would be Abby Ruth."

"Well, we didn't argue. But if that were the case, Abby Ruth Cady would've stomped up a good ol' goodbye storm on her way out the door."

"You've got a point," Jenny said. "Mom isn't one to tippy-toe around."

"Which is why she and Lil are always sparking friction. They're so much alike in that way." Maggie got up and poured herself a cup of coffee. "Warm up, Lil?"

"No. I'm good." It made her blood run cold that her very best friend would think she could be so rude as to run off a houseguest, even if said houseguest had been invited while she'd been away. Water under the bridge. She and Abby Ruth had found a way to peacefully cohabitate.

Maggie sat back down at the table. "Jenny, can you help us bring your mom's stuff back in from her trailer? No need to tell her that we stored it out there and rented out her room while she was gone. If we think she sounded grumpy before, that ought to make her feel really unwelcome."

"Sure thing." Jenny pushed back from the table.

Maggie led the way out of the house toward

Abby Ruth's twenty-four-foot horse trailer. The fancy white gooseneck with a turquoise-and-red flame down the side sat beside the carriage house. The hitch was supported by a big block of wood to keep it from sinking into the red Georgia clay.

She grabbed the bolt cutters leaning against the old magnolia tree stump in front of the carriage house. "That's odd. Did one of y'all use these? I could've sworn they were hanging inside the door next to the rakes."

"Pffft." Lil shrugged. "Those things weigh more than I do. I don't know how you swing them around like they're nothing."

"Shouldn't leave them out. They won't work worth a toot once they're rusty." Maggie headed to the carriage house and disappeared inside to put them away.

Lil reached under the fender well of the trailer to pluck out the hide-a-key. But as she stepped in front of the rear door, key in hand, the heavy-duty chrome Master lock was hanging open. "Someone forgot to lock this."

Maggie closed the door to the carriage house behind her and stopped in her tracks. "Oh, no. When I was putting things in the trailer I was sidetracked by the mailman delivering the new set of socket wrenches I ordered. I must've forgotten to come back out and lock it up." The color drained from her face. "I can't believe I did that."

Jenny snatched the padlock off the back of the trailer and slid open the door. There was a loud collective sigh as they all stared at the undisturbed boxes inside. "No worries," Jenny said. "Probably best Mom never hears about this, though."

"Thanks, y'all. She'd never trust me again." Maggie raised a foot into the bed of the trailer and pulled herself up inside. "Thank goodness. Everything looks just like we left it."

It took fifteen minutes to move the few things Abby Ruth kept inside the house back into the Sweet Vidalia Room. The rest of the trailer was filled with boxes neatly marked with their contents. A rolling storage unit.

"Good as new," Jenny said.

"I'll lock up the trailer," Maggie said. "Y'all go on inside."

But before they made it to Summer Haven's front door, Maggie yelled from behind them, her voice as high-pitched as a lassoed pig. "Come quick!"

Lil turned. "What's wrong?"

"You're not going to believe this." Maggie shouted from inside Abby Ruth's trailer. "And someone get Teague!"

"I'm on it," Jenny called back and leaned inside the front door.

"What's the matter?" Lil asked when she made it back across the yard. "You look like you saw a ghost, for heaven's sake."

"Worse." Maggie stomped in a circle. "So much worse."

"How can things be worse than seeing a ghost?" Lil asked.

Before Maggie could answer, Jenny came jogging toward Abby Ruth's trailer.

Maggie took a visible gulp of air. "You know how Abby Ruth never let us in here alone?" She closed her eyes. "Well, I was curious and wanted an unchaperoned peek at her gun collection."

Jenny chuckled. "We won't tell."

"No. That's not the problem. Look!" Maggie hitched her thumb toward the inside of the trailer. "The space at the front is empty."

"What?" Jenny stumbled back, and Lil took her arm to steady her. "Are you saying all Mom's guns are gone?"

Teague joined them at a dead run but wasn't even breathing heavy when he skidded to a stop at the back of the trailer. "What happened?"

Jenny pointed inside.

Teague didn't waste one moment. He jumped into the trailer and marched straight to the front. The echo of his boots against the aluminum floor sounded like a drum roll.

Lil, Maggie, and Jenny quickly followed. At the gooseneck end of the trailer, the carpeted dressing area Abby Ruth used as her personal gun safe was stark naked except for the fine linens on the bunk.

Not one pistol. Not a rifle or shotgun hung from the hooks on the wall.

"Damn," Teague said under his breath.

"Maybe she moved them or took them with her," Jenny reasoned.

Teague peered at a U-shaped piece of metal.

"What's that?" Lil asked. "It looks like a ring like they put in a bull's nose. Wouldn't surprise me one bit if Abby Ruth rode a big ol' bucker and saved this as a souvenir."

When she reached out to touch it, Teague blocked her way. "Please don't contaminate the crime scene. The bull nose ring is actually the other half of this lock. Someone cut the thing off."

Properly chastised, Lil covered her cheek with a hand, trying to cool her hot embarrassment over her investigative faux pas. The other gals probably would've known better than to touch evidence.

"Bolt cutters," Maggie said. "They used my bolt cutters. It's all my fault."

"It's no one's fault," Lil said. "But someone will have to tell Abby Ruth."

"She'll come unglued," Maggie moaned.

Jenny blew out a breath. "I guess it should be me."

"No, Sera is the only woman for this job," Lil said. "Because we'll need all the Zen and balanced chakras in the universe to settle your mom down." Sera was the only one Lil knew who had enough patience. Plus, it was likely Sera would be returning to California, a safe distance from Abby Ruth's backlash.

Teague held up his hand. "Now, let's not get ahead of ourselves. I'll start working on this. Maybe we'll recover the guns before you have to tell her anything. I'll get my guys to come out here and fingerprint everything. Now, everyone out."

Jenny's shoulders sagged as she backtracked, and Lil felt pretty much the same way. With all these Hollywood-types invading Summer Shoals and making a ruckus, it was highly unlikely that Teague would have free time to hunt down missing guns.

"What are we going to do?" Maggie said.

"I can't lie to her," Jenny said. "She's like a human lie detector, always knows when I'm not telling her the whole truth. But if we tell her the truth, all hell will break loose."

"Mmm-hmm," Teague said. "About like a bull with a flank strap tied one notch too tight."

"Well since she's not here and we don't know when she's coming back," Lil said, "I say what she doesn't know won't hurt her."

"You mean we should hide this from her?" Maggie's eyes were wide with horror.

"I like to call this tactic *justified omission*."

AS IF SHE hadn't already been heartsick over the earlier conversation with her mom, now Jenny's stomach was a mess of worry and confusion. All fifteen of her mom's guns. Missing. Jenny plopped down on the running board of the trailer. The sun was setting, the graying clouds matching the color of her mood perfectly. "Maybe keeping quiet for now would be smart. Mom will go crazy when she finds out."

"Can't say that I blame her," Lil agreed.

"Those guns had to be worth a fortune. I don't know if my homeowners' insurance will cover something like that."

"I highly doubt it. Her guns are pretty rare." Jenny ran a hand through her hair, snagging strands on her beautiful engagement ring. She plucked them out of the setting and let them fall to the ground. "Why did this have to happen when she's out of town?"

"It's all my fault. I'm so sorry," Maggie said. "If I hadn't forgotten to lock the other door, no one would've ever been able to get this far. I feel awful."

"Who knew, besides all of us, that she had guns in the trailer?" Teague rubbed his hand across his five-o'clock shadow. "Anyone?"

Although she longed for him to put his arms around her and comfort her, Jenny knew Teague was already in cop mode. Exactly what they needed right now. "This horse trailer hasn't held horses one day since Mom bought it back in 2005. Travel and a rolling gun transport. That's all it's ever been to her. Regardless, she didn't go around advertising what she had inside."

Teague's radio went off. "Sorry," he said as he stepped away, and Jenny felt the loss of his calming presence.

"Do you know what kinds of guns they were? If we can get a list of them, or at least some of them, maybe we can start asking around," Lil said. "Help Teague out."

Jenny cast a glance at the trailer. "Mom has a detailed accounting of those guns. Trust me, sometimes I think they mean more to her than Grayson and I do."

"That's not true," Lil said with a frown. "You couldn't possibly believe that."

"Oh, wait until you see where and how she keeps her gun inventory," Jenny said with a panicked laugh. "You might change your mind about that." She hopped to her feet and scrambled into what used to be her mom's gun room. "She keeps important papers in a locker in here."

"Teague told us not to touch anything," Maggie said from behind her.

"The thief wouldn't have known this area existed." Jenny said. "It's like a secret compartment, looks like a wall panel, unless you know what you're looking for."

Lil and Maggie followed Jenny, filing back into the trailer. They marched past the boxes holding her mom's remaining household belongings to the dressing area in front. Jenny stepped inside and pushed against a wooden panel on the left. A compartment popped open.

"Very nice," Maggie said. "That's clever."

Jenny pulled out a vertical file and flipped through it. Then she reached inside the compartment to the right. "Here it is." She lifted out the square maroon photo album her mom had always kept on her bedside table back in Texas. "This isn't your average brag book."

Maggie flipped through the pages. "Seriously? This is like a baby book. Only for guns!"

Each page held pictures, facts, and target practice dates and scores. Detailed history. More details than the average mom would've ever filled in about her kid.

"I know." Jenny tried to keep her voice level. "Isn't it a shame her guns rated a nicer baby book than I did?"

"Stop that," Lil scolded. "You know she loves you."

Teague poked his head inside the small area and sighed. "Didn't I tell y'all not to touch anything?"

Uh-oh. "But I remembered Mom keeps an inventory of her guns." Jenny hustled the other women out of the trailer. Once they were back outside, she pointed at the book in Maggie's hands.

Teague rubbed his temples the way he did when Grayson's pup Bowzer piddled on the floor and let his head drop for a few seconds. When he looked up again, he said. "Get me a copy of all the information. Sorry, Jenny, duty calls. Problem down at the grocery store. Someone's pitching a fit over something called truffle oil. I know all these rich folks are spending a lot of money, but I'll be glad when they leave and we can get back to sleepy Summer Shoals." He leaned down and gave Jenny a kiss that made her want to throw her arms around his neck and never let go. Instead, she released him and watched him leave.

Maggie pulled a carpenter's pencil from her shirt pocket and a small spiral notebook from the pocket of her cargo pants. "I'll jot down the details."

Jenny started reading off the specs for each gun, each detailed on a two-page spread. When they reached the sixteenth set of pages, Jenny said, "Well, sorry, Maggie. That was all a big waste of time. Look, here's an insurance list of all of her guns."

Lil grabbed the paper from Jenny. "This is

exactly what we need. I bet the gun club guys could help us out."

Maggie thumbed through the pages of the album. "Well, look here. I found some interesting snapshots." She spun the leather book around and placed it back in Jenny's hands.

Jenny couldn't hold in the grin that spread across her face. "I didn't know she had these." She ran a finger across a picture of her mom looking so young, holding Grayson when he was hours old. Her hand covered her heart as she flipped the page and saw the collage of pictures immortalizing her childhood. Cheerleading, AAU softball, and the prom picture of her and Teague with him down on bended knee, offering her a corsage of white roses.

"If there's any way we can recover these guns before she gets home, I'll be forever indebted. There's no telling what she'll do if she finds out they're gone. Lil, she's liable to take a lesson from Grayson's castle-building book and dig a moat. Maybe build a watch tower."

"As long as she doesn't stock up on alligators." Maggie pulled out her phone. "Here. I'll take a picture of the inventory and send it to everyone in a group text. That way, we can split up and make better time on the gun hunt."

"You know Teague wouldn't be happy about y'all getting involved with this," Jenny said.

"Are you saying we should wait?" Maggie asked.

"No, but you might want to keep it on the DL for now. And I'll hope he doesn't ask me about it."

"First thing in the morning, Maggie, Sera, and I will stop by the gun shop. You okay with that?" Lil said, looking to Jenny for agreement.

She should say no. Knew she should say no. Teague was the sheriff of this county and her fiancé. She should tell them to let him handle it. "Yep."

So much for good intentions.

CHAPTER 8

*A*lthough Sera had felt bad about leaving the table last night after the strange phone conversation with Abby Ruth, she'd figured it was a situation the others could mull over, since she couldn't always put her friends before Marcus. But when they'd all trampled in the house hollering and moaning about Abby Ruth's missing guns, not to mention the mess Teague's guys were making of the horse trailer in the fingerprinting process, Sera had vowed to do whatever it took to help find them.

So this morning, she jumped behind the wheel of her sunshine-yellow VW van, feeling the familiar exuberance she'd so often experienced by teaming up with these ladies. "Come on, girls. Load up."

Lil hopped in to ride shotgun, and Maggie slid the van's side door closed with a grunt. "Where is Marcus anyway?"

"He was out of bed and gone before the sun came up. But I'm not thinking about him right now." Because if she did, she might worry about why he hadn't asked her to go along. Sera waved a hand. "We've got more important things to do. Like hunt down a gun-nabber."

"Yeah," Maggie shouted from the back seat.

"Hope we get lucky," Lil said quietly, her brows knitting together.

"Don't worry, Lil. Those gun fanatics stick together. I'm betting that the people down at the gun shop will be able to point us in the right direction if they haven't already heard something about Abby Ruth's guns themselves."

When Sera pulled into the lot for Bull's Eye gun shop, she parked on the far side of the building. Marcus seemed to be everywhere in Summer Shoals these days, and no matter how terrible it seemed, even to herself, he was not invited to her investigation party. He'd catch one whiff of the missing guns and either tell her she shouldn't be involved or come up with some movie idea.

They walked inside, and a tall man in a Bull's Eye logo T-shirt and camo ball cap looked up from behind the counter, his eyes full of excitement. For a moment anyway, because once he focused in on them, his expression faltered. "Ladies, what can I do for you?"

The man's disappointment in spotting three normal women meant only one thing. "Had a lot of big names in here the past few days?" Sera asked.

That light in his eyes sparked again. "You best believe it. You'll never guess who was in here looking for guns for his collection."

Easy. "Brad Huffman." Sera tilted her head slightly, casting a smile in his direction. *I'll play your little game.*

His mouth moved, but nothing came out. He blinked. "How in the world would you know that?"

She batted her eyelashes. Being Marcus Johanneson's wife did come with a few perks. She knew lots of intimate things about the Hollywood rich and famous. When she was living here in Summer Shoals, she'd kept up through the tabloids at the Piggly Wiggly checkout counter. Those tell-all newspapers held more truth than the average person realized.

The guy grinned a toothy smile. "Yeah, well, you won't believe who else stopped by recently."

Oh, game on, Sera thought. But Maggie took the bait first. "Who?"

The man tugged on his ball cap and smirked. "Marcus Johanneson. Bigger than life. Know who *he* is?"

Sera choked.

Lil slapped her on the back. "You okay?"

Her face hot, she nodded.

"He might shoot part of a movie right here in my store," the guy said proudly. "He's a big-time Hollywood producer and director. Used to be an actor. Heartthrob type. Surely you ladies would know him, right?"

"Of course we've heard of him," Lil said. "We were with him at Jessie Wyatt's funeral. Why, in fact, he's almost like family."

Sera elbowed her for name-dropping.

Lil elbowed her back and said to the gun shop owner, "Nice guy, isn't he?"

Sera shot Lil a glare and plucked the inventory sheet from her hand to pass it to the man behind the counter. "We're looking for guns. Very special guns. Can you help us?"

"This is your lucky day because special

guns are our business here at Bull's Eye." Then he looked closer at the paper he held between his long fingers and let out a long, high-pitched whistle that sounded like the air being released from a balloon.

"You've seen them?" Sera asked hopefully.

"No, but you're in luck."

"How so?"

He wagged a finger over the list. "Because you can't get those types of guns just anywhere. They're collectibles. Very high-dollar ones at that."

"These were stolen."

"Oh, no. I got no use for stolen property." The man winced and ran his hand across his chin. "Guns the likes of these should be kept in a safe."

"They were locked up."

"Hope you called the cops." The man's eyebrows shot up. "Guns in the wrong hands, that's how people get hurt."

"Yes, which is why we need to find them."

"May not be that easy."

If they couldn't find the guns fast enough, maybe there was another way to keep Abby Ruth from having a meltdown. Sera hitched her purse on her shoulder. She was willing to pull out the platinum card if necessary.

"Maybe we could replace them."

"You won't happen into a shop and buy these off the shelf." The man pulled out a spiral notebook, scribbled something, then tore out the page and slid it her way. "Here. Do some surfing on these websites. If anyone has seen something on your list, this is where you'll hear chatter. Depends on if whoever has them knows what he's got or not. Give me your information and I'll call you if I hear anything."

"Thank you so much." If there was one thing Sera wanted to get done before she had to figure out her own life, it was to help Lil and Maggie solve this problem with the guns. These two ladies had given her a home and purpose when her life was a little off the rails. She wouldn't trade their friendship for anything.

This gun thing was much more than a petty theft. It was a personal attack on their sacred space. And Summer Haven had been her safe place for over a year. Now, the more she was faced with addressing her situation with Marcus, the tighter her ties to this town and its people felt.

"This is helpful." Not completely, but at least they knew one place the guns weren't.

She pulled his spiral notebook over in front of her and wrote her name, Serendipity Johnson, and phone number on it.

With Maggie and Lil on either side of her, Sera left the gun shop. No one said a word as they walked to the van.

Maggie was the last to climb inside. "Y'all thinking what I'm thinking?"

Sera glanced over at Lil and then back at Maggie. "I'm thinking Operation Remington is now in progress."

SERA WAS FINISHING up an impromptu early evening yoga class on Summer Haven's lawn— a welcome relief from thinking about her future and stressing about the missing guns— when Abby Ruth's huge white dually came rambling up the drive. The strange weight Sera had been carrying around her heart since Jessie's funeral eased slightly.

Oh, thank goodness. She's home safe and sound.

That wasn't fair, though, because Sera had no idea if Summer Haven was home for either Abby Ruth or her. But it would be good to have Abby Ruth helping hunt down Jessie's missing gauntlets. The whole team back together again.

Sera smiled at her yoga students. "And release that last breath to clear away all the burdens on your mind. Remember, nothing good comes of worrying about something in the future that may never happen." Something she needed to remind herself on a regular basis these days, because she'd done more than her fair share of worrying about what her tomorrows would look like—with or without Marcus. Whether in California or back here in Summer Shoals. Not to mention she'd spent the past hour pretending to focus as she silently brainstormed ways to put Operation Remington into play. And that did anything but relax her.

By the time Abby Ruth parked and climbed out of her truck, the yoga students were scattering, and Sera had texted Jenny to let her know her mom was home.

Sera couldn't help but notice Abby Ruth's swagger was a little less swaggery than normal. She jogged over to her, the bells around her ankle tinkling lightly as her bare feet bounded across the grass. "Need help with anything?"

Abby Ruth withdrew a small duffel bag from the backseat and handed it over. "I wouldn't mind if you took this in the house."

"You look tired."

"I drove all the way from Ho...uh...New Orleans today. That's a lot of hours for this old butt to be in the driver's seat." She reached back into the truck and pulled out something else.

"Oh, what did you..."

When Abby Ruth swung back around, she had two guns and her grin, though tired, was wide. "Did some shopping while I was on the road."

"And to think some women like shoes," Sera teased.

"It's hard to scare off an intruder with a ballet flat."

Sera wanted to protest, say they didn't need to worry about intruders in Summer Shoals. But the recent disappearance of Abby Ruth's gun collection had blown a hole in that. "Why don't we go inside and get something to drink? I know Maggie and Lil are eager to see you."

"I had a feeling that Lil might not cry big ol' tears if I never returned to her precious Summer Haven. In fact, I thought about just—"

"You know what?" Sera grabbed her arm.

"You're home now, and that's all that counts. Last I heard, Maggie was planning to make her special chicken pot pie, and you're right in time for dinner."

"Supper will wait." Abby Ruth turned the other direction, the one leading directly toward her horse trailer. "I want to introduce my new babies to the rest of the family."

That absolutely wouldn't do. When they'd discovered Abby Ruth's guns were gone, they'd all agreed it would be best to break the news to her gently after they'd fixed her a couple gallons of Maggie's special iced tea. All hell would break loose if Sera let Abby Ruth walk into that trailer now to find her other babies missing. Not to mention the black fingerprinting gook smeared all over the place in there. *Think fast, Sera.*

"Jenny will probably kill me for saying this." She darted out in front of Abby Ruth and pivoted so she was walking backward while Abby Ruth was striding forward. "But she was the one who was so worried when we called you the other night."

That stopped Abby Ruth in her tracks. "My daughter? Worried about me?"

"You make it sound crazy."

"Cady women take care of themselves."

Sera did a do-si-do move that lured Abby Ruth back toward the house. "I'm sure that's true, but I'm telling you what I saw the other night, and Jenny was concerned. Don't you think you could spare a few minutes to call her? It would probably hurt her feelings if she found out you prioritized your guns over her." After all, Jenny had already endured the sting of Abby Ruth's guns taking up her brag book's premium pages.

And goodness knew Sera needed Jenny as backup when she broke the news to Abby Ruth about the guns. In fact, they probably should've booked a couple of Teague's off-duty deputies because this was going to be u-u-ugly.

"I don't remember raising such a sensitive daughter, but fine. She must be getting soft now that she's all googly-eyed in love again." Abby Ruth laughed and stowed her guns back in her truck, pressing the key fob to lock them up. "Or she could be getting hormonal." She rubbed her hands together as she and Sera headed for the house. "Oh, what I wouldn't give for a Castro-Cady baby."

Based on the glass of wine Jenny had tossed back after discovering her mom's guns were missing, Sera was certain that wasn't the case, but what was the harm in leveraging a soft spot? "Could be."

They made their way inside, and Sera called out, "Guess who's home, girls?"

Lil and Maggie came rushing out of the kitchen, but Maggie looked as if she wanted to turn and hightail it back in the other direction when she laid eyes on Abby Ruth.

Sera dodged around Abby Ruth to wrap her arms around the paling Maggie and steady her. Poor thing didn't have much of a poker face.

"Abby Ruth," Maggie said. "It's good to have you back. We've missed you." Sera shoved Maggie in Abby Ruth's direction. She wrapped her in big hug, which always tickled Sera's funny bone because Maggie was much shorter and only came up to Abby Ruth's shoulder. Sometimes less when Abby Ruth was wearing her cowboy boots with the taller heel. Abby Ruth patted her on the back. "You'd think I'd taken a trip to Antarctica and been gone for months."

Lil said, "Well, when you traipse off and don't tell anyone where you're going, we have a right to worry."

Abby Ruth shot Lil a raised-brow look over Maggie's shoulder. "Do you need me to tell you the story of the pot and the kettle?"

She had a point. When Lil had turned herself in at the federal prison camp, she hadn't said a word to anyone. Granted, that had been before Abby Ruth came to live at Summer Haven, but Lil's duplicity all those months ago was still a sore spot with Maggie.

"Guess we all have our reasons," Lil said.

Thankfully, the front door swung open and broke the tension between the two women. And as if he'd lived at Summer Haven every day of his life, Marcus strolled in like king of the manor. "Ladies."

"Who in hell's blue bells is this hot hunk?" Abby Ruth said, her swagger suddenly back and in full force.

Sera stopped Abby Ruth before she embarrassed herself. "Abby Ruth Cady, I'd like you to meet my...my...husband, Marcus Johanneson."

Abby Ruth's expression changed from flirtatious to impressed. "Well, if that don't beat all I ever stepped in. I pictured you a lot older looking. And shorter. Guess I should've put two and two together. The funeral. Sera. You being in the business and all." She reached out to take Marcus's hand, pumped it up and down like she was trying to get water from an old-fashioned well. "Sure is nice to meet you. I loved what you did with your movie *For Guns or Country.*"

Oh, if Sera didn't nip this in the bud right now, Marcus would stand there all night and talk about filmmaking. She gave him a move-it-along look.

Apparently, they hadn't lost all their marital mojo because he nodded. "Abby Ruth, it's a pleasure to meet someone who likes a good war movie. But if you'll excuse me, I have some...ah...calls to make."

Both Sera and Abby Ruth watched him climb the stairs to the second floor.

"You know, I've seen pictures of him all these years," Abby Ruth commented. "But he's a damn sight sexier than I ever imagined. Don't let that get away from you, Sera."

Definitely not a discussion Sera felt up to having tonight. "It's complicated, but when I get it worked out, I'll let you know. But enough about him. Did you hear that someone made off with Jessie Wyatt's gauntlets?"

"It was on the local radio when I was coming in. That must've been a fiasco," Abby Ruth said.

"It's been interesting, to say the least. Would you like something to drink before Jenny gets here?"

Abby Ruth struck her notorious pose with her hip cocked out. "I don't know why she's all fired up to see me tonight."

Lil shot her a disapproving look.

"What?" Abby Ruth lifted a shoulder. "It's not that I don't want to see my daughter. I just needed...wanted...some time to get settled again."

A few minutes later, Jenny rushed through the door. "Mom!" She pulled Abby Ruth in for a tight hug and mouthed over her shoulder to the grannies, *Does she know yet?*

All three of them shook their heads vigorously.

"We want to hear all about your vacation." A slightly forced grin on her face, Jenny released her mom. Then she hurried into the parlor and planted her behind on the velvet divan. Abby Ruth glanced at Sera, her question clear in her expression: *Has my daughter been drinking?*

"I'll get us some tea." Maggie made a beeline for the kitchen.

Yes, they would break the conversational ice with some chitchat and Maggie's tea, then they would tell her what happened. Sera said, "I bet you ate some fabulous food. What was your favorite?"

Abby Ruth sprawled her long form on the velvet divan beside Jenny and propped her boot heels on the turned leg antique ottoman. "Oh, you know that thing at that place."

"Bananas Foster at Brennan's?" Sera asked.

"Yeah, that's it."

"And what about Bourbon Street?" Maggie said, setting a tray of tea on the piecrust table. "I love Bourbon Street. Although most folks were drinking lots of things aside from bourbon. What'd you have?"

"I had that drink at that bar." Abby Ruth dropped her foot to the ground.

"A hurricane at Pat O'Brien's, I bet," Sera said. "Marcus loves those."

Abby Ruth snapped her fingers. "That's the one."

"Are you sure?" Lil asked.

"Why wouldn't I be?" Abby Ruth scowled. "I was there, wasn't I?"

"It's just that..." Lil glanced at Sera, but she had no idea what the message was supposed to be. "Brennan's has been closed for renovations and isn't due to reopen for at least two months. And I read on CNN a fire broke out in Pat O'Brien's block of Bourbon Street and caused enough damage that they evacuated all the businesses until an investigation could be done."

Abby Ruth jumped up from her slouch and strode toward the doorway to the entry hall. "What's with y'all? I feel like you're a pack of jackals chasing after a half-lame baby gazelle. What does it matter what I did or didn't do? Quite honestly, I'm not sure it's any of your business."

That brought Jenny to her feet, and she squared off with her mom. "You know what gives us the right? We love you and care about you, even though you're the most hardheaded, most jackass stubborn woman we all know."

Abby Ruth pulled her hands up on her hips. "Excuse me?"

Jenny kept right on. "And when you take off without a word, it makes us worry. And dammit, Mom, that's not fair. In fact, it's downright childish."

Abby Ruth's face paled, but within seconds, her color came back with a vengeance and flooded her face. "Fine, you want me to tell you that you're right? That I didn't visit either of those places?"

"You didn't, did you?" Sera's voice came out soft. A bad feeling crawled up her spine, and she swallowed hard. Did she want to know where Abby Ruth had actually been?

"I'll admit it. In fact, I wasn't in New Orleans at all."

"Then why would you tell us—"

"If I'd wanted you to know where I was going, then I would've shared. But if you feel the need to know my every move, then here's the truth. I was in Houston. Does that satisfy all of you?"

Jenny held out her hand as if to calm her mom. "If it was only a visit back home, then why all the—"

"Because there are some things a woman needs to do alone," Abby Ruth said, her tone high and tight. "And one of those things is hearing a doctor tell her she has breast cancer."

CHAPTER 9

*B*reast cancer? After Abby Ruth's blurted revelation, the parlor went silent. And no matter how many times Sera heard that diagnosis, it set off a primal fear inside her. Too many women were dealing with cancer.

The space was a complete vacuum, as if every smidgen of air, thought, and emotion had been sucked away. Only the television made any noise, but no one was paying any attention to it.

Sera glanced over at Jenny. *Stunned* wasn't an accurate description of her expression. *Devastated* was more like it, and the same feeling was reflected on Lil's and Maggie's faces. Sera had seen people wearing it a few times while traveling with Marcus, especially in countries hit by civil war or natural disaster. It was as if the cosmic carpet had been ripped out from under them.

"Mom?"

"Hellfire," Abby Ruth muttered. "I didn't mean to say that."

Sera didn't know which woman needed a hug more right now. She stood there wishing she could press a reverse button.

Jenny took two stumbling steps forward and cracked her shins against the ottoman.

Sera grabbed her arm. "You should both sit."

But Abby Ruth remained on her feet, her mouth a stubborn line even though her face was drooping with exhaustion. "Are we done with all this show and tell now? I'd like to go out to my trailer."

"You can't be serious." Jenny's voice shook in a way Sera had never heard before. A vibration hinting that she was seconds away from meltdown. "You lay a bomb like that on us and then plan to stroll outside and play with your guns like nothing happened?"

"What's wrong with—"

"My God, I have called you hardheaded and stubborn on plenty of occasions, but I've always believed you weren't as self-absorbed as some people made it sound. But, Mom, now I'm not so sure." Jenny's voice broke on the final word. "Maybe you could stick around for a few minutes and fill us in on this little cancer thing."

Although Jenny might not be able to see it through her anger and hurt, Abby Ruth's weariness and confusion were clear to Sera. They hovered around her in an oval of dark muddy yellow.

"Jenny," Sera said quietly. "Your mom is tired, and I don't think this is helping."

Jenny whirled toward Sera, obviously about to bite off her head and spit it on the floor. Sera raised her chin but softened her eyes, and Jenny seemed to get the message.

"I...uh...okay." Her voice steadier, she turned back to her mom. "But if you're so tired, and I can imagine you are, then I'm asking you to please go up to your room and get some rest. I don't want to fight tonight. Sera's right, this isn't the time."

Abby Ruth's eyes closed. Her nostrils flared as she inhaled. "Jenny, I'm sorry. I..."

Sera could feel the weight of pain inside Abby Ruth right now.

"Can you make it upstairs by yourself?" Jenny slipped an arm around her mother's waist and turned her toward the parlor door.

"I think so."

"Well, that won't cut it. I'm coming with you. I'll help you get unpacked and settled in. I won't ask another question. I promise." She led Abby Ruth into the main hallway but shot Sera a look over her shoulder that wasn't hard to interpret.

Whatever she, Maggie, and Lil did, they absolutely could not let Abby Ruth know about the missing guns.

Sera sat with Lil and Maggie in complete silence. Soft conversation floated down from the second floor, and with every one of Abby Ruth's and Jenny's footsteps, the tired old boards of Summer Haven creaked overhead.

The rainbow of color that usually filled any room these girls were in had turned to black and white and gray so quickly.

The sound of Abby Ruth's door clicking closed was followed by Jenny's footsteps on the stairs. She descended, ever so slowly, as if any distance between her mother and her right now was too far.

"I think we all could use a good night's sleep after that," Jenny said.

Sera's heart felt as if it would break into a million pieces. The story wasn't a new one.

Almost every family had been attacked by cancer. But that didn't make it easier when you were the one in the disease's crosshairs. The emotional toll it took on the victim and their families was so personal. Made a person feel so incredibly alone.

Even those who survived had a rough run of it, bearing a scar. The sick, the caretakers, and every friend and loved one shared in that journey.

Sera should know, losing her mother to colon cancer. All the healthy eating, nature loving, and good living hadn't protected her.

"This is one bad day," Jenny said.

"Uh...uh...oh," Maggie stammered. "I think it might have just gotten worse. Looks what's on TV."

They all swung around to the massive flat-screen Abby Ruth had, as Lil liked to say, *desecrated* her parlor with.

Sera dropped to the ottoman to watch. "That's footage of Jessie's funeral." Those damn newshounds. They'd made a mockery of her friend's final farewell. Well, the paparazzi and Jessie's family had.

Maggie grabbed the clicker and turned up the volume. "I hope I didn't see what I think I saw."

"What?" Sera asked.

Maggie pointed to the television.

The newscaster's voice was full of drama. "It's no secret that Jessie Wyatt's famous gauntlets disappeared during her funeral. But tonight, we bring you exclusive footage of the moments just prior to the theft." They cut to a clip of a family member talking about the true worth of the gauntlets. "Those rumors about Jessie's gauntlets? All true. They're worth a fortune and they belong to this family!" The newscaster leaned forward as if looking into every home across the country. "You tell us, America, do you think an old Southern belle wanted Jessie's gauntlets for her very own?"

The screen zoomed in, showing a crowd around Jessie's casket, but with one woman touching the gauntlets. And there was no mistaking that blue-blond hair. "Oh, no," Sera breathed.

"That's what I thought I saw," Maggie said. "Good Lord, Lil."

"Who the heck does he think he's calling old?" Lil protested.

"That should be the least of your concerns. This could be serious," Maggie said. "Your hand is right there."

"When will this night end?" Jenny groaned

as the newscaster transitioned to a story about a zombie crawl happening in Atlanta.

Sera walked over and wrapped Jenny in a hug. "For you, it ends right now. Do you need me to drive you home? Or you can stay here."

"I can drive. I've got to pick up Grayson from his friend's house." She turned and headed to the door. "I'm so glad you are all here for Mom."

"And for you, dear. We're here for you too. Don't you forget that. Goodnight," Lil said.

Sera walked Jenny out, and Jenny said, "Mom can't find out about those guns. Not yet."

"We're on it," Sera said, hoping like heck they could come up with a plan that would recover the guns in a hurry. Jenny drove off, and Sera stood there wondering how so much chaos could swirl up like a cat-five hurricane in such a short time.

She went inside, and Maggie and Lil looked as frazzled as she felt.

"We need to clean the fingerprint mess out of Abby Ruth's trailer pronto," Sera said.

"At least we can fix this part even if we haven't been able to track down the guns themselves," Maggie said. "I'll go get the cleaning stuff and meet y'all out there."

It took all three of them nearly an hour to get the mess cleaned up. "I hope those fingerprints help Teague and his people find Abby Ruth's guns, because otherwise I'm not sure a clue is worth this kind of mess," Lil said.

Maggie collected the soiled paper towels into a trash bag, and they made their way back to the house.

Inside, there was only a meager good-night between them as they went their separate ways to call it a night. Sera tiptoed into her room. Marcus had fallen asleep with his phone in his hand. As usual.

Unusual was the Spotify playlist playing softly. She took the phone from his hand and closed the app. She placed the phone on the nightstand then undressed and climbed into bed. Marcus's warmth and the steady pattern of his breathing against the Cherokee Rose Room's frilly cabbage rose wallpaper soothed her.

She laid her head on his chest.

Marcus wrapped his arms around her, his big frame engulfing her. She'd always felt safe in his arms—a familiar calming place, but not one that could chase away the sadness she was feeling tonight.

"I didn't mean to wake you," she

whispered.

"Mmmm. It's okay." He sifted his fingers through her hair. "You sound sad again."

He knew her so well. She tilted her chin up, looking into his eyes. "Abby Ruth has breast cancer."

His brows lowered, and he pulled her closer. "I'm sorry."

"I knew something was wrong. Her aura started shifting before I went back to California. I thought it was all the crazy stuff going on around here at the time. What if I'd mentioned it to her? Maybe I could've—"

"Sera, you're not a psychic. It's not like you have a crystal ball."

Which was seriously too bad.

"Let me help you forget about all that gray stuff. Let me make you see pretty colors." He ran his hand down her back, his normal prelude to sex. "I love you."

"Love has never been the problem." Sex had definitely never been the problem. Their problem had always been lifestyle, and right now she didn't know how to break it to him that she would never leave Summer Shoals while Abby Ruth might be fighting for her life. Would he understand?

Marcus sighed, a gust of warm air against

her hair, and his hand stilled. "But you love these women too."

"Like family." She reconsidered. "No, not *like* family. They are family."

"I thought I was your family."

"Does it have to be one or the other? Try to understand that they need me. Now more than ever." Abby Ruth didn't deserve a one-two punch of stolen guns and cancer. Too much for anyone, even a woman with Texas-size strength.

Suddenly missing the comforting and arousing stroke of Marcus's hand, Sera snuggled closer, which was her normal sign to him that she was in the mood too.

But he didn't immediately take her hint. Instead, he said, "Sera, I don't want to lose you."

She lifted her face to his and kissed him, filling it with all the pent-up emotion she'd been harboring for so long. Minutes later, when their lips parted and they were both breathing heavily, she whispered against his lips, "Then let's see if we can find each other again."

WHEN LIL SHUFFLED into the kitchen the next

morning, she was surprised to see Sera standing near the coffeemaker in one of her flowing gauzy skirts and a T-shirt, a soft smile on her face.

Lil sniffed the air. "That smells an awful lot like real coffee." She couldn't help but hope.

"I thought after last night we might all need a cup of something inspirational, and I figured it was too early for shots of Abby Ruth's whiskey. Plus, we don't want to have to tell her that's missing too."

Lord, if that wasn't the truth, Lil didn't know what was.

Maggie stumbled in, looking like a pinball bouncing off the doorjamb and a chair. "Caffeine," she croaked.

"How did you sleep?" Sera asked.

"Like hell," Maggie muttered.

"Then it's good everything looks brighter and clearer in the light of day."

Lil and Maggie settled in at the farmhouse table while Sera bustled around and placed coffee and bowls of oatmeal in front of them.

Maggie eyed her bowl suspiciously. "This doesn't have any weird stuff in it, does it?"

"Organic peanut butter and a splash of pure maple syrup."

"Yum." Maggie's spoon immediately delved

in.

She'd already shoveled in a big bite when Sera added, "Oh, and maybe a few chia and flax seeds."

"Thammmit, Therra," Maggie sputtered, then swallowed with a grimace. "I let my guard down because you made real coffee."

"Tell me the truth, did that bite taste bad?"

"No," Maggie said, "but those little seed thingies popped in my mouth. Like eating a spoonful of roly-polies. Yuck."

"Girls," Lil cut into the breakfast debate, "we need to talk about Abby Ruth's guns. Finding them is priority number one."

Maggie sloshed back a big sip of coffee, swishing it like mouthwash before she swallowed. "Even after what we saw on TV last night? Because I think keeping your butt out of jail may trump the guns."

The thought of that footage during the celebrity segment made Lil's insides turn mushier than Sera's oatmeal, but she had to put her friend first. "Yes. With Teague busy dealing with all the chaos in town to make much progress on the investigation and Abby Ruth sick, we need to step it up."

"We'd better work fast then," Sera said.

"We'll knock that out quick and then shift

back to those dad-burned gauntlets." Lil sure hoped it was as easy as it sounded in her head.

Maggie blew out a breath. "I know the guy at Bull's Eye said guns like Abby Ruth's can't be bought and sold just anywhere, but I keep thinking we should hit the pawn shops."

"You're right, Mags," Lil said. "But not because we expect to find the guns. What we're after is information."

"I saw a sign for a pawn shop off the interstate when Marcus and I were coming in from the airport. We could stop in there."

"No, ma'am." Lil patted the tabletop twice. "Those pawn shop folks can be a sketchy lot. There's only one place I trust. It's in Atlanta, but I promise it'll be worth the drive." She'd had her own taste of pawning stuff after Harlan died, and Rick at J&R Pawn had done her right.

But before they could all scatter to get dressed, the front doorbell rang. Lil glanced down at her nightgown and robe. "How I wish we could go back to a time when people asked before they called on you."

Sera hopped up from the table. "I'll get it."

Perfect, she could handle the visitor while Lil put on her face and made herself presentable. She was tiptoeing across the main hallway to her bedroom when Sera called, "Um...Lil? Someone is here to see you."

"I'm indisposed at the moment. Can you show them to the parlor and get coffee?"

"Ma'am," a gruff male voice rolled back to her. "I need to talk with you. Now."

Although the man clearly wasn't Teague, there was something similar in his tone. That commanding, I-am-the-law-around-here timbre.

Oh. Oh, dear.

Lil patted at her hair and straightened her shoulders. Goodness gracious, if Momma had ever caught her accepting a gentleman caller in her nightclothes, she would've had a conniption fit.

"And a Margaret Rawls too."

Maggie peeked out of the kitchen, her eyes wide. "Oh, Lil. I know we didn't do anything, but this is scary."

Lil grabbed Maggie's hand and swept into the parlor as if she had on a ball gown and diamonds. Attitude and bearing were everything. "Good morning, Officer. How may we help you?"

"I have a few questions about the—" he checked his notes, "—gauntlets stolen from Jessie Wyatt's casket."

"Young man, do you even know what a gauntlet is?"

"Some kind of armband." He cleared his throat and tugged at his knife-creased khaki uniform pants. "Can you tell me what you saw the day of Jessie Wyatt's interment?"

"A lot of people, a beautiful if slightly over-the-top ceremony, then Jessie Wyatt's crazy cousin hollering like a banshee."

"Specifically, what you saw on the casket?"

"A big spray of flowers, bluebonnets, and Jessie's iconic cowgirl outfit."

"Anything suspicious happen while you were near the casket?"

"No." Lil held up a finger. "Actually, as we walked inside, I saw a rose on the ground and picked it up."

"Was that significant?"

"I didn't think so, but then I'm not a trained professional like you."

He cut a glance her way. "You said the casket spray was a blanket of bluebonnets. So where'd the other flower come from?"

"People were placing roses on top of the casket as they left."

"On top of the gauntlets?"

"All over the casket," she said. "She was very loved. Young man, if you want to know if

I stole those gauntlets, why don't you come out and ask me? It's not good manners to beat around the bush."

The deputy's ears turned red, and Maggie bumped Lil with her hip.

"Ma'am, did you take the gauntlets?"

"If I took the gauntlets, would I tell you to ask me about it?"

"That's not exactly an answer," he said. "Did you touch them?"

Maggie sent her a warning look, but it wasn't as if Lil could lie about it. The proof was all over the gossip news. "Yes."

"Why would you do that?"

"Because they were out of alignment."

"Out of what?"

"You know, out of kilter. One was at a forty-five degree angle. The other at...oh, I'd estimate thirty-nine."

"Ma'am, are you OCD?"

"Oh sea what?"

Maggie leaned over. "He means obsessive compulsive disorder. You know, like Nash Talley."

"Ooooh." She gave a definitive head shake. "No, I'm not OCD. But a lady's clothes should always look their best, whether or not she's alive."

"No one would believe that story. Why would you expect me to believe you touched the gauntlets, but didn't steal them?"

"I didn't touch them."

"But you just told me you *did* touch them." His eyes bugged from his face. Lil checked his finger for a wedding ring and found it empty. Not surprising if his eyes often performed that unattractive trick.

"No, I said I adjusted *one* of them." My goodness, where was Pitts Country training their deputies these days—at a drive-thru?

"You know this looks bad, don't you, Ms. Fairview?"

"In all my years, I've certainly learned that just because something looks one way doesn't mean it is that way. Do you go around harassing innocent people simply because they were in the store when someone shoplifted a can of beans?"

"Lil," Maggie said in a low tone, "do not antagonize him."

"But you're not exactly innocent, now, are you?" Once again, he checked his notes. "In fact, you served fourteen months in federal prison camp for a crime you confessed to."

That set Lil to shaking, half from fear and half from deep red anger. How dare he? But she held it together and smiled. "Well, using that logic, if I were guilty of what you're accusing me, wouldn't I say so outright?"

He snapped his notebook closed. "Were the gauntlets on the casket when it was taken inside the mausoleum?"

"I can't say for sure. I was behind the workers who were pushing it. And when we went inside, they raised the casket in the air. It was hard to see much."

"The only reason I'm not putting you in handcuffs right this minute is because you told me about the rose you'd found and because, at your age, you're not much of a flight risk."

Oh, the rebellious part of Lil wanted to tell him she was as much a flight risk as anyone else and that she planned to march upstairs and pack her bikini for a tropical vacation as soon as she tossed him out on his behind. But she held her tongue. "I understand completely."

"Don't travel beyond Bartell County until we clear you." He stood, and Lil joined him. The sooner she had him out of her house, the better.

Once she'd seen the deputy to the door, Lil leaned against the foyer wall. When would life around Summer Haven ever return to normal?

Her world used to be orderly and simple. Volunteer work, some quilting, and if she snuck in an MMA bout on TV once in awhile, no one had been the wiser.

Now, every day was a bit of craziness. Reminded her of the time her momma had gone a little berserk over an old mattress her daddy had refused to replace. Lil could still see the stubborn line of her momma's mouth as she dragged that thing down the stairs and out the front door. *Bump, bump, bump.*

She'd put a match to the mattress, burned it right there on the front lawn. The flames shot so high someone had called the volunteer fire department, but momma had refused to let them put out the fire until only piles of springs were left.

For months, a circle of charred grass and earth had decorated Summer Haven.

But Daddy had run out and bought a new mattress lickety-split.

"Bartell Schmartell. We've got things to do." Lil straightened and strode back into the parlor. "Okay, girls. Since we already planned to hit the pawnshop today, I figure we can make a quick stop by the mausoleum on the way. See if we can pick up any clues. We'll just have to work both cases. How does that sound?"

"What about Abby Ruth?"

Lil glanced at the ceiling above them. "Jenny planned to come back over this morning, so she'll be here to entertain—"

"You mean *distract*."

"—distract Abby Ruth while we take care of business."

CHAPTER 10

"Okay, girls," Lil said from her jouncing seat in the back of Sera's van. "We have to accomplish a ton today. All we have to do is find Jessie Wyatt's missing gauntlets and Abby Ruth's guns. Surely we can do it."

She saw the quick raised-brow look that Maggie shot toward Sera, who caught it even though she was driving sixty miles an hour down the county road toward the Holy Innocence Mausoleum.

Darn it, she wanted those two to stop elbowing her out of their investigative insider secrets. "Just say it, Mags."

"What?"

"Whatever it is you were communicating to Sera via mind meld."

Sera glanced back to her right, her lips pressed together, and Maggie sighed.

"See." Lil aimed her fingers toward them both like an airline attendant pointing out exits. "That. Right there."

Maggie twisted in her seat to look at Lil. "It's just that you make it all sound so easy, like you plan to snap your fingers and everything that's missing will suddenly run and jump into your arms."

"Goodness, with that attitude, how did the three of you solve these other little crimes around town?"

Sera glanced in the rearview window, and for once, her face wasn't a study of sunshine and happiness. In fact, she looked downright fierce. "First of all, theft and fraud aren't little crimes."

"I only meant—"

"Second, if you're insinuating we don't believe in our ability to find anything we set our minds to, that's silly. I'm the most optimistic person around. But Lil, Rome wasn't built in a day, and crimes aren't solved in a day either."

"Fine, so maybe tracking down everything today isn't completely realistic, but between the mausoleum and the pawn shop, surely we can get some solid leads." Wasn't that what the CSI people called them—leads?

She needed to get Abby Ruth to show her how to use that darned DVR so she could start recording all those crime shows. She could probably learn a few tricks that way.

Once they were inside the mausoleum, Lil realized all the bouncing in Sera's backseat had rattled loose her two cups of breakfast coffee. "Why don't y'all start looking around up here? I'm going to the ladies' room, and I'll check out that area while I'm there. Let's meet back here in twenty minutes for a quick debrief."

"Should we synchronize our watches?" Maggie asked.

Lil had a feeling there was a touch of sarcasm behind her BFF's words, but she simply smiled. "I think we can wing it." Lord, as loosey-goosey as Maggie's and Sera's methods were, sometimes she wondered if their past successes weren't all just dumb luck.

Not that she would say such a thing, of course.

The tiny brass sign for the restroom pointed her to the stairwell.

Her knee popped as she turned, but she caught sight of the elevator across the hall. She walked over, pressed the button and waited. The chug-chug-chug of the elevator took its own sweet time and then finally with a thud, the heavy metal door slid open like the sigh of a giant.

Well, she supposed no one was in a great hurry around here anyway. What did it matter if it took the thing ten minutes to go from floor to floor?

Once she was on the lower level, a flash of hot pink caught her eye. She spun around to see what she'd caught in her peripheral vision, but it had disappeared.

She walked down the empty hall, her shoes echoing against the shiny marble floor.

The rows of dearly departed—stacked one upon the other clear up to the ceiling like Campbell Soup cans on the grocery aisle—were disconcerting. Small alcoves held special memorials, which was nice, but those touches didn't cancel out the place's creep factor.

On her search for the restroom, she spotted a large wooden bureau tucked into a small alcove. Although her bladder was complaining, she had to stop and look through it because it seemed like a perfect place to hide something. Something like a pair of priceless cowgirl gloves.

With a quick look to the left and right, she walked over and carefully slid open the top drawer. Her pulse bunny-hopping, she quietly made her way through every one of the twelve drawers of varying sizes.

She slid the last drawer closed, and the excitement inside her burst. The entire chest was empty.

Well, that would've been too easy, wouldn't it?

Although it would've been terribly fun to waltz back upstairs and show the other gals she'd found exactly what they'd come for.

Since that wasn't the case, her only direction was onward.

Finally, she spotted the bathroom door. Shoot, she'd already spent six and a half of her twenty minutes hunting down the potty.

Inside the ladies' room was a well-decorated anteroom. It held a plush couch and chairs positioned around a high-quality area rug. Slender vases, nearly as tall as she, stood in the corners, their plumes of foliage giving the otherwise stark space a softer look. Lil pulled out a drawer on the antique makeup table with an ornate mirror hanging above. Nice, but it was a reproduction, not the real deal.

Inside the restroom itself, the smell of ammonia and a sickeningly sweet freshener hung in the air. She went into the last stall, locking herself in to do her business. As she did, quick-heeled footsteps entered the anteroom.

Those couldn't be Maggie's footsteps. Maggie walked with purpose, not with a flurry of quicksteps that tapped out the tempo of a good foxtrot.

"Sera?"

No answer.

"Hello?"

Nothing.

She cleared her throat, hoping whoever it was would make themselves known, because being alone in this place gave her the creeps. And being alone with her panties down was darn-right unnerving. On a positive note, those hadn't been heavy men's footsteps. Then again, if the footsteps weren't a man's and they weren't a woman's, then what else could be out there? Visions of ghosts, or worse...hot pink zombies...made it impossible to relax.

Maybe those footsteps had been her imagination, but her heart rate still seemed to be convinced otherwise.

At the sink, she washed her hands and

glanced up to catch another flash of hot pink. Florescent zombies?

Lord, where was Daryl Dixon from the Walking Dead when she needed him?

ALTHOUGH STILL SLIGHTLY SORE FROM her lumpectomy and the long drive from Texas, Abby Ruth dressed herself and headed down the stairs, half expecting to be ambushed after what she'd let fly last night. But Summer Haven was strangely quiet.

Almost disappointingly so.

Just like that anonymous Houston hotel room had been last week.

More than once, she'd wished one of her friends or Jenny had been there with her. But why burden people? What they hadn't known hadn't hurt them.

Which was the reason she'd gone back to Texas in the first place. Otherwise, they would've been fluttering around her asking things like "Do you need help?" and "Can I bring you some water?"

She'd been perfectly fine handling the procedure all by herself.

Or had she?

Maybe her memory of feeling scared and

alone could be blamed on the knock-out drugs she'd been given.

"Anyone here?" she called out.

Silence.

Fine. Perfect, actually. I didn't want to talk about it anyway.

What she really wanted to do was go organize her guns, introducing the old guard to the newest family members, so she headed outside.

Before she could unlock her trailer, Jenny's BMW came hauling butt up the driveway, a dusty rooster tail pluming behind it. She executed a tight turn, and the car's rear-end arced around before she came to a rocking stop. If Abby Ruth hadn't known better, she might think her daughter was competing in a professional fishtailing competition.

Jenny jumped out of her car. "I turned your phone to silent last night, but I expected you to text me when you woke up today."

"Honestly, Jenny, I never checked my phone. It's still upstairs."

"What're you up to?" Her daughter slid between her and the back of her horse trailer, much like Sera had intercepted her the evening before.

Abby Ruth held up her hands, the sweet

Slotter Derringer in the right and a Spanish Miguelet in the left. "Getting my new babies settled in. It was careless of me to leave them in the truck last night."

Rolling a hand in the general direction of Abby Ruth's bustline, Jenny said, "I think we should talk about this...the...your..."

"You can say the word. Believe me, I've heard it plenty lately." She set the guns on the back step rail of the trailer and dug in her pocket for her keys.

Jenny launched herself at Abby Ruth and wrapped her in a hug, pinning her arms to her side.

Abby Ruth let a humiliating high-pitched squeak escape her, and Jenny immediately pulled away. "What is it? What's wrong? Did I hurt you?"

Sidestepping her daughter's fluttering, the kind she'd hoped to avoid, Abby Ruth said, "I'm fine. Just a little sore."

"From what?"

"You won't leave this alone until you know every detail, are you?"

"Mom, I'm seriously torn between hugging you and strangling you right now. Of course I want to know everything. Now why did you flinch when I touched you?"

Maybe she should've stayed in Texas. Then again, Jenny, Maggie, and the others probably would've marched their happy heinies all the way to Houston if she'd stayed there for radiation treatment.

But she hadn't decided about that yet.

"I have what's called DCIS."

"Ductal carcinoma in situ."

"How did you know?"

"What do you think I've spent the past twelve hours doing?" Jenny rubbed her forehead, the line between her eyebrows attesting to the stress Abby Ruth had caused her.

"The internet can be a dangerous place." Hell, she knew that from the online dating ring she and the gals had busted up a while back.

"That's good news, though, right? Stage 0 cancer?"

"Which is the reason I didn't feel the need to blab my business all over the place." She turned her back on Jenny and started messing with the lock on the trailer, her nerves suddenly twanging like a two-bit banjo.

"Blab? Telling your daughter and best friends that you have cancer is *not* blabbing. It's called sharing."

"Fine. You want me to share? The reason

your hug hurt was because I had a lumpectomy while I was in Houston."

"You did not." Jenny glanced at her chest. "You did not have surgery without telling me."

"Sugar, it was a day thing."

"And then you drove back to Georgia by yourself. My God, sometimes I think you shouldn't be let loose alone. Even Grayson would know not to do something so stupid."

"I should remind you that Grayson doesn't have a driver's license." She stuck her key in the lock and clicked it open.

"Don't go in there!"

"What? Why?"

"Because...um..."

"If I find out Maggie has taken to storing her tools in here while I was gone, I will give her a talking to." She opened the door and hopped up.

When she turned to grab the guns, Jenny was frozen except for her lips, which looked like the goldfish Grayson had recently begged Abby Ruth to buy him. *Gulp. Gulp. Gulp.*

"Are you okay?"

"No," Jenny moaned and dropped her face into her hands. "I've failed."

"You *are* pregnant. I told Sera that was the reason you've been acting so crazy." She stepped back down out of the trailer. "I remember when you got knocked up with Grayson, I swear it was like your brain had been sucked out by aliens and replaced with Jell-O salad. The kind with a bunch of nuts in it."

"I am not pregnant. I'm not married yet."

She lifted her eyebrows. "I can't believe you just said that. You know how that whole pregnancy thing works, right?"

"Dammit, Mom. Listen to me!"

"Then say something worth hearing."

"They're gone."

"The aliens?"

"No, the guns."

Abby Ruth glanced down at the guns she was holding. "They're right here."

"No, the rest of them. You see, they were here, and then Lil and the others rented out your room. Then they were gone," Jenny babbled.

"So someone squatted in my room and then they left?"

"No, every last one of your guns is missing."

What? A hazy film covered Abby Ruth's eyesight, and she swayed against the trailer door. Her guns were gone? No! That was almost as bad as if someone had snatched up Grayson.

"I'm sorry. We didn't want to tell you last night because—"

Carelessly, she dumped her new babies into Jenny's arms and hightailed it toward the other end of the trailer.

Sure enough, when she opened the door to the compartment that normally held her most precious treasures, it was empty. She sucked in what felt like her last breath.

This time, the sound of pain that came from her was low and mournful.

CHAPTER 11

*H*and to her thumping chest, Lil spun around to see a chestnut-haired woman about her same height, dressed in highlighter pink from the top of her hat to the tips of her pumps, sitting in a Queen Anne chair in the anteroom. A half-smile on her lips, she rotated her pointy-toed shoe in a slow circle.

A light chuckle escaped Lil. This lovely woman was anything but a zombie. "You startled me." Lil balled up the paper towel and dropped it into the waste bin.

"I'm sorry," the woman said. "I didn't mean to."

Well, then why hadn't she answered when Lil called out?

"Unless a service is in progress, usually

there aren't many people around Holy Innocence except for the occasional cleaning crew." The woman leaned forward and picked up a dainty teacup from the glass-and-chrome table in front of her.

Tea? Well if this wasn't the oddest place for a such a beautifully dressed woman to take tea.

"I'm clearly not part of the cleaning crew." Lil stood taller, glad she'd taken the extra time to dress in a nice blouse and skirt for the visit, unlike Maggie and Sera who came as they were in jeans and yoga pants. A resting ground should command a certain amount of respect. Clearly she and this woman had the same philosophy. "And it's a shame that more people don't visit their loved ones here."

Even though Harlan hadn't left this world on a high note, Lil still placed flowers on his grave and paid him due respect for the many wonderful years they'd spent together.

"I find most people aren't as dedicated as we'd like to think they are in honoring their dearly departed. I seem to be a minority." The woman took a sip of her tea. "Are you here visiting family?"

Not wanting to tell the complete truth about why she was here today, Lil said, "Not exactly. I attended a service recently but didn't get the opportunity to see the beautiful stained glass. I thought I'd do a self-guided tour."

"The Jessie Wyatt funeral?"

"The exact one."

"You knew her?"

"Do I look like a funeral crasher?" Lil said, reluctant to admit that she was a friend of a friend of Jessie's.

"Not at all."

Well, that was certainly a relief. "I saw Hulk Hogan." Now, why in the world had she blurted that out? This woman probably didn't know who he was.

"You don't say," she said. "I spotted Michael Douglas and Sam Elliott."

"You were here?"

"I'm here almost every day," she said with a serene smile. "My husband, Ronald, didn't much care to be alone when he was alive, so I try to spend several hours with him each day. Seems only right."

Goodness, now that was devotion. "How nice."

"The gauntlet theft has been all over the news."

The woman seemed to be looking Lil over. Had she seen the footage the paparazzi had taken from the chopper? Did she recognize her as the woman touching the gauntlets? Lil's stomach swirled.

"Seems so odd that they could go missing in plain sight. Don't you think?" The woman in pink sat back and thrummed her fingers on the arm of the chair. "But I doubt it was personal."

"Stealing at a funeral? That seems *terribly* personal."

"You'd be surprised what drives people to do things you'd think they would never, ever do."

Lil felt a flush creep up her body to her cheeks. If this woman only knew the lengths some people would go, she certainly wouldn't be sitting here sipping and chatting with Lil.

"People will do crazy things for money. It's a master manipulator." The woman's lips pursed as if she'd sucked on the lemon floating in her tea cup. "Can tempt those you'd never think would harbor a bad thought. But then maybe someone couldn't bear the idea of Jessie's precious items being locked in that vault for eternity. Nostalgia is powerful too."

She was right. Lil had crossed the line herself to keep up appearances when Harlan had let her down. And if someone was willing to steal from the dead because they wanted a memento, rather than money, maybe one of those Jessie Wyatt lookalikes was guiltier than they'd thought.

"Last week was my first time in a mausoleum," Lil said. "I'm curious if you've ever seen anything strange happen around here?"

"What do you mean?"

It wouldn't do to make her suspicious, so Lil said casually, "Oh, it's such a large and fascinating place, I figure all kinds of people pass through."

"Well, there's plenty to see. Did you know there's a vault in the outdoor pavilion the size of a garage because someone wanted to bury her husband with his John Deere tractor?"

Lillian could picture stuffing Harlan in a huge vault with those darned scratcher tickets. Somehow that would've been just deserts to have him half-suffocated in the middle of those black trash bags. She stepped forward and extended her hand. "Oh, I'm Lillian Summer Fairview. From over Summer Shoals way."

The woman tipped her head to the side, her hat shading her face. She hesitated for only a moment then took Lil's hand. "Rosemary

Myrtle."

"As in Myrtle Knolls?"

"One and the same."

No wonder Lil felt such a kinship with this woman. They were both matriarchs of their respective communities. "Perhaps we could have lunch one day. I have a feeling we have a great deal in common."

"I'd like that."

As Lil shook Rosemary's hand, she noticed it was past the time to meet up with Sera and Maggie. "A pleasure. I must be off," Lil said, then rushed out and back toward the elevator. With each step, she thought of the woman she'd just met. Why weren't there more ladies like Rosemary around? Wouldn't it be nice to have a civilized tea once in a while? Tiny sandwiches, decadent desserts, and reminiscing about how things used to be.

Yes, that would be a wonderful way to spend an afternoon.

As she hurried past, the door to the loading dock was open and something caught her eye. She turned and walked back to find a bluebonnet lying in the middle of the floor.

How on earth had that gotten down here?

WHILE SHE AND Maggie waited for Lil to return from the ladies' room, Sera glanced around at the mausoleum's granite walls. The place had seemed safe enough a few days ago when they came for Jessie's service, but today, all that cold stone felt foreign, foreboding, almost menacing.

Maybe the feeling was a reflection of her nagging guilt about not letting Marcus know what she and the other ladies were up to. He deserved to know, but she didn't want him to tell her she shouldn't get involved, because that would feel like a step backward when it seemed as if they might be finding each other again.

Besides, he hadn't told her everything about his goings-on lately either. But today was about helping her friends, so she pushed her thoughts of Marcus aside and focused on her surroundings.

Huge murals of stained glass told stories from the Bible, but still the place felt like trouble.

Which was crazy.

Many of the panels etched with names, birthdates, and death dates were also labeled with nice sentiments like "She will be missed" and "His light shines on." But most reduced a person's entire life to a name given to them by someone else, two dates, and a dash.

"It's all in what you make of the dash," she said wistfully.

"What?" Maggie said.

Sera trailed her fingertips across Cecil K. Clementine's vault, traced the curve of the Cs and the edges of the K. "Cecil's dash lasted from 1948 to 2015. What do you think he did with it?"

"We don't know Cecil." Maggie pulled Sera's hand down. "Do we?"

"Well, no."

"Sera, did you sneak some of my iced tea before we left the house this morning? Because I have no idea what you're talking about." She whispered, but her voice still carried in the stark stone space.

"Have you ever thought, really thought, about the fact that we only get so much time to walk this earth? And we don't get to say when or where our time is up?"

"Abby Ruth. The big C. I know. It's got me shaken up too." Maggie joined Sera in standing before a stranger's last resting place. "But what's with all this *dash* talk?"

"I want my dash to mean something."

"Why in the world would you think it

won't? Sera, you're one of the most giving, most loving people I've ever known. You've probably had an impact on hundreds, if not thousands, of people. People you have no idea you've touched in a special and meaningful way."

"Sometimes I've just been a bracelet."

Maggie placed a cool palm on Sera's forehead. "Hon, are you feeling okay? This isn't the first time I've had a hard time following your logic, but even for you, all this talk of dashes and bracelets is weird."

"Did you know the Gypsy Cotton Gallery is up for sale?"

"Oh." Maggie's face fell. "I guess I shouldn't be surprised. Does this have something to do with your dash?"

Yes, it definitely did. "Wouldn't it be wonderful to make that space something that would benefit the community? I had this picture of it as not only a gallery but a place where people could gather for events. And I could teach yoga there."

"Only if you're here in Summer Shoals."

Maggie was right. And that wasn't something Sera had time to mull over now, when they were here on a mission and had two important cases to solve. She released a pent-up breath. "Okay, if you were going to steal part of a priceless costume, where would you stash it?"

"That's a trick question, right?" Maggie waved an arm that encompassed the vaults that rose twenty feet high to the ceiling. "It's not like this place lacks hiding places."

"The culprit could've been one of the guests. Maybe those Jessie Wyatt wannabes. Or one of her family members. They're a greedy bunch," Sera said. "It wouldn't surprise me to find out her family is involved."

"Maybe so, but this is the only lead we have, so we start with what we've got. The cops looked inside the vault. The gauntlets are gone. With all the hubbub, maybe whoever took them hid them here in the mausoleum and hasn't come back yet. We have to look in case the gauntlets are still here. Let's start by checking for any crypts that have loose granite or don't have caulk around the edges."

"But if there's no caulk, wouldn't they..." Sera trailed off because it was too horrible to contemplate. There were people in those crypts! She gave the air around her a sniff test, but all she got was a snootful of elegant floral arrangements, made of roses and lilies.

"There are plenty of empties, so let's not

worry about whether or not that outfit is hidden in an occupied one. We'll cross that...bridge...if we have to."

Although Sera wasn't exactly keen on the idea, it made more sense for her and Maggie to split up for the search. "Why don't we each take a row and we'll leapfrog each other until we make it to the opposite side of the building? If we don't find anything suspicious among the ones we can reach, then we'll go from there."

"Works for me."

She and Maggie split up, and as Sera did the push test, one vault at a time, she tried not to picture her own dad behind one of the granite squares. Which was ridiculous, since he would've hated being stuffed in a 32-by-26-inch rectangle. He would've said, "That's no way for a man to stay wild and free." If she had to guess, with the course of the tides, he was probably somewhere near the Aleutian Islands by now. Hopefully, he'd caught up with her mom out there in the ocean.

She smiled, remembering the man who'd taught her how to grow vegetables and clear her mind while striking a proper balasana pose. What she wouldn't give to pick up the phone and hear his voice.

"Any luck?" Maggie stage-whispered from the end of the row.

Sera wasn't certain which would be luckier, to find something that moved or not. "Everything's in place so far."

"Darn it. Nothing here either." Maggie pointed to the next row. "Moving on."

A twinge of guilt threaded through Sera. Part of her was hoping Maggie would find the open vault if there was one...not her. But she had to do her part. She turned to face the vaults head-on but caught a glimpse of something from the corner of her eye. *What in the world?*

At the end of her row, a glowing yellow orb about the size of a basketball hung three or four feet off the ground. Sera blinked, her eyelids doing a hummingbird impersonation. Surely that round thing was an optical illusion. She glanced up at the huge stained-glass window behind the orb. Maybe the sun was simply shining through the apostle Judas's robes.

She examined the details of the stained glass. The intricate artwork was gorgeous and colorful, but that orb couldn't be explained away. Judas wasn't wearing a speck of yellow. So how? What? A ghost?

She supposed if someplace was going to be haunted, a mausoleum was a pretty good place to haunt.

"Maggie?" Sera's voice quavered slightly.

Maggie's tennis shoes made a swooshing sound across the low carpet as she ran to help Sera. "You found something?" Maggie's eyes danced with excitement.

"I'm. Not. Sure."

"Whatever you found, is it gold and sparkly?"

"Kinda?" Sera wanted to point, but her arms hung heavily at her sides.

"Goodness gracious, Sera, are you scared? I thought you'd find this place peaceful." Maggie rubbed Sera's arm. "You okay? You've gone pale."

"Look past me," Sera said with a gulp, "and tell me what you see."

"You're not looking in the right direction. You're supposed to be—" Maggie drew alongside Sera and followed her gaze, stopping as abruptly as the flow of her words. "Wha...what is that?"

"I was hoping you could tell me."

Maggie fumbled around in the pocket of her khaki pants and pulled out her cell phone. "Whatever it is, we need a picture of it." Snap,

snap, snap.

As Maggie clicked away, Sera watched the orb change shapes and become longer, almost as if it were growing legs.

Sera's heart sped up. She never should've indulged in a cup of real coffee this morning instead of her normal chicory substitute. Hopefully whatever—or whoever—that orb was, it was friendly.

As quickly as it lengthened, the orb contracted again, became smaller and smaller until it disappeared with a pop of light.

Maggie dropped her arm until her phone rested against her thigh, but neither she nor Sera made a move. They stood, watching the spot for several minutes.

"Do you believe in ghosts?" Maggie finally asked.

"I don't not believe in them." Sera's voice was regaining its steady tone. "I think there are plenty of forces in this world we're not always open-minded enough to recognize or see. My dad always said that the world shows you what you need when you need it."

"I think I would've liked your dad."

"He was the absolute best." Her dad would've loved Maggie. Too bad they never got to meet. But then had he not died, Sera never would've ended up in Summer Shoals.

Everything happens for a reason.

Maggie's lips contorted into a half-smile, half-frown. "I know this sounds crazy, but do you think it's possible that was Jessie Wyatt's ghost?"

"Gold *was* her signature color, and I can see it would be hard for a ghost to manifest gold sequins, fringe, and bugle beads." Sera wrapped her arms around herself. "Maybe yellow light is the best she could do from the other side."

"And what if Jessie wanted to take her favorite cowgirl outfit to the other side with her?"

"Honey, you can't take it with you," Lil said as she strolled up. "No one is going to buy that Jessie took her own stuff. But I just saw something interesting. A bluebonnet on the floor near the loading dock."

Sera and Maggie shared a look that said they weren't planning to tell Lil about what they'd seen...yet. "Wouldn't the flowers have been delivered there?"

"I don't know," Lil said. "Maybe."

"Did you look around for the gauntlets downstairs?"

"I did. Nothing."

"That would've been too easy. We only have those rows left to check on this floor," Sera said.

Lil followed along on the search. "I met a woman while I was downstairs."

"Maybe she's returning to the scene of the crime," Maggie said. "This could be our first real lead."

"No, she was lovely. Definitely not the kind of person who would steal."

"You're making friends here?" Maggie said. "I haven't seen a living soul except the security guard."

"It isn't as if I went looking for her. She was in the ladies' room. Rosemary Myrtle, a well-to-do widow, who had on the most marvelous pink outfit," Lil said. "Anyway, I think we're going about this search all wrong. And I have a clue."

"To where the missing gauntlets are?"

"Yes. We're looking in the wrong place." Lil spun around. "Lordy, this building is like a mirrored funhouse. Let's go over to where Jessie's interment was."

Maggie shot Sera a look that said it was better to follow along than argue.

"Do you know how to get back there?" Lil asked.

"You returning to the scene of the crime? I don't like it one bit," Maggie said. "If someone sees you there, it could further implicate you. Maybe Sera and I should go look and you wait here."

"Don't be silly." Lil put her hands on her hips. "No one knows I have a prison record."

"Except the cops," Sera blurted and regretted it immediately when Lil turned to her with a regal look on her face.

"The police have no reason to set me up. Now let's go."

"Fine. This way," Maggie said. Near Jessie Wyatt's resting place, flowers still stood at varying heights, the arrangements in random states of wilt.

"Maggie, you check the trash bin over there and around all of those flowers. Sera, you come help me push on the crypt fronts."

"Why do I have to check the trash?" Maggie asked.

"Because Sera is stronger than you and me put together."

Maggie shoved at her bangs and walked away mumbling.

As she and Lil made their way down the aisle where Jessie had been interred, pushing on each facing they could reach, Sera kept an eye out for the glowing orb. But everything was quiet and in place.

"Darn it," Lil huffed. "I thought this area was our best bet."

Maggie rounded the corner, hands empty of gauntlets.

"Did you find anything?" Lil asked.

"Several pages ripped from a magazine, three well-used tissues, and half a melted chocolate bar, which is a complete waste of good candy."

"We haven't found anything either," Sera said. None of the vaults were loose in the slightest. And even if it had seemed appropriate, they didn't have enough time to start prying off slabs of granite. "I think it's time to head out."

Lil's mouth turned down into a half pout. "I thought for sure we'd find something here. Can't we stay and—"

"We need to get to the pawn shop," Maggie glanced at her watch, "but I've got to go to the ladies' room before we drive all the way into Atlanta."

"It's downstairs." Lil waved toward the door to the stairwell. "Go on. I'll keep looking."

Sera joined Maggie and whispered, "Should we tell her about the orb?"

"Lord, no. We can only track down so many disappearing things today."

CHAPTER 12

*W*hile Maggie was using the facilities, Sera entertained herself in the anteroom with a little dance, a cross between ballet and bullfighting. Maybe a solo *paso doble*, like she'd seen when she'd had tickets to *Dancing With The Stars*. She flung her arms as if waving her mighty cape, then spun around just as Maggie stepped out of the restroom.

"You keep that up and Valentin Chmer-what's-his-name will be knocking on your door," Maggie said.

"Chmerkovskiy. Actually, I was supposed to be paired with Derek Hough the season I left California," she said, ending her solo with a curtsey.

Maggie's eyes went wide. "Sometimes I'm

not sure I really know you, Sera."

Sera looped her arm through Maggie's and pulled her close. "You may not know everything about my life, but you definitely know the real me. I promise."

Maggie cut her a sideways look that insinuated she wasn't completely convinced. "Think we have a few minutes before Lil comes looking for us?"

"She should be busy upstairs for a while. Seemed like she wasn't going to give up until she found something. We'll probably have to drag her out of this place."

Maggie dug her phone from her pants pocket. "I want to take a few pictures down here. In case Lightning Bug Jessie likes to roam the range."

"We've named the orb now?"

"Why not?"

They tiptoed around a corner to see if they could spot the ghostly orb again. To their right, a door was open, and Sera peeked inside.

"What is it?" Maggie asked.

"I think it must be the shipping dock Lil mentioned." The room was poorly lit, but Sera made out half a dozen caskets. Five were constructed from what appeared to be bronze or copper, but one wasn't anything like the others. It looked as if it was fashioned from rough pine, which surprised her.

But maybe a lower-grade casket wasn't completely unusual. It probably cost a mint to be interred here, so it wouldn't be surprising to find some people skimped on the condo itself so they could have a more upscale zip code.

"Look." Maggie clicked off another quick picture. "There's the bluebonnet flower Lil was talking about."

"We should search. She's new at this." Sera was about to dart inside the room when she heard someone whistling. She and Maggie froze.

Then a man wearing coveralls and carrying a broom turned the corner at the end of the hall. When he spotted them, the whistling stopped and his eyes narrowed.

The best defense was a good offense, at least that's what a 49ers quarterback had once told her. "Excuse me, sir? Thank goodness someone else is here."

His shock of white hair was mussed like he'd been out in a windstorm. "You're not supposed to be near the shipping docks."

"We didn't mean to be. We were trying to

find our way back upstairs. I think we've gotten ourselves all turned around."

"No problem." His face relaxed and he pointed down the corridor. "Head down the hall and the elevator is across the way."

"Thank you. You've been helpful."

"Sure thing," he said, stepping inside that dark room and closing the door behind him with a finality that said Sera and Maggie wouldn't get inside.

"Let's keep looking for LBJ," Maggie said.

"Don't tell me his ghost is here too," Sera whispered.

"Not Lyndon Baines Johnson. Lightning Bug Jessie."

"Whew."

They made their way down the hallway with Maggie continuing to snap pictures with her phone.

"Margaret Rawls, are you taking snapshots inside this sacred resting place?" Lil's voice came from near the elevator, causing Sera and Maggie to stop and look in her direction.

"Oh, I...uh...of course not." Maggie pointed to an eight-foot tall robed and winged figure lording over an alcove. "I was getting a shot of that angel."

Lil eyed her suspiciously.

"I think we've done all we've come to do."
Sera took Maggie by the elbow and pointed her
toward the elevator. "And if we're going to run
down Abby Ruth's guns before she finds out
they're missing, we better get to that pawn
shop before it closes."

"Maybe there's nothing here to find." Lil
pressed her lips into a fine line. "Those gloves
are probably long gone, which means I have no
way to clear myself."

"There's always a chance the pawn shop
might know something about Jessie's stuff
too," Sera said.

"I can only hope," Lil said.

As they strolled into the elevator, a flash of
yellow blinked in the hallway, and Sera leaned
back out to see if she could catch another sight
of the orb. But the corridor was empty.

*Jessie, if that was you, are you trying to
tell me something?*

"MAUSOLEUM WAS A BUST. I guess my hunch
wasn't so good," Lil shouted over the clanking
and creaking of Sera's van. Sera and Maggie
had been right about this investigation being
tough, and Lil was disheartened by their lack
of success. "What if the pawn shop is a bust

too?"

Pulling out of the parking lot, Sera glanced over her shoulder. "Don't let any negativity leak out to the universe. We'll find something. I just know it."

"What if we don't?"

"Then we keep trying," Sera insisted, steering the van onto the interstate ramp. "Only positive thoughts."

"Maybe we need a list of suspects," Maggie said, turning to Lil. "When we've done these cases in the past, we've worked up a list of suspects and motives."

"Okay," Lil said. "I guess my name is at the top of the cops' list, but who's on *our* list?"

"Good question," Sera said.

"Should we brainstorm?" Maggie pulled out a tiny spiral notebook from her pocket. "I can take notes."

Sera shook her head. "No. That's double work. We should make our list when we get back to Summer Haven. It'll be easier to focus."

"With the paper on the wall!" Maggie's excitement couldn't be mistaken. "Oh, Lil, that part is so much fun. You're going to love it."

"All I know is I need to clear my name." Lil folded her hands into her lap and leaned back in the seat.

Nearly an hour later, Sera pulled the van into the front parking spot at J&R's Pawn Shop.

Lil led the way from the van with Sera and Maggie on her heels. She opened the heavy barred door, trying to avoid looking at the bright yellow measuring stick that had mocked her all those months ago when she'd come here the last time, right before her stay at Walter Stiles Prison Camp.

It still made her sick that she'd been forced to use this place as a dumping ground for precious items from her past, like Daddy's pocket watches, which were now lost for good. But thankfully, Maggie had been able to save Lil's wedding rings.

J&R's owner Rick had never asked too many questions, and he'd done right by her. Hopefully he could shed some light on one of their problems today.

Rick's face lit up when he spotted her. "Miss Lillian?"

"Hello, Rick." She walked over to the counter and shook his hand.

"It's good to see you. You look great. I wondered whatever happened to you." He leaned his thick forearms on the glass countertop, giving Sera an appreciative up and down, and then a spark of recognition hit as he saw Maggie. "You. You're the one who came in and picked up Miss Lillian's wedding set."

"That's me."

"You bring me some good stuff today?" Rick asked Lil.

His face was so eager, she almost felt bad that this was purely a fact-finding mission.

"Afraid not." Lil glanced into the cases where so many people's memories were lined up under the LED lighting. How many pawned items ended up here? Rick had given her extensions several times to keep her from losing her valuables, but he couldn't possibly do that for everyone. "I'm looking for something."

Rick spread his arms. "Possibilities are endless. What's your pleasure, ma'am?"

"A couple things actually," Lil said, glancing around the large space. Chock full of stuff, the pawnshop appeared to be a prosperous business all year long. "Has anyone brought in a pair of ladies' Western gloves bedazzled with gems and edged in gold fringe?"

"Can't say they have."

Although she'd known it was a long shot,

disappointment settled inside her. Then a thought occurred to her. They couldn't look at this as an either-or scenario. Maybe someone had taken the gauntlets for both a memento *and* money.

"How about a handful of sapphires, rubies, and diamonds about yay big?" She made a quarter-inch opening between her thumb and forefinger.

He laughed. "Now that, I would remember. Haven't seen anything of the kind."

Shoot. "Didn't figure so, but if you do, let me know."

"Not the style I'd picture you wearing, Miss Lillian," Rick teased. But he glanced over at Sera as if he was imagining her in a little cowgirl outfit, probably with a whip.

Lil pulled out the list of Abby Ruth's guns. "I'm actually hoping you've recently seen this collection or anything from it."

Rick's brows pulled together as he dragged his finger down the page. "Nice set here. Yours?"

"No. A dear friend's. Stolen from my property, but the local authorities haven't been able to track them down yet. I thought maybe you'd be able to help me."

"Haven't seen anything like this in my

place, but we're required by law to register all guns passing through our shops on the Pawn Tracker Alert database. I can check that for you."

"Would you?"

"Anything for you, Miss Lillian. It's so good to see you. I was worried something happened to you. You were here like clockwork for such a long time."

Boy, wouldn't he be surprised to know where she'd been all that time. "Tell the truth. Gal my age, you thought maybe I kicked the bucket and you missed out on the estate sale." She gave him a wink and he blushed. "Guilty. I can read you, Rick."

"Well, you did always have neat stuff. So where have you been?"

"Folks my age are always checking items off their bucket lists. I went somewhere I thought I'd never, ever visit, much less spend over a year."

"Wow," Rick said. "Sounds like a place I should take the missus. Where'd you go?"

Maggie coughed, and Sera grabbed Lil's arm. "Oh, Lil, don't make us listen to all that vacation stuff again."

"Well, I'm glad you're back," Rick said.

"No one is happier than me."

"Let me check the database for these guns." He tapped on a keyboard at the end of the counter as Sera, Maggie, and Lil meandered through the shop.

Maggie rounded the corner with a teal plastic box. "You won't believe what I found. Look at this. Only forty dollars. Do you know what one of these costs new?" She plopped the carrier on top of a table and opened it up.

"Looks like a giant turkey carver," Lil said.

"A Sawzall, Lil. Do you know how many times I could've used one of these over the past year?"

"Gracious, no."

Rick said, "I'll give you ten percent off today for bringing my old friend back in."

"Sold," Maggie said, carrying the item to the counter.

"Sorry, Miss Lillian. No luck on those guns, but do you have an internet connection back home?"

"Of course we do. We're old, not dead."

He laughed. "I've jotted down this website you can check. Guns like those on your list may show up here. You can keep an eye out for them, but you promise me if they do pop that you'll call your local authority to make the contact. They should be watching this website, but let's be real, they're busy."

Lil smiled. "Thank you. I knew you'd help us."

"Don't be a stranger."

As they left the shop, Lil lagged in the doorway. When she glanced at the ruler along the edge of the door this time, unlike the weekend before she headed off to the big house, she seemed to be back to her same old five feet.

CHAPTER 13

Sera was eager to get the brainstorming process underway. They needed to gather a list of suspects and work this case quickly. If they didn't get started as soon as possible, Marcus would be ready to leave Summer Shoals, and she'd be left out of the investigation. The thought of that ate at her because she'd missed the excitement of solving cases with the girls.

But her mood fell as she pulled into the long driveway leading to Summer Haven. The Maserati that Marcus had rented was parked right out front. "I don't think Marcus will understand our interest in solving these cases," Sera said. "We might have to put off our brainstorming until he leaves." She slammed the gear shift into park and then followed Lil and Maggie inside. "I'm sorry."

Maggie's eye narrowed. "Wait a minute. Where's Abby Ruth? Her truck's been missing so much lately that I didn't notice at first."

"I bet she's with Jenny, but I'll shoot a text to be sure," Sera said.

"Since we have to delay talking about the case, I'm going to make a quick run to the market." Lil took the list from the refrigerator then headed out the door. But there was no spring in her step even though she normally enjoyed grocery shopping.

They had to get Lil's name cleared. It was hard to see her feeling so down. And the last thing Sera wanted was for her safe and happy world here at Summer Haven to feel as if it was beginning to unravel at the edges. They needed to set everything right.

So rather than seeking out Marcus, she took her laptop out to the front porch. Settling into one of the rockers, she began looking up information about that eerie orb, and she checked out the website Rick mentioned.

She'd already been sitting on the front porch for an hour when Marcus came outside. She didn't have to turn around to know it was him, because his familiar ocean-scented aftershave wafted with him. Was it awful that she hoped he didn't want her to join him on a scouting mission this time? She lowered the screen on the laptop to keep him from asking questions about her research.

"I better get a move on or I'll be late for my appointment to see an old cabin north of here." He glanced at his watch. "I'll see you in a while."

"Potential location for the romantic comedy you were telling me about?" she asked.

"Yes, that or the thriller I'm also considering," he responded as he headed for his car.

She watched him leave. He loved his work, and when he had a fresh idea, he reminded her of a six-year-old with a frog in his pocket. Any other wife would probably be worried that her husband was off running around to parts unknown. But she'd never worried about Marcus like that.

Relieved to have alone time with the girls, she tucked her laptop under her arm and made a mad dash inside.

Maggie stood at the kitchen counter stirring up another batch of her tea. At the rate they'd been drinking that mix since all this crazy gauntlet and gun stuff had gone down, they might need to consider a group membership to AA.

Sera set her laptop on the counter next to the pitcher of tea. "I haven't been able to stop thinking about that glowing orb from the mausoleum."

"I know what you mean. I haven't been able to shake it either," Maggie said.

"At first, I thought it was Jessie trying to communicate with me because we were so close, but after my research, I'm not so sure."

Maggie stopped stirring and set the spoon in the sink. "What did you find out?"

Sera tipped back the laptop's screen so Maggie could see it. "Lots of information about similar sightings."

"At our mausoleum? Not ours, but...oh, heck, you know what I mean."

"Not only there. Apparently there's a history of those sightings all over the place, but I found several accounts of them right there at the Holy Innocence Mausoleum," Sera said.

Maggie moved in closer. "Really? I'm surprised we never heard anything about it. Stuff like that usually spreads pretty quickly around here. What does it say?"

"Unfortunately, the orb won't get us any closer to finding Jessie's gauntlets, but..." Sera held up a finger and broke into a grin. "It could be a miracle." She clicked a bookmark to YouTube and pointed at the screen. "See. It looks exactly like what we saw."

"It does." Maggie watched intently. "I thought you couldn't record ghosts."

"Well, maybe orbs and ghosts are different. I don't know, but it says the orb is believed to be Katherine St. Simon, Lady of Sorrows and Healing."

"Sorrows and healing, what does that mean?"

"She's rumored to have healing powers. There are several more recorded accounts on the internet of people who've visited her, let her energy surround their bodies, and whatever disease or ailment they suffered from began to get better."

"Oh my goodness! Are you thinking about Abby Ruth?" Maggie grabbed Sera's arm. "This is big."

"I think so too. We'd be crazy not to at least try it."

Maggie's grin faded. "She'll never go for it."

Sera chewed on her lip. "She has to. I wonder if Jenny would help us get her to the mausoleum?"

"She'd be as skeptical as her mother."

"You're right, we'll have to get clever. We'll get Abby Ruth there, one way or the other."

She heard Lil call out from the front door over the sound of plastic bags rustling, "Home from the grocery."

"Coming," Sera called back, but Lil had already made her way halfway to the kitchen, so Sera grabbed a couple of the bags she had looped over her arm and carried them to the counter.

"Did you hear back from Jenny? Abby Ruth's with her, right?" Lil asked Sera. "I couldn't get this whole mess off my mind while I was at the Piggly Wiggly. I almost missed that cantaloupes were on two for four dollars."

"The cancer mess, gauntlet mess, or gun mess?" Maggie asked.

"All of it," Lil said.

Sera leaned against the counter as Maggie and Lil went through the normal routine of unpacking the groceries and putting them away. "Well, the good news is Jenny took the bullet and told her mom about the missing guns."

"Oh," Lil and Maggie breathed together.

"The not-so-good news is she said her mom was so spun up that it scared her. She wants us to keep her mom out of the investigation."

"That could be a challenge, but Jenny has a point. The last thing Abby Ruth needs right now is another burden on her mind," Maggie said as she dumped grapes into a colander in the sink and began to wash them.

Sera plucked a grape from the strainer. "You're right. She should concentrate on her health. We can take care of the rest."

Looking livelier than she had earlier, Lil pulled a piece of paper from her purse. "When can we start that suspect list?"

"I say we get down to it right now." Excitement streaming through her, Sera tossed the grape in the air and caught it in her mouth. She chewed and grinned. "I think it's time to break out the paper and markers."

Lil gawked at her. "I don't think this is an appropriate time for an art project."

Maggie grinned at Lil and motioned toward the formal dining room. "Watch and learn, my friend."

LIL SETTLED into one of the chairs at the table and rested her hands on the arms. It was obvious Maggie and Sera had some type of ESP system, and it sometimes hurt to be on the outside, but she was learning that their silent communication was helpful when it came to solving crimes.

Maggie left the room and came back in wearing a roll of duct tape like a bangle bracelet.

Sera skipped back into the room, her arms loaded with brightly colored markers and a roll of newsprint.

Lil thought she might swallow her tongue as she watched Maggie help Sera unroll the paper, then yank a wide length of duct tape and slap it against the beautiful flocked wallpaper to secure the paper. She'd taken no more care than if she'd been posting flyers in the Piggly Wiggly's front window.

Lil forced down her protest at the ill treatment of her wall coverings. That stuff was sixty years old anyway, so she tried to keep perspective. What was a little adhesive among friends?

Besides, it was time to get serious about all these problems. It was like the universe was suddenly against Lil. Abby Ruth's guns being stolen from Summer Haven and Lil being caught on film as the last person to touch the precious Jessie gauntlets. A shiver crawled her spine. *I hope all this isn't a sign I wasn't supposed to get out of prison early, because going back would be my undoing.*

"Okay, what do we know for sure?" Sera brandished a big purple marker, and Lil prayed silently it wouldn't bleed through the paper.

"The guns went missing before last Sunday," Maggie said.

Sera wrote the date on the paper. "And Abby Ruth left when?"

"Doesn't matter, because we know that whoever stole the guns cut the inside lock, which means it couldn't have happened until after we moved Abby Ruth's things into the trailer and forgot to lock it." At Maggie's wince, Lil smiled gently and patted her hand. She knew her dear friend was still beating herself up over that mistake.

Sera's eyes lit up. "Perfect. A tight timeframe. Much better. Good job, Lil."

A swell of pride flooded Lil's chest.

Maggie piped up. "All the guns were unusual enough that they can't be pawned easily."

Sera wrote, RARE GUNS, and then drew an arrow. "So we could be looking at someone who needs money or is a gun collector."

"If we're looking for a collector, that would be the reason we haven't come across them in the Pawn Tracker Alert Database. Because they wouldn't be looking to sell the guns."

"Or," Lil said, raising her hand in the air, "like us, the thief didn't know those guns would be hard to get rid of."

"Good point. Only that broadens things out again." Sera tapped the pen against the palm of her hand. "How about we add known thieves? Maybe Jenny can get some insight from Teague on that. And Lil, you know everyone in this town. Certainly we can dig up known baddies around here."

Lil got up and grabbed a pad of paper "I can do that."

Sera pulled in a deep breath. "You know, it wouldn't be so farfetched to suspect Jessie's family. They were always so jealous of her fame. Always tapping at her door for money."

Maggie said, "Maybe you could talk to them since you were so close with Jessie. See what they're thinking."

"I can take that one," Sera said. "Who else?"

Lil chimed in. "A memorabilia collector? And those Jessie lookalikes still seem suspicious to me."

"Yes, Lil. Good one." Maggie grabbed another marker and walked over to jot that on the paper. "Anyone else?"

A grin spread across Sera's face. "Maybe a crossdresser with a fringe fetish?"

"For goodness sake," Lil exclaimed.

"Hey, it's not that farfetched."

"Maybe not in Los Angeles," Lil said. "But it is in these parts."

Maggie wrote CD w/a FF down at the very bottom of the page. "Who all was around the house between the time we moved Abby Ruth's things to the trailer and when we discovered the guns were missing?"

"The mailman left a package at the front door," Sera said.

"I think Teague had at least one Little League practice on the field out back," Lil added. "So anyone connected with the team."

"Goodness gracious." Maggie blew out a slow breath. "There are at least twenty kids on Grayson's baseball team, which means thirty to forty parents."

"Was there anyone else here at Summer Haven?" Lil said, then noticed a strange expression on Sera's face. "What are you thinking?"

"N...nothing." She quickly looked away and concentrated on the paper in front of her.

"Lil," Maggie said softly, "I think we have

to add Charlie to this list. I know how much you liked him, but he spent two nights—"

"I'd sooner suspect Angelina herself than Charlie." Her shoulders rolled in and she slumped in her chair. "I'm telling you, that boy had manners. Something you don't see much of these days."

Sera *hmmed* and drew a little star next to Charlie's name.

"Anyone else?" Maggie asked. "There have been a lot of strangers in town lately."

Lil sent Maggie an appreciative smile. Yes, she might be throwing Lil a bone, but the intent was nice.

"What about Brad Huffman? He stopped by one day to see Marcus." Sera wrote Brad's name above Charlie's on the paper under the heading SUSPECTS. "The gun shop owner reminded me that I read about Brad's collection in one of the entertainment magazines. It stood out to me because most people living in California think guns are Satan's sticks."

"But he's so handsome." Lil frowned at Sera as she jotted down the famous actor's name.

"He was here during the window of opportunity," Maggie said.

Window of opportunity. Lil committed the phrase to memory.

"Yes, he was."

Marcus knocked on the doorframe, but the adoring look he usually wore around Sera was nonexistent. "Sera, what's going on here, and why are you discussing Brad? "

"I thought you were out scouting more locations," Sera said. "How long have you been standing there?"

"That cabin turned out to be a cheap gardening shed, and I've been here long enough to hear a few things I don't like. You need to let the sheriff take care of those stolen guns."

Sera capped the marker and let out a breath. "I'm afraid we can't do that."

Marcus stepped into the room, his hands on his hips and elbows out, taking up more than his fair share of the space. "What? You ladies suddenly think you're Charlie's Angels or something?"

Lil rather liked picturing herself as Bri, the Kate Jackson angel. Smart and no-nonsense.

"Marcus, you don't understand. These are Abby Ruth's guns and we have to—"

"I think I do understand. But what I don't understand is how you'd think Brad, an old friend of ours, would steal your new friend's guns. Have you completely lost it?"

"No. We're just following all leads, hon."

"Do not embarrass me with my colleagues, Sera. I get it. You're having a little fun, but stolen guns are serious and dangerous business. This is real life. Not television. You can't honestly believe Brad would break into a horse trailer and scrounge around for guns. First of all, how would he have known they were there? And second, the man has plenty of resources. If he wanted a gun, he could damn well buy it for himself."

Sera lifted a shoulder, but it was clear she wasn't backing down and she wasn't intimidated by her husband's skepticism. "First, this is a small town and people talk, so Brad could've heard about Abby Ruth's eccentric collection that way. A few of the guns were quite rare. And you know as well as I do that many of the Hollywood types aren't particularly good about hearing the word *no*."

He scowled at Sera. "You used to think everyone was good at the core. What's happened to you? I've indulged your need to be back in Summer Shoals. Hell, I'm starting to see why you love the place. But now you're turning your new life against our old one.

From one day to the next, I'm not sure where we stand."

"It's not personal, Marcus. That's the way this private investigation thing works. We have to explore every possibility even if it makes us uncomfortable or sad. We've brought down criminals who were members of this community. It doesn't make us happy, but it does expose the truth."

"I said I don't know where we stand, but the reality is I'm afraid it's worse than that. I don't know who you are anymore." He shook his head and left the room. Then the sound of the front door opening and closing filtered to the dining room.

"Oh, Sera—" Lil started.

But Sera held up her hand. "Can we table that little scene for now? I know Marcus is upset, but I *will* go talk with Brad. Let's finish our brainstorming session for now and figure out what else we need to do."

Unfortunately, Lil was fairly certain the next thing she needed to do was pay a visit to Angelina Broussard.

CHAPTER 14

*O*h, Lordy had the poop hit the propeller when Abby Ruth returned from Jenny's the evening before. She'd stomped around in those boots of hers, mumbling and grumbling, even pulling at her short hair.

Had Abby Ruth not already dropped the bomb about her cancer, Lil might've been inclined to chastise her for clomping around like that on the heart pine floors, but Abby Ruth had clearly been devastated, and seeing her like that was like meeting a stranger. At one point, her eyes had filled with tears. Those guns meant the world to that woman.

When Maggie tried to wrap her in a hug, Abby Ruth pulled away and blew her nose like a foghorn, claiming seasonal allergies. They'd let her get away with the fib.

But this morning, it was clearly time to investigate further. And although Lil was having a hard time believing Charlie could've had a darn thing to do with Abby Ruth's stolen guns, she had to do something to cross him off their suspect list.

So she selected a nice pantsuit from her closet—one with elastic for the back of the waistband since she'd yet to lose all the weight she gained in prison camp—and applied her signature pink lipstick.

It didn't do to go into a lion's den without the proper precautions.

When she walked into the parlor, Maggie and Abby Ruth were watching television.

"Well, don't you look nice," Maggie said to Lil. "Where are you off to?"

"To talk to Angelina."

Maggie's lips went tight, and she shook her head and glared at Lil.

"Why are you looking at me like that, Maggie?"

Abby Ruth's back went straight, and suspicion swarmed her face. "Are y'all talking code behind my back?"

Oh. Oh, no. Lil, would you like to allow any other cats to stroll out of the bag?

She felt like a big old dope because she'd

been so focused on her visit to Angelina to clear Charlie's name that she hadn't thought about Abby Ruth sitting there.

"What?" Abby Ruth demanded. "What are you two up to?"

"You're being paranoid," Maggie said.

Maybe it was better to stick with the truth as much as possible, and it might soothe Abby Ruth to know they were doing something to get her guns back. "I'm going to talk to Angelina about the young man who rented your room. I don't believe for a moment that he's got anything to do with your missing guns, but I can see that it would be irresponsible not to—how would you phrase it?—pull that string of possibility."

Abby Ruth muted the TV and looked at Lil, one of her eyebrows doing a move Lil had only seen when Sera folded herself into a yoga contortion. "Why *wouldn't* you suspect him? Or did you rent my room to more than one person while I was gone?"

Lord, would this woman forgive Lil for running her own house the way she saw fit? "We very carefully packed up your belongings and stored them with thought."

"You might've *thought* to lock my trailer," she grumbled.

"You're absolutely right. That was careless of us. Which is exactly the reason we're trying to make this right by finding every last one of your guns."

"You should've told me what happened the minute I drove up. Or texted me while I was gone." Abby Ruth turned and gave Maggie the stink eye. Lil didn't have a fancy phone, so she couldn't be held responsible for that oversight.

"Do you really think you were in any shape to hear the news then?" Maggie asked gently.

Abby Ruth ignored her and looked Lil up and down. "You sure put on the dog for Angelina. That woman. I don't trust her further than I can throw her with my left arm. And you know how well that damn thing is working right now."

Lil picked up her purse and looped it over her arm. "Regardless of how any of us feel about her, I'm hopeful she'll make this as painless as possible."

"Wait a minute," Maggie said. "This is important to all of us. Why are you the one talking to Angelina?"

"Because I'm the one who said yes when she asked for a favor, and that's when this whole mess started."

Abby Ruth pushed against the divan and

rose to her feet. "I can promise that you're not going to interrogate Angelina Broussard without me."

As Abby Ruth stalked toward the front, Lil said to Maggie, "Maybe we shouldn't tell Jenny about this."

"You think?"

Lil hurried outside, her chest tight from having made such a misstep.

Of all the reasons she still mourned the fact that she'd been forced to sell Daddy's Tucker 48 lookalike to Angelina, Abby Ruth's jumbo-size truck was the biggest of them. She tried half a dozen times to climb into that Goliath without success. Finally, Abby Ruth came around and gave her a boost with her good arm. And not a gentle one. She put a palm under Lil's fanny and shoved her up like she was a human shot put.

Now, they were headed down Main Street toward Angelina's, with Abby Ruth driving like she was competing for pole position and Lil sitting in the passenger seat, her feet hanging off the edge like Lily Tomlin in those old rocking-chair skits. Something about being unable to touch the floor made an old woman feel silly and small.

She wrapped her hands around the

seatbelt, trying to stay upright as Abby Ruth took the turn onto Angelina's street.

"If we get to Angelina's alive, I'd appreciate it if you would stand back and let me ask the questions," Lil said.

"Would you let someone else do that if your children had been kidnapped?"

"It's not like we're talking about Jenny and Grayson here. Please try to keep this all in perspective." Lil looked out the side window to disguise her eye roll. If she'd ever been fortunate enough to have children, she wouldn't have named them Glock and Ruger. It was surprising Jenny wasn't named Kimber after that fancy gun Abby Ruth loved so much. "I shouldn't have to tell you that you and Angelina have a history of rubbing each other the wrong way. This isn't about making a power play. It's about getting information in a friendly way so we can get your belongings back with the least possible fuss."

Abby Ruth didn't do much more than grunt, but when she approached Angelina's house, she pulled the steering wheel slightly to the right, just enough that the wheels on Lil's side of the truck ended up over the curb and in the front yard. Lil sighed to herself.

If Angelina caught sight of Abby Ruth's

parking job, she'd have a fit, but the positive side was Lil wouldn't have far to step down from the truck.

They rang the bell, and a few moments later the front door swung open to reveal Angelina, dressed in a pair of silvery jeans that looked as if they'd been sprayed on her legs in an auto body shop. Her blouse was a riot of abstract colors with sleeves so full she looked as if she might take flight at any second. "Hello?"

"Angelina," Lil said, "we need a few minutes of your time."

Angelina cast a quick look past Lil, toward the house next door that matched the blue-and-pink color of her own, except in reverse. "I still have guests at the B&B. I was about to run over and—"

"It won't take a minute." Lil stepped forward and put on her best society smile as she slid past Angelina and into the foyer.

When Angelina turned to protest, Abby Ruth stalked inside as well. Angelina's face scrunched up like she'd eaten a big bowl of peeled kumquats, but she quickly waved an arm in welcome as if she'd been the one to invite them inside. "What can I help you with?"

Goodness, just like young people these days, always wanting to get right down to business. What happened to the days when a hostess asked if she could take your bag or if you'd like a cup of tea? Manners never went out of style, but they'd certainly been forgotten by many. Surely this investigation stuff would be much more pleasant over tea and cookies.

Maybe Lil needed to write a handbook: *Lillian Summer Fairview's Guide to Crime Investigation Etiquette.*

"We have a few questions about that lowlife you brought over to Summer Haven," Abby Ruth said.

"Excuse me?"

First copy of that handbook will go directly to Abby Ruth.

"What Abby Ruth means is we'd like to send a thank-you note to Mr. Millet. We wondered if you might have his address."

Angelina's eyelashes, thick with mascara, looked like moth wings as she blinked slowly. "You want his contact information?"

"Don't you send all your customers a follow-up note?" Lil asked. "It seems like good business sense to me."

"Are you insinuating that I don't know how to run my own B&B?" She crossed her arms, making her colorful shirt's arms flap like a bat heading out at sundown to find her dinner. "Or maybe you're planning to try to give me a run for my money? I hate to tell you this, Lillian, but Summer Haven isn't zoned for commercial use. If you have a mind to start accepting paying boarders—" she shot a scathing look in Abby Ruth's direction, "—then you can think again. That would be illegal."

"Then why were you so hot to foist ol' Charlie off on them in the first place?" Abby Ruth shifted her weight and rested a fist on her cocked hip. "Didn't have a problem with it when it suited you, I see. Maybe that was because you and Charlie have a little something-something going on the side."

"Excuse me? My husband is the most successful doctor in Summer Shoals, why would I need—"

"Not that kind of something-something," Abby Ruth snapped. "But how can we be sure you didn't stash him at Summer Haven to do recon for you?"

Abby Ruth's face was darned near the color of her flaming red boots, and sweat was forming at her temples. If she fell out right here on Angelina's floor, Jenny would never forgive Lil. *Take a breath, Abby Ruth.* Jenny was right. Keeping Abby Ruth out of this stuff wouldn't be easy, but it was necessary. She didn't need this kind of stress on top of her health concerns.

Lil placed a hand on Abby Ruth's shoulder, hoping to calm her.

Angelina swung her head around like she was part owl. "Why would I care what's happening at that old place?"

Her dismissive tone hit Lil right in the pride. Still, she tried to keep the peace. "Abby Ruth, why don't we—"

"Maybe because you wanted him to scope out any valuables," Abby Ruth cut in.

Angelina slid a sideways look at Lil. "The way I hear it, there's not much of value in that house anymore. So not only is what you're insinuating ridiculous, it's insulting. Having Charlie stay at Summer Haven was an emergency. A one-time thing."

"Maybe she's worried you're better at this inn-keeping thing than she is and wanted Charlie to spy on your breakfast menu," Abby Ruth said to Lil.

Angelina huffed. "That's silly—"

"Angelina, I promise I have no intention of turning Summer Haven into some revolving door boarding house." But if Lil took in the occasional business traveler, who would ever know? "If you'll simply give me Charlie's home address, phone number, and email, Abby Ruth and I will be on our way." Lord, these two women were exhausting. The rate this was going, she'd need a senior citizen's nap when she returned home, and it was only ten in the morning now. "In fact, I'll be happy to sing your B&B's praises in my note to him."

Angelina sniffed. "I've worked too long and hard to put Broussard B&B on the map to let someone snatch it all away from me."

Lil glanced at Angelina's perfect gel nails. She'd bet a hundred dollars—money she didn't have to spare—that Angelina had hired others to work long and hard for her. Good grief, her B&B only had half a dozen rooms, yet she had a full-time manager on staff. "I understand completely. You should be proud of what you've built here."

Behind Angelina, Abby Ruth opened her mouth wide and poked her finger inside, mimicking making herself sick. When the other woman whirled around to reach for a pad of paper on the entryway table, Abby Ruth quickly dropped her arm and stood there as straight and innocent as a choir boy.

Angelina quickly jotted something on the

paper. "Here's all his pertinent information. Charlie Millet. 555 Duffer Mill Way in Minden, Louisiana. And he always calls so I don't have his email address."

"That's fine. I think those electronic thank-you notes are tacky anyway. I'll send him a personalized notecard."

Angelina handed over the page with Charlie's details on it, and Lil folded it twice, sharply creasing the edges before slipping it into her handbag. "Thank you so much, dear. We'll get out of your hair now."

When they were outside on the sidewalk, Lil said to Abby Ruth, "See what you can catch with sugar instead of vinegar?"

"If I know Angelina—" Abby Ruth never slowed her purposeful stride toward the truck, "—then I'm pretty sure what you caught was a big ol' pile of stinking hot bullcrap."

CHAPTER 15

When they returned to Summer Haven, Abby Ruth stomped upstairs, and Lil huddled in the kitchen with Maggie and Sera to give them an update. "I got Charlie's contact information from Angelina."

"I'm surprised Abby Ruth didn't call him from the truck."

"No telling what she would have said to the poor man. I didn't give her the chance." She tapped her handbag. "The information is safe right here in my bag, but I do think it's time to clear Charlie once and for all. I'm calling him right now so we can move forward finding the real culprit."

She picked up the landline and dialed. *Ring, ring, ring.* Finally, the call clicked to connect. Unfortunately, all she got was a recording.

"Hello, Charlie. It was so lovely to have you at Summer Haven. After you left, I realized I'd love to have your mother's Brunswick stew recipe, the one you were telling me about. If it wouldn't be too much trouble, I would appreciate a return call." She recited the phone number then set the receiver back in its cradle.

"No one home?"

"I got voicemail, but the message was recorded by a woman who said her name was Robin Polaski," Lil said.

"That doesn't sound good," Maggie said.

"It could be his girlfriend's number," Lil protested, then turned to Sera and held out the piece of paper. "Angelina didn't have his email, but she gave me this address."

Sera whipped out her tie-dyed cheaters and studied the page. "I can do a Google search on his name and the city."

"It's that easy?" Lil asked. "Whatever happened to the white pages?"

"These are the white pages, but better. They don't have to be recycled." With her normal lightning typing speed, Sera tapped away on the keyboard. As she continued, her forehead creased in a way Lil had rarely witnessed, which did not bode well. Sera looked up. "Are you sure this is the right information?"

Lil looked past Sera's shoulder at the address she'd typed into the website. "Angelina wrote it down herself."

"Could she have been mistaken about where he lived?"

"I don't think so. She looked it up while we were standing right there." Lil sat down. "Why? What did you find?"

"That's just it," Sera said. "I didn't find a thing. And although his name isn't as common as Smith, it isn't uncommon either. I Googled him. Then I used my favorite people finder website, findpeoplenow.com. I typed in Charlie Millet and Minden, Louisiana. No results. Then I tried Charles Millet. Heck, I even tried Chaz. Nada. If this search engine says there isn't a Charlie, Charles, or Chaz Millet in that town, it's probably accurate."

"What do you think that means?"

Maggie sighed. "It means your darling Charlie was a liar."

Lil's heart crumpled. "But he was so nice."

"Lil, can you remember anything about Charlie that might help us run him down?"

"Just that I was a better cook than his

momma, but that she makes a mean Brunswick stew."

With her pointer finger, Maggie rubbed a circle in the center of her forehead. "George and I used to attend a hardware conference every year. Luckily, it moved from place to place. It was actually in Shreveport once."

"If I remember my geography correctly, that's not too far from Minden," Lil said.

"Then we know he was either lying to you about the stew or where he's from."

"You should never lie about family recipes."

"I think he was probably telling the truth about his momma's cooking, but that means he's not from Louisiana. We might think Brunswick stew goes with barbecue like jelly goes with peanut butter, but I never saw it on a menu anywhere in Louisiana."

"Interesting," Sera said. "This is one of those times when it would be helpful to have our resident Texan in the room."

Lil cast a quick glance toward the kitchen doorway to make sure their resident Texan wasn't listening in. "I think we all know that's not a good idea. The last thing I want to do is set back her recovery. And she needs her strength for when they do the radiation."

"She hasn't decided on that yet," Sera told Lil.

"Well, of course she'll get the treatment." Lil hadn't even considered she might not. That frightened her.

"We don't know what she'll decide, but it's up to her. And you're right, no matter what she decides, she's going to need her strength," Sera agreed. "So it still looks like Charlie is our best bet. Problem is, we need to find the man."

"Well, if he was telling the truth about his momma's Brunswick stew, then we know it's likely he's from here in Georgia, North Carolina, or Virginia."

"That's not a lot to go on."

Something occurred to Lil. "One of the evenings he was staying here, he ventured out for some dinner and entertainment."

One side of Sera's mouth lifted. "And we all know what *entertainment* is a code word for. I hear that Gary's Gallery of Girls place just over the line in Pitts County does a pretty swift business."

"Sera!" Lil scolded. "Charlie might be a thief, but he was respectful. I don't know how things work out there in LA, but this is a small town and our nice gentlemen don't go to...um..."

"Gentlemen's clubs?" Maggie offered. "Maybe, because it's not like there are a lot of evening entertainment options around here, Lil."

Lil covered her face with her hands. Well, at least she hadn't caught Harlan partaking in that particular vice.

Sera rolled the marker between her hands. "We definitely should talk to folks at the diner and Earlene's Drinkery. They've been good sources of information before." She turned and started another column, listing both places and the gentleman's club, too.

"Why don't we start at the diner and go from there?" Maggie said. "I bet Dottie could tell us if Charlie met anyone for dinner or happened to say anything helpful while he was there."

"Sure wish I'd taken a picture of him." But how was Lil to know she'd be hunting down her guest a few days later? "And I'll talk to Angelina and confirm his contact information."

"I have an idea." Maggie hopped up and hurried to the kitchen. A few minutes later, she returned with a large russet potato and an armful of kitchen gadgets.

"What in heaven's name?"

"Give me a minute." She laid out all her cooking supplies. "Now, what can we remember about Charlie?"

"He had dark hair and a mustache."

"Perfect." Maggie grabbed the potato and speared it with a basting brush so the bristles drooped down over the potato. Then she unwrapped a chocolate cupcake Lil hadn't been aware was in the house. With a sad look, Maggie contemplated it for a few seconds and muttered something that sounded like, "Sometimes sacrifices must be made." With a definitive movement, she shoved the cupcake onto the top of the potato.

Sera hooted with laughter. "I loved this as a kid. I had the set—Mr. and Mrs. Potato Head. My favorite was attaching Mr. Potato Head's lips to Mrs. Potato Head's butt."

Lord, that sounded more likely to be right up Abby Ruth's wicked alley. "Mags, why are we playing some warped version of a cooking show?"

She frowned at her creation. "I know it won't actually look like Charlie." She glanced at Lil. "But it will get us thinking about the specifics of his features."

"With a potato?" Lil asked. "Besides, he looks less like Charlie and more like Adolf

Hitler if you ask me. We need something a little more realistic. Sera, you painted all those backdrops for the July Fourth parade a while back. Can't you do something?"

Still chuckling, Sera grabbed Maggie in a one-armed hug. "Have I told you lately how much I love you? But if you'll both hang on a minute, I think Lil's right. We can do better."

She went upstairs and came back carrying an iPad. "Check this out." She sat down next to Lil and waved Maggie over.

Maggie cast another glance at her Charlie lookalike creation, then gave a small shrug. She brought it with her to the table and used her finger to scoop off bits of chocolate frosting and pop them in her mouth. When she caught Lil looking at her, she said around a mouthful of cupcake, "If a gal can't indulge herself now and again, there's really no reason to keep on living."

True enough.

Sera did a little chair dance and tap-tapped on her screen to bring up what Lil now knew was called an app. "This is the coolest thing. I found it while I was in California, and I hoped we'd get the opportunity to use it."

The screen opened up with a big blank spot in the middle and a row of what looked like shrunken heads in an assortment of shapes and sizes. "Would you say he had a square head, a round head, or something else?"

"Maybe more oval."

With her index finger, Sera selected a head that looked a bit like Bert from Sesame Street and dragged it to the middle of the screen. She clicked again and outfitted the head with dark hair and a bushy mustache.

"Much better. Less like Hitler and more like Groucho Marx," Lil told her.

Little by little, Sera added what they could remember about their guest—tiny earlobes, a nose that crooked slightly to the left, and a softish chin—until after a series of clicks and resizing features, the picture in front of them looked enough like Charlie that Lil said, "That's him."

"It is," Maggie agreed. "It looks just like him."

"Great," Sera said. "I'll send a copy of this to each of our phones." She paused and looked at Lil. "Since you don't have a cell phone, I'll print one out for you."

For the first time, Lil regretted that she'd stubbornly refused to get one of those newfangled smart phones.

Before, she'd never understood why

someone would want to listen to music from her pocket or type short messages to a friend. Seemed like one more way the modern world was intruding on the good ol' days when calling on someone meant traveling to their house and paying them a civilized visit. But it could also mean she'd have a phone-a-friend option if she ever needed it.

But today, that was neither here nor there. They needed to get out in the community and do what they could to track down the man who had most likely stolen their friend's beloved guns.

LIL AND MAGGIE flashed the picture of Charlie around town most of the afternoon and got absolutely nowhere. When they spoke with Dottie at the Atlanta Highway Diner, even she had no insider info for them. Nothing much ever got past the longtime waitress, so that was disappointing. Wherever Charlie ate when he was in Summer Shoals, apparently it wasn't at the diner.

This investigation was not going well at all.

Maybe Lil was messing up the girls' mojo.

Maybe she wasn't meant to be part of the team.

She and Maggie came back to Summer Haven no closer to the truth than when they left. Lil bristled at the thought that she might not fit in, and she dropped her purse on a chair in the parlor as Sera and Marcus came downstairs.

Sera rushed into the room ahead of Marcus. "I'm going to run over to Angelina's with Marcus." She lowered her voice. "He's still mad, insisting if I plan to talk with Brad that he's going with me. I'm hoping I can investigate and soothe Marcus all at the same time. Maybe you girls can get a good lead at Earlene's Drinkery. We were lucky there before, remember?" she said. "But wait until Abby Ruth goes out or somehow keep it from her. We don't want to upset her again."

She shot Lil an okay symbol, then draped her poncho over her arm and left with Marcus.

No. Lil didn't remember, because she hadn't helped them crack that case. And danged if she didn't sometimes feel like the last one picked for the kickball team, and she didn't like that feeling one bit. But she wasn't about to be left out this time.

So Lil followed Maggie outside and climbed into her little red pickup. At least she could get herself up into this truck, unlike Abby Ruth's beast.

"Earlene's it is," Maggie said.

No surprise the parking lot was full. Dollar draft night always brought a crowd to Earlene's. Harlan had cozied up to the bar regularly when he was alive, but Earlene's wasn't a place Lil normally frequented. Especially now that she knew the bar had sold Harlan plenty of lottery tickets over the years. On principle she'd waged a personal boycott on the joint.

Maggie slid out of the truck and headed for the door. "Someone in here has to have seen Charlie."

"Just because a man drinks doesn't make him a thief," Lil said, hearing the sulk in her own voice.

Maggie slowly turned to Lil. "After all we've all been through over the past couple of years, you're the last person who should believe all people who seem good are good." She placed her hands on Lil's shoulders. "Repeat after me. Bad Charlie."

"Bad Charlie?"

"Yes. That's right. Say it again."

"Bad Charlie?"

"Charlie isn't a good guy."

"He was nice."

"He lied. Lying is bad. He's Bad. Bad, bad Charlie."

"Oh stop it. Besides, we aren't all that much better. We were keeping the truth from Abby Ruth about her guns and now we're investigating without her."

Maggie swung open the bar's front door and walked inside. "Well, we had good intentions, and we can manage this perfectly well without her now that you're back."

Oh, that certainly made her feel like a first-string kickball pick. In fact, being as good as Abby Ruth was better than being a simple team member. That woman was fearless, so if Maggie thought Lil was just as good, she was like the team captain.

"Crud." Maggie said, throwing a hand out in front of Lil, nearly clotheslining her.

"Ouch. What was that for?"

"Look who's at the bar."

Sure enough, at the far end of the bar sat a tall, slender woman rocking a pair of skinny jeans stuffed into boots the color of a Hawaiian sunset and a white blouse starched as sharp as that wit of hers. Unmistakable even from the back. Abby Ruth Cady.

"Well, let's circle around to this end of the bar. She won't see us. We'll flash the picture of

Bad Charlie then get out of here."

"Do we have to call him that?"

Maggie's mouth thinned to a stubborn line. "Yes, we do."

Lil nodded and tucked herself behind Maggie. "And what's Abby Ruth doing here anyway? She shouldn't be drinking."

"She could just be watching the game."

"She has a short glass filled with something dark-colored. Drinking whiskey in her condition is idiotic."

Maggie snickered. "Are you planning to tell Abby Ruth that she's an idiot? Lil, you have a lot to learn about communicating with that woman. Let's take care of our business and get out of here."

True. Taking Abby Ruth head-on was probably not a good plan. No sense ruining the détente they'd established recently. "Right behind you."

Maggie led the way, taking a wide sweep to the outside of the dark bar. Black leather couches and chairs made up small conversation pits. On this side of the room management still allowed smoking, and Lil waved a hand in front of her face to clear the smog. TVs broadcast sporting events at ear-bleeding levels from competing stations, creating a chaotic atmosphere. Couple that with the occasional crash of billiard balls, and Lil thought she probably knew how criminals felt when the cops dropped one of those noisy flash things.

Maggie approached the nearest bartender, and he called out, "Maggie Rawls, haven't seen you in a while!"

She put a finger to her lips and shifted her back to Abby Ruth. "Shhhh."

The bartender's forehead creased in confusion.

"I don't want Abby Ruth to know we're here."

He looked over his shoulder. "She hasn't said much tonight. Not like her. Of course, the Astros lost again, so a calm Abby Ruth is better than the one that breaks a pool stick over the jukebox when her team loses."

Maggie flashed Lil a see-you-don't-want-to-mess-with-her look.

"Point taken," Lil said. She pulled the printed copy of the Charlie sketch from her purse and handed it to the bartender. "Have you seen this man in here?"

He glanced at the picture. "Don't have my glasses, but ask Sasha. She knows the customers better than anyone."

"Thanks." Maggie worked her way to a corner booth and took a seat. "Abby Ruth won't be able to see us over here."

Sasha weaved through the crowd with precision, never dribbling a drop from her full tray of drinks. Anywhere else, three waitresses would be working a bar this size, but Sasha handled the capacity with ease and a smile. "Hey, ladies. What can I get ya?"

"We don't need a drink, but keep this as a tip, dear." Lil slid a twenty across the table along with the sketch. "Have you seen this young man in here?"

Sasha studied the picture. "It's a little dark in here, but he does kind of look familiar."

Maggie whipped out her iPhone and handed it to Sasha. "This better?"

"Oh yeah!" The waitress tapped the phone with a polish-chipped fingernail.

Lil cringed at the sight. Didn't take much time for a woman to keep her manicure in check, or at the very least remove the polish when it began to chip. Seriously, didn't these young girls take any pride in themselves?

"That's Charlie," Sasha said. "Strong, silent type."

That surprised Lil, because the Charlie she'd met seemed very outgoing and likable.

"Been coming here a long time. About every three weeks or so."

"Bingo." Satisfaction streaming through her, Lil winked at Maggie. "Recently?"

"A few days ago. He always seems to just be passing through on his way somewhere. Business, I guess. Important business probably, because he's one big tipper."

Maggie asked, "He ever say what business he's in?"

"Transportation and logistics."

Lil pondered that for a moment. "What does that mean? He could be anything from a truck driver to an air traffic controller."

Sasha shrugged. "As long as he tips me in fifty and hundred dollar bills he can be whatever he wants."

"Do you know how to get in touch with him?"

"No. Never asked."

"Has he ever had company here at the bar?"

"Yes. But his friends were quiet, like him, only not big tippers."

"Did he ever say anything about guns?" Maggie asked.

The waitress paled. "Never. Why would he talk about guns?"

A woman came sauntering up behind Sasha, and Lil's heart clenched. She swept the composite sketch off the table and into her lap, and she tried to kick Maggie, but she couldn't reach. Lil gave a hearty over-the-top laugh. "Oh, Maggie is just joking with you."

The waitress shot Lil an are-you-crazy look. "I got tables to wait on," Sasha said. "You need anything else over here, flag me down, okay?"

"They don't need a damn thing," Abby Ruth said, waving her off.

The waitress took the escape route.

Eyes squinty and chin in the air, Abby Ruth asked, "What are y'all doing here?"

"Chatting with Sasha about drink choices."

"What did you scoop into your lap?"

"Nothing." Lil had never been a good liar, but she tried by saying, "We were talking about some repairs at Summer Haven."

"With the waitress? You want me to believe that Sasha does construction work on the side?" Abby Ruth's fist found its favorite spot on her cocked hip.

"I meant Maggie and I were discussing it."

"You expect me to believe you got in the car and drove all the way over here to talk about home repairs and you don't even have a drink? That makes no sense at all. I'm a regular here, but you two? Y'all could probably count on one hand how many times you've been here. Doesn't add up, ladies."

"Just as much sense as you being here drinking does." Lil was sorry she'd said it before the last word came out of her mouth, because Abby Ruth was already turning three shades of magenta.

"Excuse me?" Abby Ruth rose to her full height, close to six feet tall in those danged boots of hers.

Lil had already rolled out the grenade. She couldn't just sit there now. She took in a deep breath and blurted it out. "You shouldn't be drinking. It's not good for you in your condition."

"Oh, Lil," Maggie said, dropping her head into her hands.

"My condition is fine, thank you very much." Abby Ruth snapped her fingers in the air above Lil's head. "Quit treating me like I'm dying. If I choose to drink, bar brawl, or bungee jump, it's my damn business." Abby Ruth's nostrils flared and her spiked-up hair suddenly gave the illusion of an insulted dark-headed cockatoo. "And for the record, I was drinking root beer and watching the game. Now, what the heck are the two of you really doing here?"

It was time to stop with all the lies, so Lil pulled the sketch out from under the table. "We stopped in for a few minutes because we thought someone might have information about Charlie."

Abby Ruth scooted into the booth next to her and plucked the portrait from her fingers. "So this is what that no-good bum looks like. I could've spotted him as a crook from a mile away." She tossed the picture on the table.

"It looks like he might not have been quite as good as he seemed on the surface," Lil said.

"Those over-the-top nicely mannered men always raise my suspicions. Probably a sociopath. The nicer they are, the warier I am. That contact information Angelina gave you was useless. Dead end, wasn't it?"

Abby Ruth had been right. Clearly her radar was better than Lil's when it came to bad guys. "Like the alley behind the market. Not a thing there of use."

"Yeah. I knew that was a complete line of BS Angelina was giving you."

Maggie lifted her arm along the back of the booth seat. "Abby Ruth has Spidey senses on that stuff," she explained. "Her intuition has been key to every case we've solved."

"Thank you," Abby Ruth said, her attitude softening a skosh. "But if you really believe that, then why are y'all leaving me out of everything?"

Lil folded her hands on the table. "You became so upset when we went to Angelina's, and we don't want to add to your stress."

"Leaving me out is stressing me out!" Abby Ruth said loud enough that heads turned in their direction.

"See, that's what I'm talking about."

Abby Ruth paused and breathed, then leaned in and lowered her voice. "You don't know anything about guns. You don't even know what you're looking for."

"But your guns disappeared from my home and we're trying to set it straight." Telling Abby Ruth her daughter was the main reason they'd left her out of the investigation wouldn't help the situation. And if Abby Ruth decided to push things, she could probably make Lil file a claim with her insurance and then that bill would go up. She was having enough trouble making ends meet as it was. This whole situation could quickly start tumbling like a pile of TNT-filled dominoes, and they'd all be in a heap of trouble if she lost the house.

"Stop it," Abby Ruth said. "It happened. It's

not on you to fix it."

"We can't just sit and wait for Teague to find them," Maggie said. "He's up to his eyeballs in rich celebrity duties. Besides I feel responsible."

"They're my guns, so I've got the most to lose." Abby Ruth's mouth turned down, an expression on any other woman that would've indicated she was about to cry. "Besides, what if this is my...my last investigation?"

Oh, Lord have mercy, how could they possibly say no to that pitiful request, even if it was melodramatic hooey?

Maggie didn't look like she was going to budge, but Lil couldn't argue with Abby Ruth's points. There were valid, after all.

"Fine," Lil said. "You're in."

Jenny would just have to forgive them.

CHAPTER 16

*T*he next morning, Abby Ruth hopped out of bed with the sunrise. She hadn't felt this much like her old self in months. Not since she'd begun keeping her own secrets from her friends. But hers were out in the open now. And maybe the confrontation at Earlene's Drinkery last night had been a bit awkward, but now her friends were no longer investigating behind her back, so things around here could get back to normal.

Granted, if Lil hadn't rented out her room in the first place, her guns probably wouldn't have been stolen. Then again, if she'd told them where she was going instead of sneaking off to Houston, Lil probably wouldn't have taken in a sticky-fingered boarder to begin with.

So the missing guns were as much Abby Ruth's own fault as theirs.

Besides, those gals needed her skills, and working these cases was one thing that made her feel young and useful.

Spidey senses. She thrust her wrists forward like Spider-Man. *Whoosh whoosh.* Yeah, not a bad super hero to be like. Better than Wonder Woman. Invisible airplane? That was downright silly.

Tucking her denim shirt into her jeans, she slipped a hand-embroidered Peruvian wool belt through the loops of her Levi's and checked the look in the mirror.

She was still sore from her visit to the gun range. Yeah, she'd rushed that a little, so today she'd just clean her Glock and work with the girls on finding her collection. She knew darn well Bad Charlie had to be the one who'd stolen her guns, and she had a bullet with that son-of-a-gun's name on it.

Okay, maybe a pellet, but she knew how to make those hurt like the dickens.

A sweet aroma wafted up the stairs and Abby Ruth sucked in a lungful. This day was getting better and better. That had to be the scent of Sera's famous vegan cinnamon rolls with soy frosting in the air.

"I've missed those cinnamon rolls," she said to herself as she descended the stairs.

More than once she'd been surprised that something Sera had whipped up tasted as good, better in this case, than the real thing. And she didn't want to know what was in the pastry because that would likely ruin the whole experience.

Her friends' casual chatter was comforting on this bright morning, and her world finally felt right again for the first time since she'd first heard the words *breast cancer.* Sure, she still had some big decisions to make, but things would be okay. She'd done everything she'd been told to do up to this point. And she'd learned one big lesson along the way.

No more secrets.

At the sound of Sera's laugh, a smile tugged at Abby Ruth's lips. Summer Haven hadn't been this alive and vibrant without Sera, and if she left again, for good this time, the house might never be the same.

"And I didn't get any good leads," Sera said from inside the kitchen. "But I did clear someone off of our suspect list."

"The actor with the gun fetish?" Lil asked.

"Yes. I spoke with Brad Huffman, and not

only does he have a good alibi, but he collects German guns, so he has no interest in Abby Ruth's Spanish collection. And like Marcus said, he has enough money to buy anything he wants. Sounds like he's off our list."

"We didn't have much luck either," Maggie said. "But Abby Ruth knows we're looking into this, and she wants to help find her guns."

At the mention of her name, Abby Ruth stopped short of the door.

Sera's voice rose. "How did she find out? I thought we said we were going to be careful to keep her out of the search."

"She saw us at Earlene's," Lil said. "And she's got a point. They are *her* guns. It's only fair we include her."

Abby Ruth felt the warmth of friendship course through her. She'd never thought she and Lil would get past amicable to truly friendly, but darned if the old Southern belle wasn't on her side today.

"She *is* part of our team," Maggie said. "And she wants to help."

"I don't care what she wants. She's obviously not thinking straight these days. I read that cancer recovery and survival chances improve significantly if the patient isn't carrying unnecessary stress. And this is clearly unnecessary. We can handle the search just fine without her."

Everything inside Abby Ruth, including the recently kindled warmth, froze. That was Jenny's voice.

Maggie said, "But her intuition is strong on these cases. If we can keep her from going off half-cocked, then—"

"We're talking about my mom here," Jenny said. "She doesn't do anything halfway."

Abby Ruth might normally take that as a compliment, but today her daughter's words felt like a slap.

"Jenny and I agreed we can't take a chance that Abby Ruth could hurt herself, or negatively impact her getting well in any way," Sera added.

"But she's a grown woman," Maggie protested. "Who are we to decide if she's well enough to help or not?"

"She drove herself all the way from Texas to Georgia after a lumpectomy," Jenny said. "She obviously can't be trusted to take care of herself, so we need to do it for her."

"I hate to lie to her too, but we have to support Jenny in this," Sera said. "So let's simply tell Abby Ruth what she wants to hear. She doesn't have to know we're figuring out this gun thing without her."

How could Sera, of all people, do this to her? The woman who was all about following your bliss and self-actualizing your...well, whatever the hell you self-actualized. Abby Ruth jammed her hands into her pockets, her fingers twisting into the seams. Not only was Sera planning to keep things from her, but Jenny believed she couldn't take care of herself.

Bull crapola.

The day Abby Ruth Cady needed to be coddled was the day the devil was hosting a house party and serving up daiquiris and frozen margaritas.

Part of her—the hurt and angry one— wanted to march in the kitchen and set these women straight. But they'd already decided she was out, and they'd only tell her what she wanted to hear.

Summer Haven had just lost its charm.

So she headed directly for the front door and took long, angry strides down the porch stairs and across the grass to her dually. When she dropped the tailgate, she ignored the stab of pain from unlatching the heavy piece of metal.

Dammit, she hated being weak.

She slid into the driver's seat, and with a quick three-point turn she had the huge truck repositioned in front of the gooseneck trailer, lined up perfectly on the first try. She hopped out, dropped the trailer on the ball, and clipped the safety chains into place.

"I don't need anyone's help." Back inside her truck, she gunned the engine. The trailer clanked along behind her as she pulled across the lawn and onto the driveway. To hell with Lillian Summer Fariview's pretty grass. "Cady women take care of themselves. Thank you very much."

Her first instinct was to drive straight out of town. Back to Houston. Atlanta. Hell, Kalamazoo would be better than Summer Shoals right now. She didn't know a damn soul there, so no one could push an agenda on her. But that was a longer drive than she planned to make today, so instead she pulled into the Piggly Wiggly parking lot.

It was time for a fresh start if she planned to leave Georgia.

She flung open the trailer doors, revealing everything she owned except for the few personal items she kept in her room at Summer Haven. She could send for those later.

Dragging a pile of horse blankets out of the trailer, she spread them on the pavement across two parking spaces, then started unloading her belongings.

On the side of a tall cardboard box full of housewares she hadn't used since she sold her house in Houston and hit the road, she scrawled EVERYTHING MUST GO.

For the right price, she might even let the trailer go. Without her guns, who needed it anyway?

Her arm ached, but that was a small price to pay for freedom. She drew a definitive arrow on another box, pointing toward the trailer. People could dig through everything she owned for all she cared. When all this crap was gone, she'd have a pocket full of cash and open road to roam.

Dragging a lawn chair out of the trailer, she plopped her butt down in it and willed herself not to cry.

It didn't take long for people to start perusing her belongings. No surprise. She had some good stuff here. Pots and pans, dishes, camping gear, more linens than she knew what to do with after dating that man who owned an outlet store, and assorted sports memorabilia. Lots of it autographed.

With a hundred and forty dollars in her pocket inside of thirty minutes, she wished she'd thought to unload this junk a long time ago.

Then Teague pulled up in the parking space next to her. She turned her back to him and kept talking to the gray-haired trucker who was interested in her autographed Dale Earnhardt hat.

"Excuse me, Abby Ruth?" Teague tapped her on the arm. "Can I talk to you for a minute?"

"I'm busy here, Tadpole. Why don't I catch up with you later?"

"I'm not sure this can wait," Teague said with a tug on his sheriff's cowboy hat.

"How about a hundred dollars?" the trucker asked.

"You kidding me?" she railed at him. "This is the real deal. The Intimidator himself sweated in this cap." She turned the hat over. "See that big splatter? That's where the champagne splashed on him on victory lane. This ball cap is worth at least four hundred bucks. But today..." She glanced back at Teague. "I'm highly motivated to unload this stuff. Two hundred. Take it or leave it."

Teague positioned himself between the

customer and Abby Ruth. "You need a permit to sell from this parking lot."

"Don't you start that mess with me." Abby Ruth waved him off and barked at the truck driver, "Fine. Give me your hundred bucks. Take that hat. I don't care."

The trucker traded the bill for the hat and ran, probably in case Abby Ruth changed her mind.

"Abby Ruth, what's gotten into you?"

Her lips were pinched so tight she thought they might split. Without a doubt, she should've headed to Kalamazoo. Except she was pretty sure Kalamazoo was someplace cold.

"How many of these lawn chairs you got?" a bleach blonde woman asked.

"That's the only one. Ten bucks."

"Five."

"Six, and it's yours."

"Done."

Teague returned to his car, but didn't crank it, just sat there watching her. Why the hell wasn't he leaving?

She ignored him to tend to the six people checking out her wares. But not five minutes later, Sera's van pulled into the lot, and out rolled Abby Ruth's so-called friends and traitor daughter.

She held up her hand like a traffic cop, aiming it directly at Jenny. "Do not," she warned. "No, ma'am."

"Don't what? Don't stop you from having an illegal rummage sale? Mom, what the heck is this all about?"

"Oh, don't you use that surprised tone with me. Just tell me what I want to hear, why don't you?"

Jenny's mouth snapped shut, and her eyes popped as wide as the bull's-eye on a two-foot target.

"Oh, yeah. Can't deny it, can you? Not a single one of you. I heard it with my own ears." Abby Ruth felt her face contort as she mimicked them. "She can't make a decision for herself. We should make all of her decisions for her," she sneered. "Well, let me tell you what I want *you* to hear. You do not know what's best for Abby Ruth Cady. None of you."

Jenny snatched four hangers with Western pearl-snapped shirts on them from a lady's hand. "Not for sale," she said.

Abby Ruth darted over, grabbed the hangers from Jenny, and handed them back to the woman. "Those aren't even your size, Jenny."

Jenny gave the plus-sized woman a once-over. "Well, they aren't her size either."

"I'll have you know these shirts are for my daughter's Halloween costume. She's always wanted to dress up as a cowgirl."

"Oh." Jenny's face softened, and she thrust the hanger holding Abby Ruth's red shirt with silver and black stitching toward the woman. "My treat."

Holding up a rhinestone-studded belt, the woman asked, "This too?"

"Sure."

"Dammit, I was asking twenty bucks for that belt!"

"I'll buy you a new one, Mom."

The woman, probably sensing a knock-down drag-out, scurried off with her prizes.

When another lady began sifting through Abby Ruth's jeans, Jenny snapped, "Get away. This is my stuff."

"Stop it, Jenny. These are my belongings. At least until I die and will them to you."

Jenny stared her down with a hot look that would've made a lesser woman pee her pants, but Abby Ruth just scowled back. Apparently realizing she wouldn't win the stare war, Jenny rushed across the parking lot to the buggy corral and came clanking back with a Piggly

Wiggly cart in tow.

"In the basket," she ordered to each potential customer as she steered the wonky cart around the lot. "This sale is over." She aimed it like a bullet toward a man holding a Houston Astros jersey. "Drop it, mister."

"I'm buying this. I'm the biggest Astros' fan around."

"No, sir. And that shirt wouldn't fit over your head much less that belly. Hand it over," she said with snap of her fingers. "Now."

He dropped the shirt, letting it fall to the asphalt, and backed away from Jenny, one step at a time, watching her like she'd lost her ever-loving mind.

Abby Ruth understood his fear, but she also felt a surge of reluctant admiration for her take-no-prisoners daughter.

With Jenny baring her teeth like a rabid bear at them, every customer made a hasty exit.

"Great." Hands on her hips, Abby Ruth stood there watching them scatter like roaches. "Just great."

"What's going on here, Abby Ruth?" Sera asked in her most Zen-like tone. "Your chakras are a murky green-brown, and I swear I can feel your blood pressure rising from here.

Were you going to let that guy buy your favorite Astros jersey?"

"Why shouldn't I? I was on target to make a cool thousand dollars before y'all crashed my sale."

"This is all a big misunderstanding." Lil urged, "Come on back to Summer Haven."

"Why would I do that?"

Lil's eyes softened. "Because we love you. You're family."

Abby Ruth was glad she didn't have other family because they were clearly a big ol' pain in the butt. "And you're humoring me. I don't need your help. I don't need your pity. And I sure as hell don't need you deciding what I can and cannot do!"

"You said yourself that the doctor said you should be taking it easy," Jenny said.

"Don't twist my words, young lady." Abby Ruth leaned in and met her daughter nose to nose. "He said to get enough rest so that I can return to my normal routine in a few days. It's a few days, and I ain't dead yet."

"But you've been so stressed out." Jenny's confrontational attitude melted like a campfire marshmallow. "Your blood pressure is probably through the roof."

"That's on all of y'all and this gun fiasco.

It's got nothing to do with my little situation."

"Little situation?" Jenny's hands clenched at her sides. "Cancer isn't a little situation, so quit making light of it."

"Well, you quit anchoring me with cement boots then. I'm going to be fine. Unless the doctor's humoring me just like y'all are. Telling me what I want to hear."

"Mom, that pity-party hat does not look good on you."

"I don't need any of this." Abby Ruth sucked in a breath and stalked toward her truck. To heck with all this junk in the parking lot. Jenny could fight people for it if she wanted, but Abby Ruth was done.

"Stop, you no-good liar!" Lil hollered.

Abby Ruth whirled around. "What did you call me?"

Lil's fist waved in the air, and her eyes were as big as hubcaps. Maggie grabbed her by the arm. "Lil! What has gotten into you? I know you and Abby Ruth have had your differences, but this is uncalled for."

"No. Not her." Lil pointed across the lot. "Isn't that Bad Charlie getting into that SUV?" She spun toward Abby Ruth and demanded, "Can't you do something? Maybe shoot out his tires?"

"Sugar, I would if I had any guns left."

CHAPTER 17

Sera ran toward her van, sweeping wide to slam her hand on the front of Teague's sheriff's car. *Wham. Wham. Wham.*

Teague looked up from whatever it was he was doing in his car and bailed out. "Sera? What the heck—"

"The guns! We have a lead! Follow us," she yelled over her shoulder, never missing a step as she jumped into her van. She started the engine and jammed her foot onto the accelerator, sending a puff of smoke out of the tailpipe, then braked hard next to Abby Ruth's trailer to pick up the girls. "Come on. Hop in!"

Abby Ruth ordered Jenny to watch her things then piled into Sera's van to ride shotgun. Lil and Maggie got into the back.

Teague pulled his car, window down, alongside the van. "What are y'all doing?"

"Dark SUV. It's Bad Charlie, the guy who might've taken Abby Ruth's guns." She pointed west. "He went that way."

"Stay put," he said, then flipped on his lights and hauled butt in the direction Charlie had taken off.

Stay put? Sera turned to Abby Ruth, sitting in the passenger seat. "Are we? We're not—"

"Oh, hell no, we're not staying put. Step on it, girl." Abby Ruth pulled the seatbelt across her lap and leaned forward to brace herself for the hot pursuit. Lil and Maggie slammed the side door of the van, and then Sera floored it.

Teague was already pretty far ahead of them, but that wouldn't keep Sera from trying to catch up. The van's engine whined as she pushed it to new limits. "C'mon, you can do it," she coaxed with a pat on the steering wheel.

"I don't see Charlie's SUV up ahead," Lil said.

"Me either," Sera said. "I hope Teague still has him in sight."

"Well, at least we know he's around. That's something," Maggie said.

"Or not." Abby Ruth pressed her hands on the dashboard. "I hope we haven't spooked him off."

"Maybe Teague pulled him over." Sera didn't slow down. "Keep an eye out at the cross streets."

Lil and Maggie had their noses pressed against the side window.

Abby Ruth's phone made the sound of a siren. She grabbed it, read the text. "Teague lost him at exit 129."

Sera lifted her foot from the accelerator.

"So close," Lil said. "I thought we had him."

"Teague's asking if we got a plate number."

Lil's mouth dropped open. "Um. No. I didn't think of that."

Of course she didn't, Sera thought. *She hasn't been on as many of these as we have. Too darned bad though.*

Abby Ruth texted Teague back. "Thanks for trying."

"Another dead end," Lil said.

"Maybe not completely." Sera sat taller in her seat. "Did you hear what that woman said earlier about why she was buying Abby Ruth's shirt?"

"It's not unusual for other women to want to be like me." Abby Ruth chuckled.

Sera slid her friend a look but decided not to comment on the truth of her statement.

"No, she said her daughter planned to use it for a cowgirl costume! What if someone sold Jessie's gauntlets to a costume shop?"

"That seems like a bit of a long shot," Lil said with a smile. "But it wouldn't hurt to check."

"Maggie, can you Google to see if there are any costume shops close by?"

"There's actually one in Myrtle Knolls."

Sera cruised through the small town then parallel parked in front of an old building. The front window was decorated with a massive lineup of mannequins dressed in everything from wedding gowns to Halloween costumes.

"I bet this is where Angelina got that stupid Wicked Witch of the West costume," Abby Ruth grumbled.

Sera and Maggie held back giggles. That Halloween party had been a fun night, and boy, had Abby Ruth made a great witch.

The four of them walked inside the costume shop. An old wrinkled man sat in front of a sewing machine putting a band of shimmery sequins on what looked like a bikini.

"Excuse me, sir?"

He pushed his horn-rimmed glasses up on top of his head and stood. "Didn't hear you come in over the sewing machine. What can I do for you?"

Sera stepped to the front. "We're looking for a Western item."

"I've got all kinds of stuff. What'd you have in mind?"

"Gauntlets. Fringy white gauntlets made of deerskin."

"I have long evening gloves. No Western gauntlets though."

Lil said, "Probably not a lot of call for something like that."

"You'd be surprised the requests that I get," the old man said. "Couples like to role play. And the strippers from down by the interstate are always coming in here with crazy ideas. They pay cash, even if it is usually all in ones, so I try to accommodate them."

"Where can we find this creative bunch of dancers?" Abby Ruth's eyebrow performed the question mark trick she did so well.

"If you came off the interstate, the bar was on the opposite corner. If you'd turned right instead of left you couldn't have missed it."

"You've been really helpful," Sera said. "Come on, girls. I think we have a bar to visit."

They all climbed back into the van, and Sera headed for the strip club. "I guess you never know where the clues will lead you."

Lil's lips were pulled so tight that they practically disappeared. "I'm not going into a strip club. What if someone sees me?"

"If they see you, it means they're at a strip club too. Who's gonna tell?"

"True," she said, her eyebrows knitting together.

Sera whipped into the parking lot, and Maggie pointed out the window. "Look over there."

"What? Is it Charlie's SUV?"

"I don't know. There are three of them, and they all kind of look like the one Bad Charlie was driving."

"I bet that skeevy jerk is in there." Abby Ruth sat tall in her seat. "Let's go."

"Can't hurt to take a look," Sera said.

"Shouldn't we call Teague?" Lil asked.

They all turned to look at her, and she shrank a little in her seat, hard for a woman as small as her to do.

"We let him in on the first part of this chase," Abby Ruth said. "We're more than in the clear to do some snooping of our own."

Sera checked out the SUVs and a few other high-priced cars. "Lil, do you recognize any of these as Charlie's?"

"I'm not sure. They all look the same to me now."

"This is the way we need to play it," Abby Ruth said. "Three of us will go inside and scope out the joint. The fourth person—" she swung around and looked directly at Lil, "—will stay out here and keep an eye on those SUVs."

"Why me?" Lil's lip poked out. Uh-oh.

"It's a very important job," Sera rushed to reassure her. "And you did such a good job being the lookout on our last case."

She slumped back in the seat, obviously not convinced.

"How about I stay out here with Lil while you two go inside?" Maggie said.

Sera and Abby Ruth hurried out of the van. At the front door a short, broad man who looked like a mini Mr. Clean gave them the once-over. "IDs?"

"You can't be serious—" Abby Ruth started.

"Just do it, please." Sera rooted around in her bag and pulled out her license.

Abby Ruth huffed but dug in her jeans pocket for hers.

Mr. Clean looked them over carefully then finally handed them back. "What're two old broads like y'all doing at a gentleman's club in the middle of the day?"

Cocking a hip, Abby Ruth shot back, "Looking for jobs, what else?"

"As bartenders?"

"Hell no, sugar, we're professional dancers."

His mouth dropped open, but no words came out.

"We've got moves." Abby Ruth executed a semi-lewd hip roll that had Sera biting her lips to keep from bursting out in laughter. And they'd thought chasing a crook would be bad for her? To a woman like Abby Ruth, these investigations were pure catnip.

"Um...uh...the person you're looking for is Rock, then. He's the owner."

With a quick pat to Mr. Clean's cheek, Abby Ruth strode past him, and Sera followed her through a purple velvet curtain. The club was dim inside, which suited them perfectly. Sera grabbed Abby Ruth's elbow and pointed toward the wall that would allow them to scope out the men in the audience without being seen. They moseyed along the perimeter, trying to be inconspicuous.

"You see that no-good gun thief?" Abby Ruth stage-whispered.

"Not yet." Because, shoot, it was hard to

identify people by their backs. "Let's circle around toward the stage."

On their way, they had to pass the bar. The bartender glanced up and caught sight of them. His eyes widened, but he covered it quickly, pulling nonchalance over him like he saw middle-aged women in this place all the time. Sera gave him a little wave and smile.

While they were making their way around, a table of four men got up and headed for the door.

"Any of those Charlie?"

"I'm not sure."

Abby Ruth pulled out her phone. "Texting Maggie now to tell her to get a bead on them." Less than a minute later, her phone beeped with a return text. "She and Lil have confirmed the men left in that fleet of SUVs, but no Charlie in the bunch."

"That's too bad," Sera said, her shoulders slumping. "I had a feeling about this place."

"Won't hurt to quickly eye the guys at the other tables, and we need to check out the costumes."

They scanned the small crowd, but none of the remaining men looked a thing like Bad Charlie. "Okay." But before they could search further, a new song came blaring through the speakers.

"I love me some Big and Rich," Abby Ruth said, doing another hip move along with some heel-toe action.

Sera turned her ear toward the speakers and tried to listen to the lyrics. "Are they saying what I think they are?"

"Save a horse, ride a cowboy," Abby Ruth said cheerfully. "Now that's a philosophy I can get behind."

Something metallic glittered from the stage, and Sera turned to get a better look. The half-moon-shape expanse held three poles, each one occupied by a cowgirl. The one on the right wore red, and blue was represented on the left.

But right there in the middle, a girl in a white outfit was shaking her moneymaker for all she was worth.

The men in the room were entranced by her tight behind, but that wasn't what caught Sera's attention. "Look!"

"Not many women can wear white and not look three hundred pounds," Abby Ruth commented. "That little bit of a girl probably weighs eighty pounds on a bloated day."

"That's not what I mean. I'm almost positive she's wearing Jessie Wyatt's missing gauntlets!"

Sera yanked out her phone and snapped a quick picture as the song was ending. Unfortunately, by that time, the dancer had struck her ending pose, and instead of catching her gauntlets, Sera's lens was filled up by a shot of the woman's tiny fringed panties.

The dancer sashayed off of the stage.

Sera quickly texted a picture to Maggie along with the message: *Go around back and see if you can find this dancer in the dressing rooms. I think she's wearing Jessie's gauntlets.*

Only Sera didn't have a good feeling about just standing around waiting. "You stay here, Abby Ruth. If that girl shows back up, you stall her and text me. I'll go help Lil and Maggie."

Abby Ruth tucked herself onto a bar stool and struck up a conversation with a young man who looked a lot like Brad Pitt.

Sera didn't have time to check for sure, so she skedaddled before he saw her. That's all she needed—for Brad to tell Marcus she was in a strip joint. She whisked past the bouncer and ran around to the back of the building.

Maggie and Lil stood next to the door crouched in a ready position.

"You didn't go inside?" Sera asked.

Lil and Maggie stood staring at the door. "We were waiting for her to come out."

Closing time wasn't for hours, and there was no telling how long that girl's shift was. Sera put her hand on the doorknob and twisted. It turned. "Wait here. If I don't come out in ten minutes, come looking for me."

Not waiting for an answer, she headed inside. The back room wasn't very big, and six girls were huddled in front of a wide mirror, dabbing at makeup and shimmying into costumes. "Hey, girls, can I ask you a few questions?"

A tall black woman looked down her nose at her.

"My first night," Sera said.

The women turned and went about their business. Not the friendliest group. The bathroom door opened, and out walked the woman wearing a flimsy robe and the Jessie gauntlets.

"Can I chat with you for a second?"

"Sure, hon."

Sera reached out to shake her hand. The woman responded to the motion, and Sera knew immediately the gauntlets were the real deal. *I found Jessie's gauntlets!* The gemstones sparkled, and one strand of thick fringe was missing. Not a detail many people would've noticed, but Sera had been on set the day it happened.

"How long have you worked here?" Sera asked, pulling out her phone and texting Abby Ruth to call Teague.

"Three years." The girl cocked a hip, the fringe on her panties swaying. "I'm the headliner. Been here longer than any of the other girls."

The tall dancer walked by and said, "Don't think you'll get any space for costumes. Starr here takes up half the lockers with her own stuff, and the rest of us are already having to fight for space."

"Sounds like they're jealous of you," Sera whispered after the other girl walked on.

Maggie opened the back door, and all heads turned.

"Somebody in trouble with momma tonight?" the black woman asked.

Maggie's eyes narrowed. "I'm looking for someone."

Sera gave her a just-wait-right-there look, and thankfully Maggie leaned against the wall as if she were waiting on someone. Sera looked at Starr and shrugged.

"Don't mind the girls. Some of them are just cranky. You'll get used to it." Starr looked her up and down. "You're about my size."

"Where do you get your costumes?"

"I make some of them. But my boyfriend hooks me up with stuff too. I have a whole trunk of things. It's like playing dress-up all night."

Sera reached out and trailed her fingertips across the fringe of the gauntlets. These were the real deal. An unexpected swell of sorrow dragged at her. Jessie had been the only one to wear them. Not even her stunt double had been allowed to put them on. "These are really great."

"I know, right?" The dancer raised both hands in the air and struck a pose. "Weigh a dang ton though."

"Are they new?" Sera gave Maggie a nod, and Maggie held her hand to her ear like she was making a phone call and then darted out the back door.

"Yep, just tried them out dancing to 'Ride a Horse.' Did you catch it?" She gestured toward the stage area. "Saw you come in. That your mom with you, or your girlfriend?"

Sera coughed, pretty sure neither was a role that would appeal to Abby Ruth.

LIL WAS STANDING with Maggie in the strip club's parking lot when Teague rolled up in his cruiser and stepped out. By the scowl etched on his face, he was not happy.

Lil put her hand out in front of Maggie. "I'll talk to him."

"What is it with you ladies?" Teague asked, annoyance clear in his tone.

"We found Jessie's gauntlets."

He dropped his head back. "Didn't you promise to stay out of it? And where are Sera and Abby Ruth?"

"Abby Ruth is holding the perimeter." She felt quite adept using the jargon she'd learned by watching television reruns. Then she said in a rush, "But no time to talk about that now. Sera is just inside the door with the gauntlets."

"Y'all are killing me," he said, then lowered his chin and said something into his radio.

He adjusted his service belt on his lean hips and entered through the back door. Lil slipped in right behind him. Sera and the dancer were a few feet away, chatting it up as though they'd know each other for ten years instead of ten minutes.

"Somewhere we can have a private word,

ma'am?" Teague said to the dancer.

"What's this about?" The Jessie-a-go-go took a step away from Teague and looked at Sera as if she'd betrayed her in the worst possible way. "I didn't do anything wrong."

He nodded toward the door. "Come with me. We can step outside where we don't have an audience."

She flushed but didn't put up a fight.

Teague held the door for her, and she walked outside in her skimpy robe, gauntlet fringe swaying. Sera pushed through right behind them and walked over to join Lil and Maggie, who'd moved up within a few feet of the door.

"I can't wait to hear what she's going to say," Lil whispered. "But I don't recognize her as one of the lookalikes at Jessie's funeral."

Teague radioed something else in, then said to Maggie, Sera and Lil, "Ladies, I'll take this from here."

Not one of them moved. This was Lil's reputation, after all. Didn't she have a right to hang around and make sure she was cleared?

"If you don't want me to call one of my deputies and have the three of you—" Abby Ruth strolled out the door about that time, "—dammit, the four of you, arrested for interfering with an investigation, I suggest you get your fannies back in Sera's van and go home."

"Tadpole," Abby Ruth drawled, "you aren't a bit of fun these days."

"That's life when you're the sheriff," he shot back. "Which not one of you are."

"But we tracked down these gauntlets, and that should count for something."

"I suppose you want some kind of commendation?"

"Nope," Abby Ruth said cheerfully, propping her hip against a car nearby in a way that indicated she had no plans to go anywhere. "But I figure we should get to stick around and hear the whole story."

"Fine, but stay quiet."

"But—"

"This is not your rodeo. Do I make myself clear?"

"Hmph," Abby Ruth grunted, but they all zipped their lips.

Teague turned to the suspect. "So, Miss..."

"Just Starr," she offered.

"Starr, what can you tell me about how you came to have these gauntlets in your possession?"

"In my what?"

"How did you get your hands on them?"

"Oh," she said. "Joe-Jack."

"Joe and Jack?" Teague jotted something on his iPad. "Are they friends of yours?"

"Just one friend. Joe-Jack. Ya know, with one of them hyphens in the middle. Apparently, his momma couldn't decide, so she named him Joe-Jack Billy-Wayne."

"Dear God," Abby Ruth muttered.

"And does Joe-Jack with a hyphen have a last name?" Teague asked.

"Williams."

Joe-Jack Billy-Wayne Williams. JJBWW—that was one heck of a monogram. Made Lil think of that Jabberwocky poem.

"Do you know where Joe-Jack got the gauntlets?"

"He always...oh..." Starr trailed off. "Maybe I need a lawyer."

"Starr, did you steal these gauntlets?"

Her eyes flew wide as she straightened to attention, all of her little fringes swinging in the process. "No, sir." She raised her right hand in the air. "Swear to goodness!"

"Then you have nothing to worry about."

"Until I get home, you mean."

"But if you choose not to cooperate, I'll have to take you in."

"But...but..." she sputtered. "My shift just started. I can't leave now. I do that and all my tips'll go to the other girls."

"Your decision."

Starr chewed on her lip, debating, for a minute or so. Finally, she said, "Joe-Jack likes me to wear nice things when I dance."

"Does he bring you nice things often?"

"About once a week," she said. "One time, he brought me this pillbox hat. Very cute. Very Jackie O. You know, until I put it on and sneezed my brains out. Who knew a girl could be allergic to mothballs? Mostly it's cool stuff though."

"Any idea where all of these items come from?"

She folded her arms across her body. "Joe-Jack has a job where that's one of the perks."

"Ladies' clothing? As a perk?" Teague's eyebrows arched. "Would Joe-Jack happen to work at Holy Innocence Mausoleum?"

Her mouth hung wide. "How did you know?"

With a gimme motion, Teague said, "I'll take those gauntlets now."

She took a step back. "Joe-Jack wouldn't like that."

"Is Joe-Jack skinny or portly?" Lil asked.

Teague turned and gave her that sheriff look. Lil smiled primly.

"Like a rail," Starr said. "I tease him about a tapeworm all the time. Eats like a cow but never gains an ounce. You know the type."

Hmm, Mr. Williams had obviously caught wind of how valuable Jessie Wyatt's gauntlets were after the service and decided to cash in. But why in the world would he let his girlfriend wear them first?

"Tell me, dear," Lil said, "did your boyfriend give you those to wear?"

Starr's head tilted to one side, making her dark hair hang down over her shoulder. "Actually, no. I found them in his closet, and he wasn't very happy when I came to the door wearing them—and *only* them. Normally me naked cheers him right up."

Teague shot Lil an *enough* look. "Did Joe-Jack mention his plans for them?"

"Not exactly. He just said his luck was turning, and that this set of fringe would make him more money than his job slinging stiffs ever would. I figured I could make a lot more tips wearing them. I put up with Joe-Jack...don't I deserve to cash in a little too?" Starr's gaze darted to Teague and then back to Lil. "You won't tell him I had them, will you?

He'll be so mad at me." She slapped her hand over her mouth. "He reported them stolen, didn't he? Oh my gosh, he knows I took them."

The tears started falling, and Teague gave one big eye roll before saying, "Calm down, miss."

Joe-Jack sounded like a right slimy person. But he was Teague's problem now. Lil turned to her friends. "I think it's time to concentrate on our other case..." She shot a quick look at Teague. "Um...our other casserole."

Once they were all inside the VW, Sera leaned back out to wave at Starr. "Nice to meet you. And great dance!"

CHAPTER 18

After the excitement of finding Jessie Wyatt's missing gauntlets, Abby Ruth needed a couple days of recuperation time. She'd promised no more secrets, but the little white lie she told the gals, that she wanted to watch the NASCAR race on TV, didn't really count. But during the race she gave in to how tired she was and changed into her PJ's to take an afternoon nap.

"Abby Ruth?" Sera knocked on the Sweet Vidalia room's door. "You awake?"

"Of course." Barely. "Why wouldn't I be?"

"We're heading to the Holy Innocence Mausoleum to check out a lead on your guns. Are you up to coming along?"

After making such a fuss about being left out, she couldn't tell Sera she was too tired to go.

So she jumped out of bed, got dressed, and off they went. Once again, Abby Ruth found herself sitting in the passenger seat, bouncing along in Sera's beat-up VW van.

She wasn't about to admit to her friends that the ride was making her slightly carsick. Because if she did, they would insist on turning around and heading straight back to Summer Haven. Then they would investigate without her, and she'd let that happen about the time pigs started chartering commuter flights from Atlanta to Austin.

"So what's the plan?" It galled her to ask, since nine times out of ten she was the one to mastermind their sleuthing. But there was a first time for everything.

"Well..." Sera dragged out the one word for so long, she almost sounded like a Southerner. Or was she stalling, once again keeping things from Abby Ruth?

She tried to push her cynical nature to the side. They'd put all that leave-Abby-Ruth-out-of-everything behind them. She had to believe that.

Sera continued, "We need to get there before the doors are locked for the day, but we'll have to hang out until afterward so we can have the place to ourselves, really scope it out."

"Never knew there was a mausoleum this close to Summer Shoals," Abby Ruth said. "Not until all this recent hype about Jessie Wyatt."

"You're not the only one," Lil said. "And I've lived here all my life."

They approached the mausoleum. One of the biggest, gaudiest damn things Abby Ruth had ever laid eyes on. And that was something a native Texan like her couldn't often claim.

Before they went inside, Sera pulled out the hemp tote bag she seemed to carry any time they went on a stakeout, and Abby Ruth eyed it. "Don't tell me we're picnicking again. I'm not sure I have the stomach for tofu salad when I know there are thousands of dead bodies all around me."

"Be honest, Abby Ruth," Maggie said, "you don't *ever* have the stomach for Sera's tofu salad."

Woman had a point. "Damn straight. Sorry, Sera. No offense."

"It's not tofu salad, so you can relax. I thought we might need a few supplies." Sera shouldered the bag and led their group of four to the entrance. "Let's take the stairs down. I figured the ladies' room would be the best place to park ourselves until closing at five o'clock."

"You don't think they'll check the restrooms before locking up for the night?"

"Best we can tell," Lil chimed in, "they don't pay much attention to that. After all, this isn't exactly Disney World, where people want to stay and play after hours."

Hard to argue about that.

They made their way to the lower level and settled in the bathroom's anteroom, surprisingly comfortable with a full-size couch, a scattering of chairs, and a small dressing table. Probably so grieving widows could fix their makeup after shoving their better halves into one of those tiny rectangular spaces out there.

At that thought, Abby Ruth couldn't stop a shudder from cruising down her back.

In front of a coffee table, Sera lowered herself to the floor in a cross-legged position and pulled a deck of cards from her bag. "How about a game of Crazy Eights or Old Maid to help us pass the time?"

Abby Ruth glanced at Lil. "How about we make a new game called Crazy Old Maid?"

"Very funny." How a woman as short at

Lillian Summer Fairview could manage to look down her nose at someone taller, Abby Ruth hadn't a clue, but the woman was a master at it.

They played half a dozen games before Abby Ruth glanced at her watch. "It's 5:15. We could probably get started on the search."

With a tug at her lip, Sera shook her head. "I don't have a good feeling about it yet. Why don't we wait another half-hour?"

Abby Ruth was wilting. If they didn't get on the stick soon, she might not have the energy to wander through all these hallways, but once again, she kept her mouth shut. "Whatever you think."

"I could use a little nap." Maggie stretched her arms high over her head and yawned so wide Abby Ruth was pretty sure she spotted her wisdom teeth.

Abby Ruth thought that yawn looked like a fake, but darned if her jaw didn't pop when she yawned too. The couch was pretty comfortable, probably even better if she stretched out on it. "I think I've had about as many hands of kids' card games as I can handle right now. If we're hanging around here for a while longer, I think I'll rest my eyes for a minute."

"Oh, good idea," Sera said brightly. She stretched out right there on the gray Berber carpet, and Lil shot her a look of proper Southern horror.

But Abby Ruth couldn't muster much interest in Lil's standards right now. She yawned again and sank down on her side into the couch's leather comfort. Oh, God, that felt good.

Sometime later, her brain slowly came online again, and she heard Maggie whisper, "Do you think we should wake up her or leave her here?"

"We can't leave her here," Sera said. "This is all *about* her."

"You sure as hell can't." With her stronger arm, Abby Ruth pushed herself to a sitting position and swiped the back of her hand over her mouth. Dammit, she hated to drool in public. "I'm raring to go."

"Let's start on the top floor and work our way down from there." Sera shot Maggie a look that meant they had something up their sleeves, but Abby Ruth didn't have the wherewithal to figure out what that something was.

When she stood, all the blood rushed from her head and she swayed. She tried to catch herself on the wall, but it didn't seem to be where she'd left it. To her ever-loving humiliation, Lil dodged under her outstretched arm and kept her upright. "Careful there."

"I'm fine," she groused.

"Of course you are."

But when they trooped out into the hallway, Sera beelined for the elevator and jabbed the up button.

Thank you, Jesus.

Once they were on the top floor, Sera once again took the lead and began skulking through the rows of vaults stretching from the heels of Abby Ruth's cowboy boots to a ceiling so high they'd need a cherry picker to store those stiffs. "Lotta bodies in here," Abby Ruth said. "Now what's the clue you got ahold of?"

Sera glanced back over her shoulder. "Shh. You might scare her away."

"Her? Her who? I thought we had a lead on the guns."

But her friends were suspiciously closemouthed about what the heck they were looking for until they made it to the bottom floor, and Sera squealed. "Oh, I think I saw something."

Abby Ruth immediately reached for the

Glock at the small of her back and threw an arm out to hustle the others behind her. "I'll take care of this." Because obviously, if someone was sneaking around this place after hours, she was up to no good.

"Only Abby Ruth would think she could solve something by blowing a hole in a ghost," Maggie said.

"Did you say ghost?" She rounded on Maggie. "The three of you have been off your rockers all evening. Are you telling me you think a ghost woo-wooed out to Summer Haven, lifted a three-pound bolt cutter, grabbed fifteen guns, and made off with them? Not only that, but she brought them back to her final resting place like some kind of spectral squirrel?"

Lord, why had she thought for a second that these three could head up a decent investigation? Thank goodness she'd discovered the truth before it was too late. As it was, her guns were likely in another state by now.

But when she looked behind her, only Lil stood there. Sera and Maggie had taken off down a side aisle, their footsteps like a herd of wildebeest. So much for covert operations.

Sera called out, "I spotted her. Maggie, you

come from that side, and we'll urge her toward Abby Ruth."

Lil looked as confused as Abby Ruth was and flashed her an apologetic smile. Something wasn't right. For this woman to pull the stick out of her proper rear-end enough to offer up a silent apology, things had officially gone down the shitter.

"I'm not going to like whatever this is, am I?"

Lil's face squinched up, making her look every one of her seventy-something years. "They only told me about all this ten minutes ago. Just keep an open mind, dear."

Well, crap.

That was when Abby Ruth spotted Sera and Maggie trailing a big ball of yellow light, patting it from behind as if they were playing a particularly lame game of tetherball.

"What the hell is that?" As they approached Abby Ruth and Lil, the orb seemed to pulse and expand tall then wide, like one of those old Stretch Armstrong dolls. "Whatever it is, I'm pretty sure I don't like it."

"Abby Ruth," Sera said, "please meet Katherine St. Simon, Lady of Sorrows and Healing."

"If you tell me I need to bow and kiss a big-ass ball of light's hand, you're out of your mind."

The glowing St. Katherine of What-the-hell-ever flickered and began to fade.

"No!" Sera blurted out. "Don't go. She didn't mean it. Stay and give her a chance."

"What exactly is she giving me a chance to do?"

"Quick, Abby Ruth. Lay down on the floor and spread your arms and legs like you're making a snow angel."

She cast a look at the floor underfoot. She wasn't sure she was as brave as Sera because no telling how many feet had tramped over this stuff. "You're not serious."

Sera jammed her hands onto her hips. "This from a woman I know has peed in the woods? Now lay down right this second, or I'm going to push you down and sit on you."

"I'd like to see you try," she muttered. But she did as Sera instructed and eased her body to the floor. When she stretched out her limbs, she felt like six times a fool, especially with her friends standing around looking down at her. "Fine, I'm here. What now?"

Sera bit her lip and stared at the light that had grown stronger again. "I'm not sure."

"I don't even know what this is about."

"Our Lady is rumored to have healing powers. There are several accounts on YouTube of people who've visited her, let her energy surround their bodies, and whatever disease or ailment they suffered from began to get better."

"So what, this is like you sending me through some kind of spiritual car wash?" Abby Ruth closed her eyes and sighed in disgust. "This trip didn't have a damn thing to do with my guns, did it?"

"No, dear," Lil said.

Great. She'd given up an evening in her comfy clothes to play Ghostbusters. Heck, not even Ghostbusters, Ghostcharmers.

She started to rock herself off the floor, but a sudden pressure skimmed across her chest, pinning her to the ground.

"Oh, something's happening." Sera's words were chock-full of excitement.

Yeah, something was happening. Something weird as hell. But as she thought it, the pull of her incision eased. Not fully, but it suddenly didn't feel like she was a Thanksgiving turkey that had been trussed up too tight.

Had to be a coincidence.

Then her arms and legs were invaded by a

pleasant tingly sensation, sort of like she'd been plugged into a happy lamp. But by God, if she wanted something otherworldly to tickle her body parts, she'd sign up with an extraterrestrial dating service.

Even as she struggled to recover control over her extremities, the tension and worry she'd been carrying in her neck and back for weeks melted away.

Though she'd never utter a peep about it, she would swear she heard Lady What's Her Name whisper, "Believe and be well."

Then, as quickly as she'd been pushed against the floor, a soft whoosh flew by Abby Ruth's ear and she was free to move again. When she opened her eyes, the yellow glow was gone.

"How do you feel?" Sera asked cautiously.

"Like a damn fool."

"Oh." Sera's shoulders slumped.

"You mean to tell me you think that Lady KitKat can cure cancer?" Although she didn't buy into that kind of hooey, Abby Ruth raised her left arm and found the movement wasn't nearly as tender as it had been earlier in the evening. She probably could make a snow angel right now.

"Maybe not, but we figured it couldn't

hurt."

Abby Ruth drew to a crouch but hadn't yet pushed to her feet when the sound of muffled footsteps in the distance hit her ears. "Someone's here, and it ain't the Lady."

"In here!" Lil pulled Abby Ruth to her feet and pushed her toward a three-sided alcove. Not exactly the best plan because now they were trapped. They all scurried behind a statue that looked like it might be the angel Michael. He was a big sucker and held a sword. She'd never been so happy to see a pair of ginormous wings. Although he was larger than life standing astride a pedestal, he was no match for four full-grown women. Sera and Maggie wrapped each other in a body-to-body hug. Which meant Abby Ruth only had one option. She gestured for Lil to step closer, so close the tiny woman was standing on the toes of her boots. They all held their breath until the footsteps crossed in front of the alcove and began to fade.

"Ah...ah..." Maggie's mouth went wide, and she squeezed her eyes closed. Sera stepped away just in time to avoid being whopped by Maggie's arm when she swung it up to block a sneeze that would've brought down the Statue of Rhodes.

Yeah, well, Maggie's arm wasn't any match for her sneeze. And Michael's wing wasn't any match for Maggie's arm. Her elbow caught a feather and the piece of that statue snapped right off.

Nimble little Lil jumped forward and caught it in her palms.

"Lord, that was close," Abby Ruth whispered.

They all slumped in relief, but apparently they slumped too soon because from behind them someone barked, "Come out with your hands up. No funny business because I have a Taser and I know how to use it."

ONE HAND NEAR HER EAR, Lil straightened her spine and slowly stepped out to face the man who'd busted them trying to hide behind one of God's soldiers. A Summer always faced her problems head on. Still, she kept the other hand behind her back and felt the weight of Michael's broken wing lifted from her palm.

"Can we help you?" she said to the forty-something man wearing a polyester uniform. And people wondered why the security profession received no respect? Get them some outfits made of natural fibers and things might be a little different. She studied his face closer. Oh my, he was the guard on duty during Jessie's service. Would he recognize Maggie and her?

His eyes never flickered with recognition. "The mausoleum closed over two hours ago."

"You don't say." She fluttered her lashes, hoping she looked innocent.

"Surely you saw the signs posted on the front door."

Oh, he wasn't easily swayed by Southern charm. Not good. Not good at all. "Surely your superior explained we were cleared to be here after hours."

"I haven't been on the job long, but I was told we don't ever make exceptions to the visitation policy. Otherwise, we'd have family members—" he eyed them with suspicion, "—like y'all taking advantage and running roughshod over the rules."

"Young man, I have the utmost respect for rules. However, we have every right to be here."

"Why don't you come up to the front and I'll call my boss. If you're here on his approval, he can confirm."

Think quickly, Lil. Mental acuity is the reason it's important to keep playing Sudoku and crossword puzzles. She might need to take up that Words with Friends Maggie had been nagging her about. "I think this will more than justify our presence."

She reached into her handbag, and the man grabbed for his belt, but all he had there was a flashlight. "Hold it right there."

She gave him her best disappointed librarian look. "I don't have a weapon in my purse. I simply wanted to show you this." From an inside pocket, she withdrew a slim leather case. She flipped it open like she'd seen them do on the cable cop shows, flashed something round and silver, and quickly snapped it closed again. He certainly didn't need to know it was one of her momma's vintage brooches. "ATF. We're here because we got an anonymous tip that some stolen guns were hidden in the mausoleum."

"That's crazy."

She waved a hand. "Is it really? Have you noticed the excess storage room in this facility?"

"Yes, but—"

"We're looking for this man." She pulled Bad Charlie's sketch from her pocketbook. "Have you seen him?"

"He's the guy that stole the guns you're

looking for?"

"Allegedly."

The security guard rubbed his chin and peered closer at the picture. "Yeah. Yeah, I'm pretty sure I saw him a few days ago. Tuesday."

Lil's heart jolted inside her chest, knocking against her ribcage. He'd seen Bad Charlie? This was crazy. She was bluffing and the guard seemed to be sitting in on her game of Texas Hold 'Em. "You're certain?"

He took the paper from her hand and studied it. "Positive."

"Do you know his name?"

His shoulder came up and brushed his ear. "Dunno. He works for one of the funeral homes around here, I think. The one time I saw him, he dropped off a casket."

Oh my goodness. This was unexpected. And so exciting Lil almost did a little jig right there. Why on earth was Charlie delivering caskets to the mausoleum? Transportation of a sort, yes, but strange. "Can you remember the name of the funeral home?"

"Can't say that I do. But you could leave me a card in case I remember anything else about him."

Yes, she certainly could if she *had* a

business card.

And if she and the other gals were actually from the ATF.

Since she didn't and they weren't, she just gave him a regal look, patted his hand, and said, "We'll be in touch."

CHAPTER 19

This morning, instead of trying to give Sera a good-morning hug and kiss, Marcus was quietly slipping into his pants as though trying not to wake her. That's the way it had been since he'd overheard her and the others talking about the gun investigation. Was he still mad about the Brad thing? He didn't understand what she and the girls had accomplished in the past. Probably never would.

And although she still wasn't sure exactly what she wanted, she knew she didn't want this chilliness between them. She couldn't lie here pretending to sleep, so she sat up and stretched. "Are you going out scouting again today?" she asked quietly. Something told her all this *exploring* Marcus was doing lately wasn't related to his movie project. Unlike many other men in Hollywood, he'd always been faithful to her. At least she thought he had.

"I have three places to check out. What I've found so far doesn't hold a candle to Summer Haven and Summer Shoals."

"Would you like me to go with you?"

He sighed. "Why do I feel like you're throwing me a bone?"

Because he was a very smart man. A smart man who deserved better than the half-truths she'd been giving him. "Marcus, do you know what it feels like to be a bracelet?"

He slumped into the chair near the window. "I have no idea what that means."

"If you think about it, a bracelet is pretty superfluous. All it does is jangle around and get in your way when you're on the computer."

"I wouldn't know since most men don't wear them."

"My point exactly. Because they're totally unnecessary and can sometimes be annoying as hell."

"Sera, what are you saying?"

"That I've been *your* bracelet on and off for the past thirty years."

"Why would you think that?"

"Because it's true." Early on, the excitement of his lifestyle and the attention she'd received as his wife had been dizzying, but she'd somehow lost her sense of self along the way, and she didn't want to do that again.

A few years ago, he'd promised it would be different, and it had been...for a while. But once the movie industry sucked him back in to do a long overdue sequel to one of his Oscar-winning movies, their marriage had rolled right back downhill. And being an accessory was not good for her health. Mentally or physically.

At first, all the travel felt glamorous and exciting. But then Marcus shot a film in a country so politically unstable that Sera and their son hadn't been allowed to leave the hotel for five weeks. One of the hotel staff had found Finn a beat-up secondhand bike and he'd ridden that thing around the sixth floor until the already threadbare carpet was in tatters. When she returned to LA, she'd informed Marcus she wouldn't raise her family that way.

"I can't help but think your extended midlife crisis drive across the country has something to do with the way you're acting now. You haven't been the same, been my

Sera, since you returned to California."

She wanted to scream at him that she wasn't *his* Sera. She was *her* Sera. "I need you to be patient."

"Patient?" His voice rose. "I didn't ask questions. Gave you exactly what you wanted. Didn't hunt you down."

"Until you filed for divorce."

"Hell, Sera, what was I supposed to do—wait forever? You have to know by now I didn't want a divorce. I just wanted you to talk to me. I love you, and you wouldn't talk to me."

"Love isn't always enough."

"Are you saying it's over?"

"No," she yelled. "I'm saying I don't want to be your bracelet anymore."

"I see." He turned away from her to gaze out the window. "So what is it you do want?"

Misery welling up inside her, Sera curled her knees to her chest and wrapped her arms around them. Trying to hold herself together. "I want to belong someplace where I make a difference. Where I'm valued for being Serendipity Meadow Blu Johnson, not Serena Johanneson."

"And that's what you feel when you're here in Summer Shoals? When you're investigating these petty crimes?"

"There's nothing petty about them. They may seem small to a man who makes movies about wars and espionage and the world ending. But to the people here, these crimes are life impacting."

He turned back to her. "Sera, tell me once and for all you don't love me anymore and I will stand up and walk out of here. I'll sign the divorce papers I was such an idiot to have drawn up."

"I...I..." She couldn't push the words past her tongue. She couldn't tell him that she didn't love him anymore because it wasn't true. But she also couldn't see how they could make this all work. Was she awful not to simply say the words and let him off the hook? "Marcus. I need time."

She watched him deflate, but in true Marcus style, he quickly shifted gears to business. Something he could control. "Although I'm looking at other locations today, I owe it to you to tell you I still think Summer Haven is the perfect place to shoot the main scenes of the movie I'm considering. I've already spoken to Lillian."

Sera released her knees, but her toes curled into the sheets. "Excuse me?"

"She's an enterprising woman. Light was

dancing in her eyes as she spit out half a dozen ideas to leverage Summer Haven as a movie set for future promotions to get people to visit."

"But she has no idea how destructive it would be for your people to come in and use her home. Make a movie in Summer Shoals if you must, but please leave Lil out of it."

"From what I see, Summer Haven would benefit from a little destruction and reconstruction."

She couldn't argue that, but people tromping through Summer Haven wouldn't be nearly as glamorous as Lil thought. Convincing her of that wouldn't be easy, but persuading Marcus was in Sera's control. "What if I could show you some places closer to Atlanta? There are tons of these old antebellum homes all over Georgia. Summer Haven isn't unique. Plus, if you choose a location closer to Atlanta, you can reduce the travel and shipping budget for supplies. Not to mention the time it will take people to get on and off set."

"That's a good point."

She knew how to motivate him. Right in the production pants. He liked his movies to run on time and under budget.

"We always were a good team," he said

simply, almost breaking her heart clean in two. "You had a great eye for location. Remember when we found that spot in the Texas Hill Country?"

"Of course I remember. You won your third Oscar for that film." She'd blown him off a lot over the past few of days to spend time with the girls, and with the investigation, there'd likely be more of that, so she said, "I'd like to go with you today. Give me twenty minutes to get dressed."

He nodded, a little reluctantly in her opinion, and left the room.

Sera climbed out of bed and glanced down at her yoga pants and the cotton tunic. For the past year or so, this had been getting dressed. Part of her wanted to go as is, but the other part of her felt it wouldn't kill her to dress the way Marcus preferred.

Twenty minutes later, she strolled down the stairs. No bells. No yoga pants. No flowing material leaving a whimsical peaceful trail in her wake. Instead she was in a pair of designer black pants tapered to the ankle, and a camel top that echoed the color of her camel Prada espadrille wedge sandals. The black diamond tassel necklace that hung low down the front of her shirt sparkled, and the charm bracelet—

a charm for every city Marcus had ever filmed in—was a bit of irony based on their earlier conversation.

She felt different when she was dressed like this. Somehow so together, so perfect, that taking a deep breath was difficult. She'd pulled her hair into a long low ponytail and secured a metal clip to hold it in place. Marcus loved riding with the windows down. She could still remember the first time he'd taken her for a ride in his convertible, a vintage Austin-Healey. Back then, the forest-green car had been his pride and joy. Most weekends, they'd driven the PCH out of Malibu, exploring the California coastline. And oh how those black seats had burned the backs of her legs when she slid inside after hours at the beach. And the glove box stuck when she tried to open it.

She and Marcus had been so in love. But she wasn't that same twenty-something girl anymore.

If only Marcus could accept her need for something more, but what man wanted to hear that he alone wasn't enough to make his woman happy? She was at a crossroads. She knew it. He knew it too. The problem was she wasn't sure she could give up either him or Summer Shoals. And yet, she had to.

"I'm ready," she said as she walked into the kitchen, but he wasn't there. "Marcus?"

She found him outside, rooting around in the back of the Maserati, covering something with what looked like a tarp. "Did you pack us a picnic?"

He hurriedly tucked in the tarp and slammed the trunk closed. "No...I...uh...thought we'd stop somewhere for lunch.

Something wasn't quite right here, but she held her hand out and said, "How about I drive?"

"No way am I wandering all over Georgia in your van."

"I meant the Maserati."

"Oh...uh..." His feet shuffled in the dirt. "I'm the only insured driver."

Fine. It wasn't worth arguing over, not after the discussion they'd already had this morning. In the car, Marcus turned on classical music, and she relaxed into the soft leather seat.

The three locations Marcus had mapped out were stair steps away from Summer Haven out off I-75. The first one wasn't anything like the picture or the description of the listing. Fine by her, because the farther he filmed from Summer Haven the better.

Sera stared out the window, taking in spring's bright green leaves and random sprigs of color dotting the yards and ditches as they rode along. When they neared the mausoleum, she thought about last night's adventure with her friends. She said a little prayer that the Lady legend had some truth to it. Even if that ball of light didn't really have healing powers, perhaps the power of suggestion would put Abby Ruth in a better frame of mind for her doctor's appointment today and allow her to heal more quickly. How that woman ever traipsed off to Texas alone, with cancer weighing on her, was beyond Sera.

SITTING in the passenger seat of her own truck, Abby Ruth tried to keep nerves from eating her up. Although she wanted to be grumpy about Jenny's insistence on driving her to her first appointment with Dr. Dempsey to discuss the details of the proposed radiation treatment, she couldn't muster up the energy. She was too darn relieved to have her daughter by her side.

After that run-in with Lady KitKat in the mausoleum, Abby Ruth had realized she had to take charge and make sure she received the medical treatment she needed. And as soon as possible.

Yes, that ghostly encounter had reduced her pain, but the only thing that would help her beat this cancer was modern science and the support of her friends and family. So there was absolutely no reason she needed to admit to anyone that a ball of light might've made a difference. Because that just wasn't something a Cady would do.

Still, the decision to move forward had been harder than getting that biopsy done. Funny that going for the lumpectomy, real surgery, hadn't scared her a bit.

Jenny reached across the seat and grabbed her hand. "You doing okay, Mom?"

Radiation seemed different. More invasive and frightening. But she wasn't about to admit that to her baby girl. "Right as rain."

She'd heard they'd tattoo her. Simple blue-gray dots, not much bigger than a freckle, marking the exact spots where the radiation would be targeted.

If she decided to do it, when this crap was over, she'd turn those marks into something that represented good, not a constant memory of cancer. Bullet holes might be funny. Okay, that would freak people out. Maybe Texas stars? Or a baseball? She had plenty of time to contemplate that over the next couple of weeks.

They parked in the underground lot reserved for the cancer treatment patients, and sweat pooled under Abby Ruth's armpits. No deodorant, antiperspirant, or powder on the most nerve-racking day of her life. She felt like she already smelled funky.

Not a recipe for a close-up pleasant interaction. Hopefully Dr. Dempsey would stay far enough away from her not to notice. Of course, the no-perfume-products was his darned rule. And if he decided she didn't need more x-rays or another mammogram or what-the-hell-ever, it'd serve him right to have to smell her stinking pits.

Jenny clung to her hand as they followed the signs into the hospital, the sound of their cowboy boots against the concrete echoing through the parking garage. "You made the right decision, Mom. Thank you for at least agreeing to discuss the radiation before making a final decision." But Jenny's shaky voice didn't reassure Abby Ruth one bit.

Abby Ruth hitched her chin, giving Jenny's hand a quick squeeze.

The big glass doors parted with a muted *swish* and they entered the hospital only to come face-to-face with a life-size cardboard cutout of none other than Red Jensen. The now retired Houston Astros Hall of Famer was grinning at Abby Ruth with that perfect smile, and she almost choked on her own spit.

That smile used to make her knees feel like she was trying to spin a hula-hoop around them.

Why in hell's blazes was Red's likeness plopped smack-dab in the middle of this lobby? She blinked and refocused, but the cardboard man was no illusion.

Thank God it was just a replica. Probably some sports medicine thing.

Abby Ruth took long purposeful strides toward the elevator, trying to skirt the grinning 2-D ballplayer as if it wasn't standing there in all its six-foot-four glory, but she couldn't resist glancing closer.

Jenny didn't seem to notice the cardboard Houston Astros player giving them the eye because she chatted on about Grayson's puppy, Bowzer, and his propensity to chew on clothes and furniture instead of his many toys.

One step beyond the cutout, and Abby Ruth breathed a sigh of relief.

Only to have it clog in her chest a second later.

Because the man who'd just turned the corner and was walking her way was completely three-dimensional. That 2-D cardboard couldn't compete on any level, because no one could duplicate Red Jensen's confident stride.

No. Hell, no. This is not happening, today of all days.

She squared her shoulders and resisted the urge to take in every inch of him. Had he aged well? Had his skin wrinkled? Was his hair thinning?

Do not look.

She laser-focused her gaze on the elevator button and used it like a lighthouse in a hurricane. No wavering. No blinking. No peeking.

Under her breath, she counted the steps that would take her to those silver doors and out of danger. *One. Two. Three. Four. Five. Keep moving. One foot in front of the other. Six. Seven. Eight.*

"Abby Ruth Cady?"

She kept walking, her heart beating so loudly she couldn't hear her boots click against the tile. Maybe her feet weren't moving. She couldn't rightly tell, because a humming whir of energy buzzed through her, blocking out all her other senses.

"Abby Ruth?" His familiar voice ricocheted through her brain like an old pinball machine. No. They didn't know each other at all. Not after all these years.

"Mom!"

At the sound of Jenny's voice, Abby Ruth stopped. Hesitated for a two count, then turned.

And no, she hadn't imagined the man dressed in a blue sport coat and an orange-and-navy tie. Of course, Astros colors.

But what made her blood go icy was watching Red cast a lady-killer smile at Jenny. Her Jenny.

"I never expected to run into Abby Ruth Cady today. What are y'all doing at the hospital?" Red asked.

"Well, my mo—" Jenny started.

Abby Ruth cut her off. "Red Jensen. What a surprise." And although the years were evident—his skin slightly leathery from all of those years in the sun, and shimmering gray streaking through his hair—he was still every bit as handsome as he'd always been.

"I take it you two know one another from

your time covering sports at the newspaper," Jenny said.

"Yep," she rushed out, still edging toward the elevator. "That's exactly right."

"She's the biggest Houston Astros fan in the world," Jenny said. Then she lowered her voice so only Abby Ruth could hear. "Even if you did almost sell your favorite jersey."

"I seem to remember that." Red held out his hand to Abby Ruth, but she just stared at it as if he had a knife in it. After a few seconds, he dropped it back to his side. "It's been a long time."

Abby Ruth could smell her own panicked sweat. Even her short hair was wilting against her head. And the weight she'd lost over the past month made jeans droop as if she'd borrowed them from a shaplier girl. Not the impression a woman wanted to make on an old flame.

"It has been a while." She forced her words out. Over thirty years. "I haven't covered a ball game in three years. Young sports journalists come cheap."

"I never was a fan of cheap imitations," Red said, and then there was that smile again. "No one could hold a candle to you. You were one of the best, but retirement suits you. You look good."

He must be going blind in his old age, because *good* wasn't a word she'd use to describe herself today.

She glanced over to find Jenny beaming at Red. Lord, she wished now she'd come alone.

"What are you doing in Atlanta?" Jenny asked Red.

He turned his attention to Jenny, but he kept glancing toward Abby Ruth as if he were afraid she'd jackrabbit. "I'm the celebrity spokesperson for MS awareness."

MS. Those two letters were like hollow-point bullets to Abby Ruth's heart. Multiple Sclerosis was the debilitating disease that had dominated Red's family life back when Abby Ruth knew him.

A disease that had, in some ways, changed *her* whole life.

But in response, she simply smiled and nodded. "We've got to run. Really nice seeing you."

She turned and headed for the elevator. Good Lord, the last thing she needed was Red back in her life. Jenny stood off to one side at the elevator bank, and Red strolled back up to Abby Ruth.

She stabbed at the button again.

"Married?" Red asked.

"Are you talking to me?"

"Yes, you. Did you get married? Is that what brought you to Georgia?"

Abby Ruth refused to face him. "No. My truck brought me to Georgia."

Red laughed. "Same old quick wit. Sure is good to see you, Ru." He stepped between her and the doors, forcing her to meet his gaze. "You never said what you're doing here. Please tell me you aren't sick."

His green eyes mesmerized her for several seconds before she broke away and tapped her watch. "I'm running late."

"Dinner?"

The elevator doors finally opened, and Abby Ruth dove between them, but Red threw his still impressive forearm out to keep it from closing as Jenny stepped inside behind her.

"Dinner with me tonight. Please. For old time's sake."

"I'd love to. But I'm in a hurry and we're headed right back to Summer Shoals this afternoon. It was great to see you."

"Summer Shoals?"

Why in the world had she let that slip? *Cady, you're getting sloppy, and sloppy is dangerous.*

Jenny spoke up. "Couple hours southeast of here."

"No problem. I have this one last talk here today, then I've got nothing to do."

Abby Ruth glanced at his left hand, specifically at his ring finger. The band he'd always worn—titanium with Houston Astros blue baseball stitching on it—was no longer there. Could he be divorced? *No. Don't go there. He would've never divorced Linda.*

And for Abby Ruth, seeing him again wasn't a simple stroll down memory lane. It was a walk off a plank into shark-infested waters. Too much time and too many secrets there.

"I thought maybe you'd heard," he said, his voice low. "Linda passed away."

"I'm so sorry, Red."

"It was pneumonia, so not a total surprise."

Years ago, Abby Ruth had read enough about the disease to know pneumonia was one of the more common complications of MS. "She was lucky to have you."

"I tried to call you. After."

A buzzing started in Abby Ruth's head, but it took her several moments for her to realize it was the elevator's open-door warning instead of her internal emotional alarm sounding.

"About dinner," Red said. "I'm not taking no for an answer."

She knew Red Jensen better than anyone, and when he said he wasn't taking no for an answer, he meant it.

"I'll find Summer Shoals and meet you there tomorrow night. I'm just one of them roamin' chickens these days, so I got nothing but time." He pushed some buttons on his phone and shoved it into Abby Ruth's hand. "Give me your number."

She let out a breath and glanced over at Jenny, who was watching them with a smile. If she only knew the truth, she wouldn't be grinning. And any argument from Abby Ruth would make Jenny ask more questions, because this was Red Jensen after all. And he sure did look fine. Better than fine. "Here." She punched in her phone number and handed it back to him.

He pressed the button and the sound of a machine gun came blaring from Abby Ruth's purse. She went for her phone.

"Don't bother. It's just me." He grinned and gave her a wink. "Making sure it wasn't the Dial-A-Prayer number. Someone did that to me once."

Yeah. That someone had been her.

324 Kelsey Browning and Nancy Naigle

He disconnected the call, and her purse went silent. "I'll talk to you tomorrow evening." He pulled his hand from the elevator door and stood there smiling as it closed.

"Mom! Oh, my God. Red Jensen is taking you to dinner. You've still got it!"

"Stop that, Jenny. We worked together. I must've interviewed him a hundred times in his career. Got him lots of press, which probably helped him land all those pain reliever and truck commercials. He's being polite, because at our age being alive is reason enough to meet for a meal."

"Oh, please. I think this is a sign you're going to be fine," Jenny said, tapping on the elevator wall. "He might be your future knocking."

"For Pete's sake!"

"Don't deny it. Come on. Any woman would be happy to go out with him. He's still as handsome as any movie star his age. I can't wait to tell Teague we met him."

Oh, seeing Red again after all these years was a sign all right, but not the one Jenny had fabricated in that romantic mind of hers. Because at that moment, Abby Ruth was convinced this was likely the worst day in her life.

After crossing paths with Red and their past taking over her whole brain like a spider wrapping its prey, she was only able to half listen to the doctor. If Red wasn't distraction enough, no one had warned her that Dr. Dempsey—who was supposed to be the best in his field—was also the best of the best when it came to good looks. With his thick blond hair and a charming smile, he was a messenger of hope today. But all Abby Ruth could think of was that if her secret with Red came out, it might be worse than a bad prognosis.

Walking out of Dr. Dempsey's office, Abby Ruth hugged the file folder of information close to her white shirt. *I have options. Good news. So why can't I think about that instead of Red?*

"Mom, I'm scared. Why didn't you agree to the radiation? You're going to do it, aren't you?"

"You need to quit surfing the internet. All the margins are clear. You heard Doc. It's my choice. I can do radiation or not and, quite frankly, I'd like to put this all behind me and forget about it."

"I know it's your life, but I need you and Grayson needs you. We all do. Cancer isn't something you can simply forget about."

Lord, that was the truth. In fact, the more people who knew about her situation, the more real it seemed to become. And the more real it became, the more strangled she felt by it all. "Although you seem to think I'm addle-headed, I don't plan to take risks. I still have plenty of kicking up my heels to do. We're Cady women, and there are no weenie women in the entire Cady family tree. We meet our problems straight on, and that's exactly what I plan to do."

"What does meeting this head-on mean, Mom?"

"There are side effects and trade-offs with continued treatments too. I'm still numb from that lumpectomy. I can barely hold my AR-15 without a constant reminder of what I just went through. There are options, but the only person who can pick the right one is me."

CHAPTER 20

The strain between Marcus and Sera was getting harder and harder for her to take since she'd voiced her concern about him shooting at Summer Haven. Lord, she wondered if that Lady KitKat orb could cure what was ailing her and Marcus these days. He was feeling it too, because he'd made himself less scarce since their outing, or maybe it just seemed that way. Sera got dressed while he snored, rolling over to hug the pillow she'd moved into her spot before she slipped out of bed. He'd been up late last night scribbling furiously in his notepad, definitely in project mode again.

Sera went downstairs feeling a little like she didn't belong anywhere right now, and she didn't like that feeling. Unsettled. That's what she was feeling, kind of like Abby Ruth and her treatment plans. Just unsettled.

In the kitchen, Maggie was chopping and dicing the ingredients for potato salad.

"Need help?" Sera asked.

"Chop." Maggie nodded toward a cutting board and celery. "You look like you have something on your mind. Chopping is good for that. And with all this stuff with Abby Ruth hanging over us, we probably could all use a chopping hour. What's wrong?"

Sera shot a quick glance toward the ceiling. "You know when Bad Charlie was here?" She grabbed a knife from the magnetic strip on the wall and went to town. "Well, he wasn't the only stranger in the house."

Her eyebrows winging up, Maggie dumped the potatoes into the bowl and started dicing hard-boiled eggs. "What in the world do you mean?"

Half ashamed of what she was about to say, Sera lowered her voice. "I mean Marcus."

Never taking her gaze from Sera, Maggie reached for the bowl, missed it twice and then finally pulled it toward her and gave it a big stir. "You can't be serious. Sera, he's your husband."

"Not once since we arrived has he let me

drive the Maserati." One of Lil's cloth napkins beckoned from the counter, and Sera put down the knife and began to fold it. A crease there, a twist here. "He keeps those keys on him all the time, which is suspicious, don't you think? It's a rental car for heaven's sake. And yesterday, he slammed the trunk in some kind of hurry as I walked up."

"Sera, you can't believe he'd do something like that."

"When the four of us are investigating, we've always looked into everyone who had motive and opportunity. Why should Marcus be any different?"

"You're my friend, Sera, and you know I will support you from here to California and back, but I don't believe Marcus would ever steal to get something." Maggie laid her hand on Sera's arm. "He could certainly afford to buy any guns he wanted, and he knows we're your friends. It doesn't fit."

"That's what my heart keeps telling me, but he's hiding something. I need to know what it is." The napkin now resembled a rabbit that had eaten a garden shot with pesticides. Sera shook it out and started again. "And we owe it to Abby Ruth to turn over every rock to find her guns."

Maggie stirred for several minutes, long enough to make the salad into baked potato soup. Finally, she slipped the bowl into the fridge, turned to face Sera, and sighed. "Let's go look. It might be unlocked, and if not we'll make a plan B."

"I knew you'd help me." She and Maggie went outside and stood next to the Maserati.

"This car probably costs as much as what George and I paid for our house." Maggie tugged on the handle. "It's locked."

"Doesn't that seem sneaky? It's a rental."

"Probably big city habits is all."

"Let's see if we can find the keys." Sera headed to the house.

"Is he a heavy sleeper?" Maggie asked.

"Very."

They tiptoed up the stairs. Marcus was sawing some serious logs. "Has he always snored like that?" Maggie asked.

"Never sounded this loud at home. Must be echoing off of the wooden floors, but yes." She laughed. "Didn't miss that while I was living here."

Maggie stopped her before she entered the room. "You really want to do this?"

"No, but I have to," Sera said, and Maggie tucked in behind her as they opened the door.

It creaked, but Marcus didn't miss a beat. In. Out. He could practically suck the wallpaper right off the wall.

They searched in all the normal spots where a man offloaded his daily detritus. Top of the dresser. Bedside drawer. In his dopp kit. Sera even dropped to the floor and lifted the bed's dust ruffle. Nothing.

Maggie patted down his pants that lay over the valet in the corner.

Sera motioned for Maggie to meet her in the hall.

"This is weird. Why does a man hide his keys?"

"That is odd," Maggie said. "I don't know what to say."

"I don't want you to say anything, but I need your help one more time. Maggie, go get your crowbar."

Back outside, they stood at the back of Marcus's rental car and Maggie stared at the trunk and swallowed. "I don't think this is a good idea."

"I have to know."

"But this is a Maserati."

"He took out the insurance on it. The company will be compensated for any damage we do."

"I want to go on record stating I told you this was a mistake."

Sera pretended to take out a pen and write Maggie's statement on her palm. "Noted."

Still, Maggie hesitated, holding the crowbar several inches from the trunk's lock. "Are you sure?"

The not knowing was about to break every one of Sera's nerves. "Positive."

Maggie sucked in a breath that expanded her bustline and wedged the crowbar in the space beneath the lock. "One, two, three." One decent push with her weight behind it, and the trunk lid swung open. She ran her hand under the metal. "Barely a scratch. They might not even notice."

"You're amazing," Sera gushed.

But whatever Marcus had stashed in there was covered with a canvas tarp wrapped over and under, like you'd roll a body. It even had curves like a woman's breasts and hips.

Sera froze. It reminded her too much of the time she was locked in a trunk and forced to ride all the way to Hilton Head. She'd climbed in herself and for a good reason, but she'd been so carsick, she'd imbibed gallons of ginger tea the week after that fiasco. Her stomach flipped now, not wanting any part of the memory either.

"You want me to look?" Maggie asked.

"I'll do it." After all, if she was strong enough to suspect and accuse her husband, she had to be strong enough to follow through. With one yank, she pulled back the tarp.

"Oh," Maggie breathed.

Oh was right. Not only was the trunk not crammed with guns. It held three guitars—one Gibson, one Taylor, and one Martin. Since Finn had learned to play at the age of eight, Sera knew her acoustic guitars.

"Sera, what are you doing?" Marcus's voice came from beyond the raised trunk.

Maggie sidled close and tried to hide the crowbar between her leg and Sera's, but it was futile.

Marcus was already standing close and staring at what Maggie held in her hand. How in the world had he gotten dressed and downstairs so quickly? "Did you two break into my car?" When he lifted his gaze to Sera's, it communicated confusion, but more than that, his expression was full of hurt. "Why would you do that?"

"Well, you see," Maggie babbled, "it was my fault, I mentioned to Sera that I needed—"

Sera cut her off. "I thought the stolen guns

might be in your trunk."

"You thought that crook Charlie stole them and then stashed them right here at Summer Hav..." He trailed off. His mouth took on the line it did when he was negotiating with a particularly stubborn or egotistical actor. That was Marcus's no-bullshit look. "You thought I took those damn guns?"

Sera regretted it. She did. Every bit of it, but she'd had to follow the lead. That was the process.

"Well, you wouldn't let me drive the car and then you've been disappearing without much explanation. Then I saw you digging around in the trunk, and you seemed edgy about me seeing whatever was in there."

"How much explanation did you give me when you hopped in that damn van and took off?" Marcus's words were clipped and cold, chilling Sera down the center of her bones.

"I told you I needed time and—"

He held out a hand palm up. "You know what? I don't want to talk about that now. It was bad enough when you were convinced Brad had something to do with the missing guns. But now you're looking at me? My God, Sera, what have I ever done to make you trust me so little?" His low laugh was rough and edged with razor-sharp desolation. "I've been a fool. I thought we could still make it work, never for a minute doubted we could find our way. I didn't realize that what I should've doubted was your love."

He pushed a button on the door handle and the doors unlocked.

Maggie whipped around to look at Sera, who simply gulped. She watched her husband jab another button inside the car and take off, spitting gravel and dirt all over them.

"We deserved that," Maggie moaned.

"No, you don't deserve anything. I'm the one he's mad at and rightfully so." Sera sat down on the ground. "I just humiliated him in front of you."

"But why does he have a trunkful of guitars?"

"I have no idea," Sera said. "Marcus and I always laughed that Finn must've been blessed by a musical fairy godmother because Marcus couldn't carry a tune in a contractor's bucket."

"That's a good memory. Hang on to it."

Why had she ever considered Marcus would have Abby Ruth's guns? He'd never owned one in his life. All this tension between them had gotten in her head and made her think crazy thoughts.

This fiasco certainly proved she could still hurt him horribly.

Oh, God. What had she done? "I love him and I don't think I want to lose him."

AFTER AN HOUR-long struggle over which darn shirt to wear, Abby Ruth showed up at the Atlanta Highway Diner for her dinner with Red in a deep purple Western shirt with tiny white pearl snaps tucked into her smallest pair of blue jeans, which still hung too loose on her.

She'd simply picked the darkest shirt in her closet to fit her mood, at least that's what she'd thought an hour ago when she dressed. Now, her nerves zinged because she realized she was wearing Red's favorite color. She'd convinced herself that her standard white blouse hadn't felt right tonight because the thought of the radiation she was facing made her feel like she was glowing.

Truth was, her mind had subliminally wanted Red to know she still remembered. Remembered everything about them and their past.

That's a dangerous game. One I'm not ready to play.

Her choice of clothing was an innocent

mistake, and if Red's ego made him think it was for him, too bad.

Things should be simple here. If there was ever a man who didn't like to make a public scene, it was Red. And although she'd promised herself there'd be no more secrets from the other gals, meeting up with Red was not part of that promise. No...this needed to be kept quiet. Just like it had been for all these years.

When she walked inside the diner, Red was already seated at a table waiting on her. Instead of a jacket and tie, now he wore jeans and a golf shirt a few shades lighter than hers.

Great. We look like a cutesy couple in our matching shirts. She cursed herself all the way over to the table.

Red's eyes seemed to sear her skin with every step she made toward him. He had a few years on her, but he still looked good. Of course, she'd seen him on TV and in magazines since they parted ways. His baseball career had been iconic, so there'd been no way to avoid catching a glimpse of him from time to time. But after he walked out on her, she'd asked to be taken off the Astros games.

But she'd be lying if she didn't admit to

herself that she could still recite every one of his stats. Lifetime ERA of 3.19, 3.09 FIP, and over 5,700 strikeouts. Or had it been 5,900?

He stood as she approached the table. Ever the gentleman. "Thanks for coming."

"You didn't give me much of a choice."

Red laughed and pulled out her chair for her to sit. "I happen to know firsthand that no one makes Abby Ruth Cady do anything she doesn't want to."

She forced herself to smile as she gripped the edge of the table.

Red reached across and pulled her hands under his. "Do you believe me, that I tried to call you...after Linda passed?"

"I have no reason to doubt you're telling the truth, but I don't know why you called after all those years."

"Ours wasn't the kind of relationship a man forgets," he said softly.

"We didn't have a relationship. We had a fling."

"What we had wasn't a fling. It was way less than what we deserved, but it *was* a relationship. I loved you, Ru. After Linda's death, I called the newspaper and they said you were on extended leave. I left a message but never heard from you. The next time I tried, they told me you'd retired and left town."

Yeah, after the newspaper management had put her out to pasture, there'd been no reason to communicate with her old employer. But even if she had, she wouldn't have returned Red's calls.

"When I couldn't track you down, it hurt."

"Yeah, well, you hurt me all those years ago."

That seemed to stun him into silence. Why had she let her true feelings come out? Being this close to him was pushing her off-kilter. And the smell of his cologne—all leather and swagger—although unfamiliar, still made her a little dizzy.

"I've missed you."

"Don't."

"This could be our time."

"That moment passed decades ago. Are we going to order dinner or not? The meatloaf is good."

"I already ordered the special."

Just like the old days. He'd always done that. Ordered whatever was on special without asking. Back then, she'd loved it. Enjoyed feeling taken care of for a few minutes. Now, it felt like an intrusion into her world. "Of course you did."

Abby Ruth fiddled with the sugar packets on the table, and her mind took a spin back to the diner she and Red used to eat at in the Montrose area of Houston.

The white sugar packets there had always stood out against the red-flecked tabletops.

Red had been Jenny's age at the time. Prime of his career. They met often in public, watching themselves to ensure they gave the illusion of a professional relationship.

But when they rendezvoused later at the condo overlooking Hermann Park, all manners were tossed like a rookie cowboy off a rank bull in a matter of seconds.

They dreamed of a life together, building a family, something he'd never done with his wife.

One night, Red made love to her in a way that was hungry and unforgettable. He was desperate for her touch, and she knew how much he loved her. After, as they lay side-by-side in the sheltering king-size bed, Abby Ruth drummed up her courage. "I have something to tell you."

Although they'd been careful, she was pregnant. He wanted children so badly, so she knew tonight would be the beginning their new life together. Why else would he have lost control the way he had? New heights. New beginnings.

"I need to tell you something first," he said, his voice low and serious. "Linda's MS is worse. Abby Ruth, she needs me. You and I can't do this anymore."

Although her heart was crushed, she knew he was right. His wife couldn't take care of herself. She needed Red more than Abby Ruth and her unborn child did.

And Red didn't need to know that in less than seven months there'd be a forever reminder of their love. That was something she would handle herself.

Black and white as newsprint.

Without more words between them, Red rose from the bed, dressed, and left. The door to the condo clicked shut behind him with a finality that made it clear their relationship was truly over.

She'd never again set foot back inside that condo.

Had he held onto it long after?

Did he still own it?

She'd kept her key, placed it in her gun safe in Texas. When she hit the road, she'd slipped it inside the case with her Destroyer Carbine.

Now they were both missing.

Between her fingers, the sugar packet split from her fiddling. The grains scattered all over the table like tiny white tears.

"Are you okay?" Red asked gently.

Her own tears pressed behind her eyes. "I'm fine."

He shifted his chair closer to her and wrapped an arm around the back of hers, then tugged her into a hug. "Us bumping in to one another. It was meant to happen." He leaned in and pressed his lips to hers.

The warmth of his touch was familiar, and the softness of his kiss still held authority over her even after all this time.

No!

She pushed away. "Stop. What the hell are you doing? We don't know each other anymore. And we're out in public."

"So?"

"So we know better."

"Those days are over. We're free to be together."

"No. We're not." Abby Ruth snatched a napkin and scrubbed at her lips as she jumped to her feet, sending her chair screeching across the linoleum.

People all over the diner turned to look,

and Abby Ruth caught sight of Jenny rushing toward the table. Of all the people to run into.

"Mom, what's wrong?"

"Mom?" Red repeated.

"What are you doing here, Jenny?" Abby Ruth tried to keep the blind panic from making her voice wobble, which made her question come out harsher than she'd intended.

Jenny stepped back. "Sorry. I was here to pick up takeout for Grayson and me since Teague is working late. I saw you jump up from the table." She glanced at Red and back at Abby Ruth. "You look upset. What's wrong?"

"Nothing," Abby Ruth rushed to say. "Well, that's not true. Suddenly, I'm feeling awfully sick to my stomach." Lord, she was rambling, and if she didn't get the heck out of here soon, she would be a puddle of memories and confusion right here on the diner floor.

Red came to his feet. "I'll be happy to drive you home—"

"That's sweet of you, Mr. Jensen, but I'll take her back to Summer Haven," Jenny said and took a few steps toward the door. "C'mon, Mom."

"She's your daughter?" he said so quietly

there was no way—please, God—Jenny could've heard.

Abby Ruth couldn't look at him. She simply turned and walked toward the diner's door, but she could almost hear the blocks begin to tumble.

Because when he asked that question, something shrewd registered in his eyes. Which scared the bejesus out of her because Red Jensen had always been a good one with stats.

CHAPTER 21

*I*n Lil's mind, there was no better time than first thing in the morning to shift gears. *Right now I can't solve Sera's or Abby Ruth's problems, but I can get to the bottom of this gun stuff. And since it all started here at Summer Haven, it makes sense for me to take the lead.*

She walked outside where Maggie, Sera, and Abby Ruth were all dressed and sitting on the porch. Just as she expected, the tension was vibrating out here.

"We have to go back to the mausoleum," she announced.

"Why?" Maggie asked.

"First, because we can't abandon an angel with a broken wing. It's wrong and I'm sure Sera's karma would not take a liking to it. Plus,

I've been thinking about the guard recognizing Charlie's picture. Something is telling me we've missed an important connection or clue."

"I don't think it's a good idea." Maggie pushed her thick bangs back from her face with agitation. "What if that security guard catches us again? We're going to be in trouble."

Sera shook her head as she looked over her tie-dyed cheaters at the rest of them. "She's got a point. It sounds risky to me too."

"We won't get caught." Lil smiled, confident in her plan. "I'm certain of it."

"How can you be so sure?" Maggie's worry wrinkle creased between her eyes.

"We'll go in broad daylight," Lil explained. "Hiding in plain sight works best." One more tip she'd picked up listening to the women in Walter Stiles. Prison had turned out to be a handy education. "Security shouldn't be so tight during the day."

"I don't know," Sera said.

"Fine. I can go by myself." Lil turned and headed for the steps, praying they'd line up behind her like baby ducks and follow along.

When they did, her breath whooshed out in relief.

Abby Ruth's toe tapped as fast as a dog's tail at a Sunday cookout. But then she thankfully strode ahead of Lil. "Let's at least take my truck. I don't think Sera's van is very inconspicuous."

"Good point." Lil had a feeling Abby Ruth's request had more to do with her preference for being in the driver's seat, but the reason didn't matter. "Works for me."

"Wait up. I'll be there in a minute." Maggie jogged over to the carriage house where she kept her tools. "I have to get something if I'm going to work miracles on angels."

They piled into Abby Ruth's truck, and before Lil knew it, they were pulling into the mausoleum parking lot. No services were in progress, and the grounds were quiet.

Once they were inside, Lil led the girls directly to the basement level where Maggie had assaulted the Michael statue. Lil stepped into the alcove and for the first time read the names etched into the monuments. "Oh my goodness gracious."

"What's wrong, Lil?" Abby Ruth followed her line of sight toward the wall.

"When we hid here the other night, I didn't even notice it."

"What?"

"This is Rosemary Myrtle's family area." She looked around the alcove and pondered. "Strange, wouldn't you expect such a cultured family to be on one of the upper floors?"

"Maybe the person who originally set it up had a fear of heights," Maggie said.

"Not important. I'm sure there's a good explanation." Lil grabbed Maggie and urged her toward the giant angel statue. "You can fix this, right?"

Her best friend pulled an economy-size bottle of Gorilla Glue out of her fanny pack, which might as well have been a darned tool belt, and brandished it as if it was the answer to every modern world problem. Which was ridiculous since Maggie's DIY holy grail was, without a doubt, duct tape.

But poor Michael's boo-boo would be pretty noticeable if Maggie wrapped it in the pink camo design she'd taken to carrying lately.

"I need a few minutes. It would be impossible to find a clamp that would hold this angle right, so I'll need to stand here until it forms a strong bond." Maggie doused the statue with glue, rose on tiptoe to press the broken wing into place, and stood there holding it.

Lil was antsy to search the place for some real clues to Bad Charlie's whereabouts. After learning that guard had seen Charlie, she had a feeling—and no, it wasn't simply her bursitis acting up—that the mausoleum had more secrets to give up.

At one point, Maggie gave Lil a sharp look. "What is wrong with you? You're dancing a jig over there. Do you need to use the ladies' room?"

It wasn't until that comment that Lil realized she'd been shuffle-ball-changing in anticipation. "Just anxious to find something that will lead us to those darn guns."

"This is all about Abby Ruth, huh?" Sera's smile was wide and knowing. "Don't try to tell us that your anticipation has nothing to do with you becoming as addicted to solving crimes as we have."

"Admit it. Sera's right." Abby Ruth's grin matched Sera's.

Lil couldn't hold back her own smile. She would never for the rest of her days forget the way it had felt to tackle the person responsible for that art fraud scheme in Summer Shoals. She'd felt strong, able, and useful. And that was a combination that could keep a gal her age alive and lively for years to come. "I admit that I can now see the appeal."

"Thought so."

Maggie gingerly released her hold on Michael's wounded wing. Nary a wobble. "He'll be good as new."

That was a relief because the last thing Lil wanted to do was use her small stash of savings to replace a statue. She pulled a piece of paper out of her handbag. "I made a list of how we might search for clues."

"Lil," Maggie said, leaning back against one of the vault-covered walls. "I'm not sure you understand the way we normally operate."

Lil waved a hand in the air, dismissing Maggie's comment. "You'll find a floor plan on the opposite side."

"Uh, Lil—"

"Since that security guard said Bad Charlie brought in caskets, what do you think about starting our search in the dock area?"

"Lil, something—"

"From there, we can move on to the employee break room, the men's room, and—"

"Lil!"

"What?"

Maggie eased away from where she'd been leaning against the wall and pointed at the vault near her rear. "This just moved."

Sera hunkered down to get a better look. "Only one of the four little screw-in rosette corner thingies is in this one. See?"

"I hardly think—"

But Maggie and Sera were already wrestling with the square piece of granite. Lil laid a hand over her chest to try to calm the palpitations that were threatening to fling her heart out into the world. "You're desecrating one of Rosemary Myrtle's family members."

Abby Ruth stepped closer. "Well, if you think about it, the family member is inside a box. Not near this marker anyway." She patted Lil's shoulder. "It'll be okay. Let's see what's going on."

They heaved the granite out and carefully set the stone on the floor. Well, at least they were being careful.

"I thought you said Rosemary seemed very well-to-do," Maggie said.

"Of course she is. She's a descendent of the Myrtle family. As in the Myrtle Knolls Myrtles."

"And she said her deceased husband's name was Ronald?"

"That's right."

"This is definitely his resting spot then," Maggie said. "But why would she have entombed him in a plain wooden casket? Not a casket so much as a cheap box." She stooped down for a better look and grimaced. "And not even good wood. It's plywood."

Maggie stepped back, giving Lil a clear view into the vault. "Is that even legal?"

"And it's missing the crypt sealer. Ya know, the plastic piece those guys caulked into place separating the space where the casket goes from the granite marker. I wonder why?"

"Why indeed?"

"Girls? I think we may have hit gold." Sera said, reaching into the vault. "Maggie, this looks just like the box in the loading area when we were here the first time."

Maggie whipped out her phone and found the pictures they'd taken. "It sure does. Look." She turned her phone to show them. "I figured it was county-funded or something. Like for a pauper's funeral."

Sera crawled partway into the crypt, which gave Lil the willies.

"I admit it seems unusual, but of all people, I know even the most prosperous families can fall on hard times. Maybe Rosemary couldn't afford better." Lil knew that feeling all too well. "We need to put all of this back the way we found it and respect their privacy."

"Um, Lil?" Sera's voice rose. "What are the odds your friend would bury her dead husband dressed in bubble wrap?" She shimmied back out, dragging a piece of plastic from the vault.

My, that did seem unusual.

"Sera, you think we can pull that casket out?" Maggie asked.

"We can do anything we set our minds to."

Half horrified and half intrigued, Lil watched her two friends contort themselves and wrestle a brown wooden box out of the vault until it teetered on the edge like a doctor's scale that couldn't quite register whether you were just right or a little on the heavy side.

A couple more pieces of packing wrap poked out from the edge of the lid.

"Do you...do you think we should..." Lil waved a hand toward the casket. As much as she did not want to see Mr. Myrtle, this was too strange not to investigate.

"It's not sealed," Abby Ruth said. "I'd say that's permission enough."

"All in!" Maggie said cheerfully. She and Sera yanked on the box and one end thudded to the floor. They dragged it out of the vault, leaving splinters on the marble floor.

I hope we're not disturbing someone's

peaceful eternal slumber.

Maggie sucked in a breath, closed her eyes, and eased open the lid.

Lil couldn't help herself and leaned forward to get the first glimpse. And there amid several cushioning wads of bubble wrap were somewhere in the neighborhood of twenty guns. "Guns?"

Abby Ruth, who'd been hanging back, lunged forward.

Lil's midsection cramped. Lord have mercy, this was big. "Poor Rosemary."

"What do you mean?" Sera, Abby Ruth, and Maggie all looked at her.

"It's obvious someone has stolen her husband and replaced him with these guns."

"Ew," Sera said. "What do you think they did with him?"

Lil didn't even want to contemplate. Anyone who was capable of hiding guns in such a sacred place obviously had no morals.

Maggie carefully sorted through guns of all shapes and sizes. She pulled out one handgun and held it up like it was a dead mouse. "Does this look familiar?"

"That's my Astra 400!" Abby Ruth's eyes sparkled with excitement, and she started unrolling the bubble wrap.

"Are all these guns yours?"

Abby Ruth stepped back with a frown on her face. "No. Some aren't mine." She lifted an AK-47 out of the box and checked to see if it was loaded.

"But are all of your guns here?" Lil asked.

"It'll take me a minute to go through them all."

"Maggie, go head off any visitors," Lil said. "If we get caught now, we'd have some explaining to do." And her own fanny would end up in one hot mess again. Terms of her probation were quite clear about abiding the law and possession of firearms.

Maggie ran around the corner and positioned herself so she could see in both directions. She lifted a hand in the air and gave Lil the thumbs up.

Lil had wanted a lead, but this was more than she'd bargained for.

Abby Ruth rummaged through the pseudo-casket. "No. Mine aren't all here."

Dang, that wasn't good news. Maybe they should search every vault in this alcove. Lil glanced around and was overwhelmed. There had to be at least fifty. Not only would it take too much time and put them at risk for discovery, but there was no way they could reach the upper vaults without special equipment. "We're not prepared to do more today. I say we put the casket back and fix it so it looks like it hasn't been touched. At least we found some of them, Abby Ruth."

Abby Ruth pushed the Astra into the back of her pants, and a smaller gun into her boot. "It's a start."

"Maybe we should—"

"If you're about to suggest we tell Teague," Abby Ruth said. "I don't think that's the best idea."

She never did, but Lil adjusted her handbag on the crook of her arm and thought. "This time, I agree. If we go to the authorities, they'll feel the need to take over. And honestly, they don't have any skin in this game."

Abby Ruth patted Lil on the shoulder, then Lil motioned for Maggie to come back to help scooch that box of guns back where they found it.

It took Lil, Sera, and Maggie all three to muscle the gun-filled box back into its proper place. Afterward, Lil was slightly winded. Crime solving was more physically demanding than she'd ever realized. Maybe it was time to add a weight-training regimen to the two miles she walked each day, trying to lose the last of the weight she'd gained in prison.

On their way to the stairs, Lil said, "Why don't y'all go on up? I need to stop in the restroom before we head home. I'll meet you in the parking lot." They didn't have to know she needed an opportunity to apply a wet towel to her sweating face.

Inside the ladies room, she splashed water on her cheeks, and as she was patting them dry when in walked Rosemary Myrtle.

Oh, what a quandary.

"Hello, Lillian."

"So nice to see you again." Not really, though. Lil was playing mental ping-pong. What was the proper etiquette in this situation? Would she want someone to tell her if Harlan's grave had been ransacked? No? Maybe? Yes, absolutely.

She forced herself to smile pleasantly at the other woman. "If you have a few minutes, I'd like to discuss something with you."

"Of course."

They settled on the couch Abby Ruth had taken a nap on, and Lil wished desperately for a cup of the tea Rosemary had been sipping the other day. Anything to make this revelation easier. "I'd like to tell you not to be upset by what I'm about to say, but I know that's impossible."

Rosemary's brow crinkled. "This sounds like bad news."

"You have to promise not to tell a soul, and I need you to keep it quiet—for a few days anyway."

"Why? What is going on?"

"It's complicated." Lil couldn't tell her the whole story, not without a lot of explaining and there wasn't time.

Rosemary paused only for a moment. "You have my word."

"I happened by your family's alcove earlier and one of the headstones was loose."

The look on Rosemary's face went from surprise to anger to sorrow in what seemed like fast-forward. "That's unusual." Her words were clipped, revealing how disturbed she was.

"You're upset. I would be too." Lil paused, hoping Rosemary would appreciate her empathy, but grief was unpredictable. "We thought it was strange too, so I felt the need to take a closer look."

Rosemary's hands tightened around her handbag. "What do you mean?"

"I hate to tell you this, but I'm afraid your husband's body is missing."

CHAPTER 22

*L*il felt terrible about being the one to break the news to Rosemary. But it seemed like the right thing to do.

Rosemary looked stunned. She made Lil promise to come see her the next afternoon, scribbled her address on the back of a brochure, and shoved it at Lil as she ran from the restroom.

It took Lil a moment to compose herself too. Poor Rosemary had to be devastated.

Making her way to the parking lot, Lil decided it would be best to keep her visit with Rosemary from her friends. She felt a special connection to the other well-bred Southern woman, but she wasn't quite sure how to tell the others that without sounding like she was putting them down.

By the time Lil and the girls got back to Summer Haven, the day had worn on them all. All except Abby Ruth, who seemed to be having quite the happy reunion with her guns, spreading them out on the dining room table and giving them a loving cleaning and polish job.

The next afternoon, Lil made up an excuse to borrow Maggie's truck. Thankfully, Maggie and Sera had decided to take advantage of the beautiful May weather and were plucking weeds from the front flowerbed.

Lil parked Maggie's truck two blocks from the Myrtle family home so Rosemary wouldn't see what she'd driven. Because this was one of those times when appearances were important. She cursed herself. Yes, she'd learned better in the past about trying to keep up with the Joneses, or Myrtles in this case, but this was a special circumstance. Once she and Rosemary knew each other better, Lil would be a bit more forthcoming about her own financial challenges.

Thank goodness she'd thought to wear a pair of low pumps. Anything higher than these one-and-a-half-inch heels and she'd be limping by the time she got to Rosemary's door.

She rang the front bell of the ornate two-story Victorian with glossy white paint, an immaculate yard, and a metal fence that had obviously been handcrafted. By the house's upkeep, Lil would've never guessed Rosemary was so strapped for cash that she couldn't afford a nice casket for her dear husband.

But then Lil knew a thing or two about keeping up appearances.

Rosemary answered the door and glanced toward the driveway. "Lillian, so nice for you to come for tea. But I didn't hear you drive up."

"It was such a pretty day, I decided to park near the Town Square and walk."

"My, that's very...enterprising of you." She stepped aside, allowing Lil to enter the foyer, a space paneled in high-dollar blond mahogany and lined with expensive-looking objets d' art.

"I'm so sorry about your husband." Lil clasped her hands together. "I've never heard of such a thing happening."

Rosemary bowed her head then placed her hand across her chest. "It's appalling. That's what it is. But I do appreciate you being so forthcoming. Let's visit for a while, please. I'm not ready to talk about that yet."

Lil could only imagine what Rosemary was

going through. Such a dedicated wife to be there every day, only to discover she was sitting with an empty box! Heavens to Betsy.

A shiny glint caught Lil's eye from across the foyer. "Is that what I think it is?" She approached a small and delicate artifact sitting in a lit niche.

"I don't like to brag, but our family is one of the few in the US to own a Fabergé egg from the pre-1917 originals. Priceless really."

"It's breathtaking." With its jewel-crusted exterior and delicate gold clasp, it was as if a multibillionaire bunny had stopped by at Easter.

"I've had my staff ready the back veranda for tea, if you'll follow me." She swept toward the back of the house.

Staff? Interesting choice of spending. Lil would've upgraded her husband's casket before paying people to wait on her.

Lil followed and tried to swallow down her envy at the beautiful furniture, tapestries, and other goodies around every corner. When she spotted a collection of pocket watches, so like her daddy's, glimmering in a lit curio, a bitter taste filled her mouth.

Stop this nonsense, Lillian. Summer Haven is still beautiful, if a little tattered.

Rosemary led the way to an expansive covered porch with a rattan dining suite sitting under a ceiling fan turning lazy circles. Fine china and crystal adorned the table.

When Lil sat, she had to hold her hands in her lap to refrain from upending her cup and saucer to look for the manufacturer's mark on the underside. *When in the world did I become so uncouth? Momma would be so ashamed.*

A woman in a well-pressed maid's uniform approached the table and poured fragrant tea in Lil's and Rosemary's cups, then she offered platters of delicate finger sandwiches and tarts. How long had it been since she'd had such a beautifully presented table? Since long before she made the acquaintance of Walter Stiles Federal Prison Camp.

She smiled at Rosemary. "Thank you for going to all this trouble. It looks and smells delicious."

"Oh, it was no trouble." Rosemary shrugged politely. "I was so delighted to meet you. Honestly, I can't believe we've lived in neighboring counties all these years and never met before. After all, I've heard for many years about the Summers and all the charitable things your family has done for your community."

"I'm sure no more than the Myrtle family has done here."

"Certainly so." Rosemary took a dainty sip of her tea. "It's lonely sometimes, isn't it?"

"Being widowed, you mean?"

Her laughter was a high tinkle. "Oh, goodness, no. I mean it's lonely being the matriarch. Having others always look to you for guidance on what's proper and allowed. I suppose that's what they mean by it being lonely at the top."

Lil nodded, but she certainly didn't consider herself lonely, not with Maggie's, Sera's, and Abby Ruth's companionship. But it seemed rude to rub that in Rosemary's nose if she didn't have similar friendships. "I suppose you're heavily involved with the Junior League and other organizations here."

"Oh, believe me, I keep very busy. It's hard work managing other people."

She and Rosemary spent the next hour chatting about everything from how to properly host a dinner party for fifty to the merits of the new iPhone as they nibbled delectable treats and sipped fine tea. Of course, Lil didn't know a thing about those smart phones, but she hadn't survived over a year in prison without learning how to fudge the truth a bit. "You know, I am sorry about your husband."

"I still can't believe anyone would disturb my dear husband's remains." Rosemary took a petit four from the three-tiered tray. "Did you tell anyone else about what you found?" She lowered her gaze, then she leveled a stare at her that set Lil on edge. "You can imagine how embarrassing that could be."

"Why? Have you?" Lil didn't quite understand the feeling she was getting, but whatever it was...it was not comfortable.

"Of course not. You asked me not to and I always keep my word." Rosemary reached across the table and laid a hand on Lil's arm. "I don't have to tell you that. We're so much alike."

Lil helped herself to another tiny tea sandwich, feeling more like a lady than she had in a long while. The smoked salmon and delicate greens were so delicious and such a treat.

"I'm so thankful you found out and told me." She lifted her teacup and sipped. "Can you tell me more about how you discovered my husband's casket was empty?"

"Well, we were at the mausoleum doing

some, shall we say, sleuthing." Lil felt a swell of pride to be part of their little team of investigators. Saying it aloud to Rosemary felt quite powerful.

"Fascinating. Do you do this often? Don't tell me you're looking for a body-stealing ring? I've heard of people grave robbing to sell body parts. I know it sounds callous, but my dear Ronald has been gone long enough that he'd no longer be a good candidate for that or any kind of scientific research."

"No, nothing like that. Actually, my friend Abby Ruth is a gun collector and had some very old and rare guns stolen from right outside my home. To my horror."

Rosemary tapped her napkin to her lips and set her teacup down. "That *is* horrible."

"So you can imagine I felt partially responsible."

"Of course." Rosemary raised her hands and gestured around her. "Our homes are supposed to be safe."

"Exactly. We'd been looking for her guns without much luck, but then one of the mausoleum's security guards recognized a picture of the man we believe is the culprit, a temporary guest in my home."

"You take in boarders?" Rosemary's

condescending tone grated over Lil's skin.

"No, but our local B&B was full to the gills with overflow of Hollywood A-listers coming for the Jessie Wyatt funeral, so one of the B&B's regulars stayed in my home as a favor to the owner."

"And how many friends did you say were with you when you stumbled across the guns in my husband's vault?"

"Oh, four of us were there. Don't you worry. I wouldn't dare put myself in the position of being in danger alone. No, ma'am. And they're great friends."

"They sound wonderful." Rosemary's phone rang. "Oh dear. I need to take this call. You will excuse me, won't you?"

"Of course," Lil said. She sat with her hands in her lap as Rosemary took the call.

With her ear pressed to the phone, Rosemary nodded. "I'm cleaning the mess up here, so you need to take care of the *three* things on your end. Yes, whatever it takes, since you're the one who made it in the first place. Toodles." She ended the call and turned her phone over on the table. "My apologies. It's so hard to find a good cleaning service these days."

Lil wouldn't know since she and the

women who lived with her took care of Summer Haven without help.

"Drink up, dear. We have plenty more." Rosemary smiled at Lil, lifting a hand in the air. Her maid rushed in to top off Lil's tea. "Maybe next time your friends can come to tea as well."

Lil experienced a small twinge. It would be nice to have a friend like Rosemary Myrtle in her life. Someone with a background similar to hers.

But did she really want to share her with Maggie and the others? Strangely, thought made her slightly dizzy.

"That's nice of you to offer. I've already overstayed my welcome this afternoon. Thank you so much for your hospitality." Lil stood and her head whirled for an instant. She was too old to sit for that long without moving around. If she didn't watch out, she was just one tea sandwich away from a deep vein thrombosis.

The goodbyes with Rosemary felt a bit foggy as Lil made her way to the door and down the block back to Maggie's truck. She slipped behind the wheel of the truck with her head reeling as if someone had blown helium into her ear.

Had Rosemary asked her about the guns in the casket?

She was quite certain she'd only told her his body was missing.

Lil's stomach convulsed. Thank goodness she'd left Rosemary's when she had. It would've certainly spoiled tea if she'd been sick in the woman's African violets.

THE FRONT DOORBELL RANG, rousing Abby Ruth from her nap on the divan. She and that fussy little couch were becoming fast friends here lately.

It wasn't like they had all that many visitors to Summer Haven. Especially unexpected ones.

Oh, no. What if the visitor was Red? Her heart picked up an extra beat and her intuition told her he wouldn't give up so easily after she'd run out on him the other night.

She dashed to the window and pulled back the parlor curtain. A dark-haired young man with a droopy mustache and a slightly crooked nose stood at the door.

Holy baloney, she recognized the guy from Sera's composite sketch. Bad Charlie, that gun-stealing egg-sucker, was standing on

Summer Haven's front porch!

"Thank you, Jesus," she said, raising her hands to the sky. Then she ran on tiptoe from the parlor to the kitchen. "You won't believe who's on our front porch," she said to Sera and Maggie.

"Teague," Maggie guessed.

"Angelina? No wait," Sera said with a snap of her fingers. "Hollis Dooley."

"No. Bad Charlie!"

Maggie jumped from her chair and grabbed her phone off the charger.

"What are you doing?" Abby Ruth asked.

"Calling Teague, of course." Maggie mashed buttons with shaky fingers.

Abby Ruth lunged over and snatched the phone out of Maggie's hands. "No, ma'am. No time for that." She pushed the end call button and slammed the phone down on the quilted placemat.

Maggie flashed her a look of panic.

"Yet," Abby Ruth added. "I promise we'll call him, but that crooked criminal is here now and we need to jump on this chance. Where's Marcus?"

Sera paled. "He left earlier."

"Good, I don't want him in the way. That's perfect. You in or not?"

Excitement hung in the room, and her friends both nodded.

Abby Ruth and Maggie huddled on the other side of the grandfather clock while Sera answered the door and invited unsuspecting Bad Charlie inside. "Oh my gosh, it's so good to see you again!" Sera leaped into his arms, wrapping him in a big bear hug and pointing him toward the dining room. "Come with me."

And like the dirty rat he was, Bad Charlie fell right in behind the colorfully dressed Pied Piper, played by Serendipity Johnson.

"Maggie, come on into the dining and see who's here," Sera sang out.

Maggie rushed into the other room, pasting a look of surprise on her face. "My goodness. So good to see you. Lil's going to be sorry she missed you."

"She's not here?"

"No. She's out running errands."

"Lil's not here, but I am. If you're looking for trouble, I'm a pretty good bet." Abby Ruth came out of hiding and strode into the room, purposefully allowing her boot heels to tap out an ominous tempo on the hardwood floor. Her last two steps landed like a one-two punch. "You stayed in my room last time you were here," she said, perching her hands on her hips. "But as you can see, I'm back."

Bad Charlie's face rearranged into what he probably thought was a smile, but he looked like a constipated weasel to Abby Ruth. "Oh, I wouldn't want to put anyone out."

"Sit, Charlie." Sera pulled out a gold-upholstered fruitwood chair from the long dining room table. "We'll worry about the exact room later, but for now you have to tell us how you've been."

The rat-weasel sat down on command. Damn, Sera had a way about her.

"I bet any room would do for you." Abby Ruth stepped forward, her legs in a wide stance in front of his chair. "Because sleep isn't what you're looking for. Is it?"

Panic flashed across Charlie's face, and his head swiveled from her to Sera to Maggie and back to her. "I...um...the B&B is full and I thought—"

"You thought you'd look for someplace more...lucrative, didn't you?"

He put his hands on the arms of the chair and began to push up.

"Oh, no you don't," Abby Ruth said, pressing her knee against his. "Not so fast. I have a few questions for you."

Maggie and Sera jumped forward to wrap a

length of colored duct tape around each of Bad Charlie's arms, strapping him to the chair. Pink camo on the right arm and turquoise with black zebra stripes on the left. Even she was fashion savvy enough to know that wasn't a good look on him.

Charlie's head bobbled back and forth. "What the hell—"

"My thoughts exactly," Abby Ruth said. "What the *hell* happened to my guns?"

"She told me to clean up this mess. Should've just done it with no warning."

"She? Who told you to do what?"

"Nothing." Bad Charlie tugged on his arms and hissed out cuss words under his breath. "You don't know who you're messing with."

"You think I'm afraid of you? Please." Abby Ruth sputtered. "You might want to reconsider that line of thought. Where are my guns?"

"No one wants those guns anyway. They're too expensive to sell on the street. Weren't worth half the hassle they've caused."

"Good, then you won't mind handing them back over." She snapped her fingers in front of his face. "Where are they?"

"I can give them to you."

"I was hoping you'd say that."

"You're going to have to let me up though."

"I don't have to do anything." Abby Ruth laughed. Being back in control of something felt good, but as she turned to share the moment with Maggie and Sera, Bad Charlie leaned forward and head-butted her right on her incision site. A burst of pain flashed inside her on impact, robbing her of breath. She slumped to the floor.

"Abby Ruth!" Sera raced across the room.

"Are you okay?" Maggie said as she knelt down next to her.

Eyes closed, she sat there on her fanny with her feet stretched in front of her, holding one arm across her chest. "That hurt, you numbskull."

"Please say you're okay," Sera pleaded.

"I'm fine," Abby Ruth puffed as she tried to stand. "Get him!"

Sera and Maggie both spun in the direction she was pointing.

Bad Charlie was making a hasty exit through the house with that chair still strapped to his hind-side.

He lumbered through the foyer and made an awkward run for the door.

The grandfather clock bonged an out-of-tune note as the chair leg hit its side and shoved it cockeyed to the corner.

From the other side of the wall, Lil's *Gone With The Wind* collectible plate in the parlor china cabinet hit the floor with a crash.

The screen door slapped closed just as Sera got to it. "I'm going after him!"

The door slapped a second time right behind Sera.

Abby Ruth was still trying to get oxygen back in her lungs and huffed out, "This would be the time to call 9-1-1, Mags."

Maggie pulled her cell from her pocket as she and Abby Ruth followed in Sera's wake. "I need the sheriff at Summer Haven. Hurry. There's a burglary in progress!"

"What's he stealing—the chair?" Abby Ruth snapped.

"Well, it *was* a burglary when he stole your guns," she said, covering the phone with her hand.

"True enough," Abby Ruth conceded.

Maggie panted into the phone, "I promise this man is a crook. Send Teague!"

When Abby Ruth and Maggie made it to the door, Sera was taking a flying leap off the porch, her limbs in all directions. Maggie punched at the door screen, pushing it wide so they could run down the steps to catch up with her.

376 Kelsey Browning and Nancy Naigle

Bad Charlie was making strides.

"Dammit, y'all should've strapped his legs too," Abby Ruth hollered.

"I'll remind you this was a last-minute takedown," Maggie said. "It wasn't like we had days to plan."

His long legs were eating up twice as much ground as Sera's. He was nearly to the curve in the driveway, and it was doubtful she would catch up unless he tripped.

Then a sedan barreled up the driveway, heading right for Bad Charlie, screeching to a stop at the last second. Sera was making up ground but was still a good twenty feet away when Bad Charlie suddenly dropped like a stone.

Abby Ruth whooped out a "YES!" as she and Maggie caught up to Sera.

The driver of the vehicle stepped out, and Abby Ruth blinked in surprise. "Red?"

He flashed that perfect smile, which hit her straight in the midsection, much more pleasurable than Bad Charlie's earlier move.

"What are you doing here?"

"You'll be seeing a lot more of me. The sheriff rented me his house."

That tidbit hit Abby Ruth almost as hard as Bad Charlie's head butt, but dammit, she couldn't deal with Red now. She glanced down at Bad Charlie, sprawled in an unnatural position on the ground and knocked out cold. What in the world? "What did you do to him, Sera?"

Sera reached over and held her hand up for a high five from Red. "This guy beaned him with a baseball."

Abby Ruth eyed Red. Surely her racing heart was a consequence of the chase and not the man standing in front of her. "You took him down?"

Red grinned. "It's what I do."

In his day, he'd had the best arm in the league. But even if he'd been a second-rate pitcher, he'd always known how to throw a cupid pitch to her heart. "We had it taken care of," Abby Ruth said coolly.

"Yeah, I noticed. Everything looked completely under control as this idiot came running toward me with a chair strapped to his ass."

Abby Ruth laughed so hard she snorted. Bad Charlie and his built-in seat must've been a confusing sight to drive up on.

But Red had come through with a single pitch. *Boom!*

"You should've seen it," Sera said, flashing

a doe-eyed glance in Red's direction. "Looked like a major league pitch."

"I bet it did," Abby Ruth said, her voice low.

"Who is he?" Sera whispered. "You know him?"

Not ready to answer the questions she knew her friends would have about Red, Abby Ruth nudged Sera with a not now message.

"I'm not sure I want to know what y'all were doing to him to make him run." He stepped closer to her, putting his arm around her waist, and she soaked up the swirl of warmth his touch sent through her. "But if I had to guess, I'd say you could spin me a pretty good story."

CHAPTER 23

When Teague arrived, he gave Abby Ruth and the others the look, the one that said "you're not off the hook and you'll be explaining this in detail later." But he cut the duct tape from around Bad Charlie's wrists and cuffed him.

"He said something about cleaning up his mess," Abby Ruth told Teague. "But I don't know what he meant."

"That's for me to worry about," Teague shot back.

"You will question him about my guns, right?"

"No, Abby Ruth. I'm planning to drop him off on Main Street the minute I drive away from Summer Haven and let him go on his merry way."

"You don't have to be so touchy about it."

"Wouldn't you be touchy if a crew of senior citizens kept trying to do your job?"

She was smart enough not to reply to that.

After Teague dragged Charlie off to jail, Marcus stopped by to pick up Sera, and Abby Ruth shooed Maggie back inside the house. But Red was still hanging around, standing entirely too close for Abby Ruth's peace of mind.

"Everything's fine now," she told him. "You can go on back to...to wherever it is you're doing."

"I just told you that I rented Teague's old house. I'll be living in Summer Shoals until further notice."

Abby Ruth tried to swallow the hunk of fear in her throat, but it wouldn't budge. "I...I don't think that's a good idea."

"Really?" Red's tone was pleasant enough, but his eyes and mouth were dead serious. "Because I think it's smart to hang around here until you're finished with your cancer treatments."

"How did you find out about that?"

"You're not the only one who knows how to ask leading questions, Ms. Journalist. I have connections at the hospital in Atlanta, and

Summer Shoals is a small town."

"Damned Atlanta Highway Diner."

"You didn't actually think I'd leave before we could settle things between us, did you?"

"There's nothing to settle."

"Then you won't mind if I go pay a visit to Jenny now, will you?" Red leveled a stare that made her shiver.

"I need some time."

"You've had thirty-something years."

Although she'd once loved this man, right now she wanted to find a stick and whack him with it. But she couldn't because he had every right to be upset. Every right to want to stay. "Red, I'm sick." Damn, she hated playing that card, but she wasn't sure she could handle him and cancer at the same time.

He reached out and stroked a callused thumb over her cheek. "Which is the reason you should let me back into your life. Think about it, Ru, and you'll realize I'm right."

The nickname swirled inside her, tickling those old memories that had once made her heart skip beats on a regular basis.

When Red strode back to his car, Abby Ruth's heartbeat was still triple-timing.

She soothed herself with some NASCAR on the big-screen TV she'd installed in Lil's front parlor. Lil still sneered at it every time she walked by the room, but she'd been known to sit down and watch an MMA bout from time to time. There was more to that Southern belle than she let on. And more to Red and their past than Abby Ruth had ever let herself think about.

"Abby Ruth, about that man outside earlier..." Maggie's voice came from the hall, her footsteps following.

Abby Ruth squeezed her eyes closed, pretending to be asleep to avoid the questions about Red's unexpected arrival.

She'd just settled deeper into the cushions when the house shook on its pier and beam foundation. Without bothering to grab her boots, she ran for the front hallway in her stocking feet, sliding across the slick wooden floors.

"What in heaven's name?" Maggie hollered from the kitchen.

"I don't know," Abby Ruth yelled back, "but whatever it is, it's out front." She jerked open the door only to find Maggie's truck halfway up the steps, one front tire on the porch and one hanging off the side, with the engine revving at what sounded like five thousand RPMs.

Maggie came flying out onto the porch behind her. "Lil!" Maggie jumped forward and started tugging on the driver's side door. "It's locked!"

Abby Ruth skidded around to the other side and jerked open the passenger door. Lil's forehead was pressed against the top of the steering wheel, and dots of blood dripped onto her lap. Without thinking twice, Abby Ruth crawled inside and wrenched the ignition to the off position. Then she reached beyond Lil's thin little back and popped the driver's side lock.

When Maggie swung open the door, Abby Ruth said, "Call 9-1-1. Now." *Good Lord, we're keeping Teague in business this week. He's going to kill us.*

THE LAST PLACE Abby Ruth wanted to be today was in another doggone hospital, but a few hours after the ambulance took Lil to the Bartell County Hospital, she was in the small waiting room along with everyone who lived at Summer Haven and Jenny's little family. Even Marcus and Red were there. Just waiting for news about Lil.

At least all of this mess was keeping the

heat off Abby Ruth's personal life. Red was not something she was prepared to discuss. Which wasn't much of a worry the way Maggie was pacing. Lord, if her heart was beating half as fast, she'd be the next one in a hospital bed. "Calm down, Maggie. She's in good hands," Abby Ruth said, taking Maggie's clammy hand into her own.

Finally, one of the nurses, a handsome strapping young man, came in and said Lil was awake. He glanced around at their entourage. "She can't handle this many visitors. Two people, three max. And only for five minutes or so."

Teague was already standing.

"Want me to come with you, Maggie?" Wouldn't hurt Abby Ruth's feelings to not have to go in a hospital room, but she'd do it for Maggie's sake. And Lil's.

"Please," Maggie said with a squeeze to Abby Ruth's hand.

The nurse led them to Lil's room then stepped aside.

"Oh, Lil," Maggie said. "You look like a marionette, with the IV line running from you like that."

Truth was, Lil had never looked so tiny and frail, and on the rolling table beside her sat a stack of those puke bowls. Poor old gal.

Maggie rushed to her side, her hand hovering over Lil's without actually touching it. "You scared the fire out of us."

"I'm sorry about your truck." Lil's voice was small and scratchy.

"Don't you worry about that."

A blonde thirty-something doctor walked in, her stethoscope bouncing against her white coat. "She was actually very lucky. That pokeweed is some mean stuff."

"So she didn't have a heart attack?" Maggie asked.

"Not even close," the doctor said. "For someone who weighs what she does, the amount she had in her system could've killed her."

"What do you mean? How?"

Lil squeezed Maggie's hand. "I was poisoned, Mags."

"I'll be damned," Abby Ruth said.

Teague's face went all serious and sheriff-like. "Lil, if you feel up to it, I need to ask you a few questions."

"I can handle it," she said.

"Only a few minutes, and don't overtire her." The doctor gave an I'm-the-boss nod and walked out.

"Do you have any idea how this might've happened?"

"I think it was something in the tea or sandwiches."

Maggie blinked and grabbed for her phone. "We probably need to contact the diner and let them know before others pop up sick."

"Not necessary. I wasn't in a restaurant," Lil said. "And this isn't food poisoning."

"What are you saying?" Teague asked.

"I'm saying that I don't think this was an accident at all," she croaked. "I'm almost certain Rosemary Myrtle meant to kill me."

LIL WATCHED confusion flash across Maggie's face.

"You were with Rosemary Myrtle? Why didn't you tell me that's where you were going?" Maggie lowered herself into the chair next to the bed.

"I don't know. I should've told you she invited me to tea." Lil closed her eyes. "I didn't want you to feel left out."

"I think I need a word with Miss Lillian alone," Teague said, shooing everyone out, and proceeded to pepper her with questions.

Lil had to hand it to him. That boy was

dedicated to his job, so much that he was willing to hold the little plastic bowl for her every time she needed a break in her explanation in order to be sick.

"I'm so sorry," she groaned after he handed her a wet washcloth for the tenth time. "This can't be fun for you."

"But catching crooks is." He smiled. "So let's see if we can get to the bottom of this. The other ladies told you I picked up Charlie Millet out at Summer Haven, right?"

"Yes." And it made her even more miserable that she'd ever believed he was a nice man.

"I didn't have long to interview him before I was called out again, but he admitted to being involved in a gunrunning scheme. He was kinda tight-lipped about the mastermind behind the whole thing, though, saying he probably wouldn't make it out alive if he rolled over."

"Rosemary Myrtle is your mastermind."

Teague slowly shook his head. "I can't believe it. A woman like that selling illegal arms is akin to a woman like you..." His head jerked up and his face went red. "I...ah...just meant..."

"Which is exactly the reason you should

believe me when I tell you I know what I'm talking about. When I was away, I met plenty of women who'd done bad things. And although I was initially blinded by Rosemary's family name and gracious behavior, it's clear now she's a snake in the grass. You have to catch her, Teague."

"Well, this isn't completely up to me. Your friend Charlie mentioned the ring operates up and down the East Coast, from Florida to Virginia. I've already called in the ATF. They're setting up a sting operation."

"I feel responsible," Lil said. "And want to help in any way I can."

"Right now, the best way for you to help is to get well."

She filled him in on every detail she could recall. "Teague, promise me you'll keep me in the loop. I don't want anyone else hurt by this horrible woman."

Teague gently patted her hand. "Leave it to the professionals now. Based on the pickup and drop-off schedule we got out of Charlie Millet, the teams will be in place at the mausoleum day after tomorrow, and I think things will get cleared up pretty quickly with all you've been able to tell us."

But as soon as Teague was out the door, Lil

rang for her nurse. When the young man entered her room, she said, "I believe my friends are still outside in the waiting room. Could you please send them in?"

"Mrs. Fairview, you've been very sick. You need to rest."

"Young man, if you don't fetch Maggie Rawls, Sera Johnson, and Abby Ruth Cady right this minute, I will get out of this bed and walk into the waiting room myself. And believe me, I will not be held responsible for the mental anguish you or anyone else suffers from seeing my wrinkled old fanny from the slit in this hospital gown."

"Yes, ma'am." He scooted out of the room so fast that Lil couldn't hold in her chuckle. Nice to know she still wielded some kind of power.

Once Maggie, Sera, and Abby Ruth were all gathered in her room, Lil said, "If Abby Ruth's guns are in the mausoleum and we want to recover them, you'll need to get back there tomorrow morning, because the ATF has figured out Rosemary's drop schedule and they'll be all over that place day after tomorrow."

ALTHOUGH IT WAS hard for Sera to shift gears back to her own problems, which seemed so small now, Maggie had insisted she needed to make things right with Marcus. Sera planned to do that tonight.

After an exhausting day at the hospital, they knew Lil would be okay. But Teague had asked them not to make her recovery common knowledge. To the rest of the world, mum was the word until the ATF could take down that awful woman.

Sera would be lying if she said she hadn't daydreamed about leaving her life with Marcus behind to move back to Summer Shoals, but it had become crystal clear in the moment she'd broken his trust that she couldn't live without him. She could visit the gals here anytime, but if she ended her marriage with Marcus, there'd be no going back.

How could she have ever thought badly of the man who'd stayed by her side after she called to tell him about Lil? He'd had every reason not to show up. Not to come. Not to care.

Please let him forgive me for the biggest mistake ever.

Before all that craziness with Bad Charlie

and Lil's poisoning, she and Maggie had already set up everything for tonight in the garage.

Now, she gave the garage where Lil's daddy's Tucker Torpedo had once been parked one last look. Everything was in place. She and Maggie had pushed an loveseat to the center of the bay. In front of it, an old trunk held an antique silver champagne bucket, two crystal flutes, and an already chilled bottle of Taittinger Comtes de Champagne.

She had more than one mistake to make up for. Since the day she'd met Marcus, she'd never missed a single one of his movie premieres. Not until she was living here in Summer Shoals. And she regretted that now.

This wouldn't be quite the same as premiere night, but she hoped Marcus felt the sincerity of her gesture. She hooked her laptop into the TV they'd moved from Abby Ruth's room and clicked into iTunes. The video immediately began to play, and emotion rose in her chest as the studio logo filled the screen. Forcing herself to stop the film before she became engrossed, she hit pause and backtracked the video.

Oh, no. The pillows weren't evenly spaced on the loveseat. She pounced on them, fluffing and shaping. Once they were perfect, the flutes caught her attention. One was out of line with the other.

She chuckled to her herself because that brought back memories of Lil's trouble with Jessie's gauntlets. Still, Sera adjusted the glasses until she was happy with their position.

Nerves. She knew her fussing was all nerves, but she couldn't seem to help herself. This night was so important.

She slipped out of her clothes and into a sequined blue evening gown that had been hanging in Lil's closet from a past charity event. It was only tea length on Sera, but it hugged her slim frame perfectly.

She swept a hand down the skirt and tried to breathe away her butterflies. *Don't wait. Go get him now.*

She went inside the house, and excitement and anticipation pushed her up the stairs with the hem of the skirt floating behind her.

Marcus walked out of their room just as she stepped on the landing. He looked her over from her up-do to the diamond earrings he'd given her for their tenth anniversary to the dress hugging her curves. "Wow," he said. "What's this for?"

"It's for you. Marcus, I'm so sorry for the

things I've done recently." She approached him, silently worried about his reception, but he opened his arms to her. Relief and pure love streamed through her. "I've been selfish. Made so many mistakes."

Wrapping his arms around her, he rested his chin on top of her head. "I've been selfish too."

She stepped back and looked into his eyes. "I love you. As much as I ever have. I'm sorry for what I've put you through. Can you forgive me?"

A slight smile played on his lips, and he tilted his head. "What do you think?"

"I think you're a smart man who loves me enough to see past my screw-ups."

Chuckling, he smacked a kiss on her lips. "That's my girl."

"Now that we have that settled, it's time for you to come with me." She tugged him down the stairs and out to the garage.

The look on his face when she sat him down, handed him a glass of champagne, and hit Play on his latest movie was nothing less than stunned. A smile spread across his face, and he drew her down to the loveseat and hugged her close. "You can always surprise me."

Her heart full, Sera snuggled close to his side, and they watched Marcus's masterpiece in rapt silence until the last credit rolled and the last chord of the music faded away.

He turned to her, his handsome face filled with contentment. "Thank you, my darling Sera."

She smoothed a hand over his cheek and kissed him. When she finally drew back from the sweet embrace, she asked, "So is that a yes about forgiving me?"

"A forever and always yes."

CHAPTER 24

While Sera was out in the garage seducing her hunky hubby last night, Abby Ruth had barely slept a minute. Anticipation about returning to the mausoleum for her guns—and if she was honest with herself, a little envy at her friend's ability to make up with the man she loved—had kept Abby Ruth flopping from one side of the bed to the other all night.

At eight forty, she waved Maggie out of the house and knocked on the garage door. Apparently, the two love birds had nested in that loveseat last night. Sera came out wearing bedhead and a very canary-ish smile.

"It's time to roll," Abby Ruth said.

"It's a beautiful day." Sera twirled a circle and held her hands up to the sky.

"Yeah, yeah. We know you got luckier than a pair of loaded dice at a craps table, but we've got to go."

They climbed into her dually and headed to Holy Innocence. When they piled out of the truck and she looked up at the building, she thought *holy innocence, my sweet hind-parts.* There was nothing innocent about running guns out of people's resting place.

"I wish Lil could be here with us," Abby Ruth said. "She deserves to help us recover my guns and take down that Myrtle woman."

"We're not taking down Rosemary Myrtle. Teague and the ATF people are. And he's going to be very unhappy when he finds out we came back to the mausoleum." Maggie looked around the parking lot as if expecting police to pop out from behind every car. Which was silly because Lil had told them that the police and ATF stakeout wasn't until tomorrow.

"Which is exactly the reason he'll never know." Abby Ruth waved away her concern.

"Won't he be suspicious when they don't find your guns and they magically appear back in your possession?" Sera asked.

"By that time it won't matter. What could he do, take away my birthday?" The boy wasn't stupid enough to give his future mother-in-law a hard time. Cop or not, he knew when to zip his lip.

Abby Ruth strode toward the front door, pushing the baby stroller they'd picked up at the thrift shop before leaving Summer Shoals. After all, it wasn't as if the three of them could simply walk out of the mausoleum with an armload of guns.

They approached the guard, different from the one Lil had hornswoggled into believing they were ATF. This guy's grandfatherly face broke out in a wide grin. "Hello, ladies." He hopped off his stool and bent toward the stroller. "And who do we have here?"

When he reached for the blanket, Abby Ruth shimmied the stroller out of his reach. "Shh. She's asleep. My poor daughter, she's struggled with a colicky baby. An angel in every way except for those tummy aches. So when we can get her into a peaceful sleep, we don't wake her up. Ever."

"Oh." He drew back. "I hear you. My grandbaby screamed his head off for the first eight months of his life."

Once he waved them on and they were inside, Maggie said, "I don't care how many times we've done this sneak-around stuff, it always gives me indigestion." She muffled a burp behind her fist.

"This one will be an absolute breeze," Abby Ruth assured her, rolling the stroller into the elevator and poking the down button. "An in-and-out job."

Sera slid her a look. "You say that, but you're not the one who'll be worming your way inside those vaults to pull out caskets. My luck and we'll end up opening one with someone's Aunt Alma in it."

"I'd bet my right leg that not one of those crypts in the Myrtle alcove has a single body in it."

"From your lips to God's ears," Maggie muttered.

Once on the lower level, they made straight for the alcove Michael guarded. Abby Ruth looked him up and down. "I used to think you were a pretty good guy, but you've sure let a lot of stuff slip by you on your watch."

Maggie lightly swatted her arm. "Hush up. You don't get a total pass because you've been sick. Have some respect."

Abby Ruth parked the baby buggy and pulled a tarp from the cargo net. Once she and Maggie had that along with a "Maintenance Work" sign hung across the alcove's entrance, they all went to work checking the granite facings. Sure enough, most of those within reach came off easily, and the crypts were missing the spacers normally between the facings and the caskets. "Let's get these puppies out of there."

They worked out a system where Sera and Maggie pulled out one casket, and while they moved on to the next, Abby Ruth cracked that bad boy open and went through it looking for her guns. "Aha! This has the Remington 12-gauge and 9mm Kurz in it."

"Is that all?" Maggie groused. "Why couldn't they all be together?"

"Obviously, this isn't as efficient an operation as it could be."

By the time she'd pawed through half a dozen, with what they'd found last time, it meant only one was still missing. Abby Ruth checked her watch. Still a little time. "Only one more, girls. We can do it."

Maggie rose to her feet and slapped at her knees to dust them off. "That's it. Those are the only vaults with easy access."

Abby Ruth eyed the row just out of reach. "There has to be at least one more."

"You're crazy. We don't have the equipment to get up there. And even if we did, we'd get caught for sure."

"Dammit, that gun is one of my favorites."

"I'm sorry," Sera said to Abby Ruth, "but Maggie is right. I know you love that gun, but we've been here long enough as it is."

Fine, she knew when she'd been outvoted. And she was damn lucky to have her hands back on most of her precious arsenal.

When they were on the main level, pushing the gun baby toward the exit, Sera said, "Is the security guard's uniform a different color?"

Although she'd known he wasn't the same guard who'd busted them under Michael's wingspan, Abby Ruth hadn't given him a thorough looking at. In fact, she hadn't had eyes for any man since Red had dropped back into her life. But what caught her attention now wasn't whether or not his pants were gray, blue, or pink polka dot. It was what he had on his belt. She'd know that original black grip anywhere.

She skidded to a stop. "Damn him, that man has my Jo-Lo-Ar pistol."

Maggie turned toward Abby Ruth and Sera. "And that's *not* the guard we saw earlier."

"Well, hell," Abby Ruth said. "Something's up."

"Think we need to call Teague?"

She absolutely did, but damned if she

wanted to risk the opportunity to retrieve her pistol. "Why don't you two take the stroller and I'll—"

"No!" they both said.

Sera grabbed the stroller with one hand and Abby Ruth's arm with the other, urging them both behind a huge potted palm, where Maggie joined them. "If you think we're going to leave you alone with that security guard, you're sorely mistaken."

"He won't hurt me. It'll only take me a minute to—"

Maggie clenched her fists. "We're less worried about you than we are him. Last thing we need is for Teague and the other cops to show up and find a dead body at the entranceway. Murder was not on our agenda today. Or ever."

Abby Ruth huffed. "I won't kill him. Lord, it's like you don't think I have any finesse whatsoever." By the look on their faces, she'd hit their opinions of her right on. "Fine. Then how do you want to play this?"

"We'll have Sera stay here and keep an eye on the fake guard," Maggie said. "Meanwhile, you and I can take the guns out to the truck and put a call in to Teague."

"Works for me," Sera said cheerfully.

Abby Ruth cast one last covetous look toward the security guard's hip. "If I don't get that gun back, I will expect a pistol-shaped package on my next birthday." Then she and Maggie headed for the door on the opposite side of the building. But when Maggie pushed on it, the thing wouldn't budge.

"Let me try." Abby Ruth put all her weight behind it with the same result. "What's going on?"

"I don't—oh!" Maggie jabbed her finger in the direction of the elevator. "That's exactly how Lil described Rosemary Myrtle." A woman dressed in a royal blue tailored suit and matching hat stepped onto the elevator.

"I'll be damned. Back at the scene of the crime. That woman is something else." Abby Ruth reluctantly admired her enterprising nature, but didn't she have something better to do, like play with her grandkids? Obviously, the woman needed a new hobby.

"She's smart and tenacious, I'll give her that."

"Text Teague," Abby Ruth ordered, then pointed the stroller toward the door to the stairwell.

"What are you doing?"

"We can't let that woman out of our sight.

If we're not careful, she could slip through the police's fingers. And we promised Lil we'd wrap this up."

Maggie hurried behind her, rapidly tapping on her phone. Da-da-beep went the sound of an outgoing text. The next sound was angrier, like a nest of hornets batted around like a piñata. "Abby Ruth, what does WTF mean?"

"It means our boy Teague is less than thrilled that we're here."

They each grabbed one end of the stroller so it wouldn't bump down the stairs and carried it to the bottom landing for Abby Ruth to ease open the door to the basement level. "Coast is clear. Let's stash Gun Baby in the bathroom while we get a handle on what's going on here."

Once they had the stroller safe and sound in a stall, Abby Ruth and Maggie crept down the hallway toward Rosemary Myrtle's family alcove.

"How many more?" A rough male voice echoed down the corridor, causing Abby Ruth and Maggie to dart into another inset of vaults.

"Another dozen at least," a woman said back. "You need to hurry it up."

"She's not very nice, is she?" Maggie whispered to Abby Ruth.

"What was your first clue—the fact that her little entourage took off with my guns or that she poisoned your best friend?"

"If they make off with all those guns before the police get here, how will they prove that woman is a criminal?"

"We have to make sure the cops can track down these bottom feeders. Give me your phone."

Maggie handed it over, and Abby Ruth poked around on it. "There we go."

"What are you doing?"

"We need to make it to the loading dock." Abby Ruth peeked around the corner and waved Maggie out of the alcove. "Go to the right and take the long way around."

They scurried down the hallway and around two more corners. Abby Ruth checked the last hallway and found it clear. "C'mon. Quick." She pulled Maggie into the storage room. With a fast stride, she headed toward the cargo van backed up to the loading dock and tossed Maggie's phone inside.

"Hey, that phone was a present from my son."

"It's also the way the cops are going to find these guns. Besides, it's probably time for an upgrade anyway."

Voices came from the hallway outside. Damn, damn, damn. Next time they were chasing down a bunch of lowlifes, it would be nice for it to happen someplace with more camouflage. Abby Ruth and Maggie ducked behind a trio of standing flower sprays and wreaths.

"Are those real flowers?" Maggie wheezed.

Abby Ruth glanced up to find the daisies and lilies brown and crunchy, which meant they weren't plastic.

Maggie's chest started an erratic rise and fall. "Oh, oh..."

"Don't you dare sneeze." Abby Ruth pinched Maggie's nose between her thumb and forefinger, pressing her nostrils tightly closed.

Like a fish someone had tossed onto the bank, Maggie sucked air in through her mouth.

From near the truck, Rosemary said, "I'll expect my normal percentage on top of what you've already paid for the guns."

"It's gonna be hard to move this many units."

She tapped his face—hard—with the flat of her palm. "I have faith in you."

Rosemary watched the truck pull out of the bay, and Abby Ruth wanted to slap away her smile of smug satisfaction. Someone needed to put that woman in her place. Teague and the others would hopefully see she was tossed in a cell, but the cavalry still hadn't arrived so far as Abby Ruth could tell. No sound of sirens or screeching tires.

The woman strolled back toward the interior hallway like she was the Queen of the Universe. No, ma'am. That wouldn't do at all.

"We have to follow her," she said to Maggie.

They made it into the hallway in time to see Rosemary Myrtle push through the ladies' room door. Perfect. Only one way in and no way out. Abby Ruth smiled to herself. She and Maggie tiptoed into the bathroom and silently backed the stroller out of its stall. Abby Ruth held a finger to her lips and wheeled it over to the other closed stall. Once she had it wedged under the door handle, she jerked her head toward the anteroom as a request for Maggie to follow her.

Abby Ruth whispered, "That stroller won't hold her for long. Help me move some of this furniture in there."

"Are you sure you should be lifting something this heavy?"

"Probably not, but this is an emergency."

They hefted the couch, and the effort did pull at Abby Ruth's still dissolving stitches, but she breathed through the discomfort. Just a few more feet. She nudged the stroller out of the way with a well-placed kick, and they let the couch drop to the tile floor.

"Who's there?" Rosemary called out.

Neither Abby Ruth nor Maggie answered but went back for another load of furniture. When they returned with a chair, the stall's doorknob was twisting back and forth frantically.

"Let me out of here!" Rosemary's voice was full of command, but it was edged with panic, warming Abby Ruth's insides.

She lifted her chin, and Maggie took the hint. Once they had three chairs plopped on top of the couch, they stood outside and listened to Rosemary screech for a minute or two.

"Who are you? I demand you open this stall. Do you know who I am? I could sue you for—"

"Somehow," Abby Ruth drawled, "I don't think you want to be threatening legal action of any type, Ms. Gunrunner."

"Excuse me?" she said, her voice full of offended arrogance. Lord, this woman could

408   Kelsey Browning and Nancy Naigle

give Lil a run for her money in a haughtier-than-thou contest.

"I'm not sure why you're acting all offended when you're the one who's been busy not only stealing, but also poisoning innocent people."

"What in the world...why would you think... You have me mistaken for someone else. Let me out of here and we'll pretend this never happened."

While Abby Ruth taunted Rosemary, Maggie made several more trips back and forth to the anteroom, each time bringing another piece of furniture. Unless Rosemary had the ability to transform into the Incredible Hulk, she wouldn't get out of that stall without police help.

"Just like Lillian Fairview is supposed to pretend you never fed her pokeweed sandwiches and tea?"

"Lillian is de—"

"Dead? Nah, Lillian will be right as rain in a few days. You, on the other hand, will be feeling pretty sick. I hear that happens when they put you behind bars. In fact, you won't have the luxury of a pretty private potty. In prison, they have those stainless steel jobs where everyone can see you poop."

"That's uncivilized."

"Sugar, that's justice."

When Maggie returned with the fake flower arrangement from the other room, she was grinning from one side of her round face to the other. She carefully balanced the vase on top of a side table. Then she and Abby Ruth high-fived, grabbed the gun baby, and headed for the door.

Now all they had to do was get her last gun back.

When they made it back to the entryway where they'd left Sera, they found her sidled up to the fake security guard, chatting with him like she'd known him for years. That girl was an asset. It would be a real blow if she moved back to California.

Sera caught sight of them and slid her eyes to the side. That's when Abby Ruth realized not only had Sera gotten close to the man, but she'd somehow relieved him of her Jo-Lo-Ar.

Abby Ruth pushed the stroller forward and said, "Sera, we've got Momma and Daddy all set with new flowers. Say goodbye to your new friend. We need to get home for the latest episode of *How to Get Away with Murder*."

"Marvin, it was so nice to meet you. Hopefully, I'll see you here again sometime." Sera squeezed his arm and gave the guy a sexy smile that would have his head whirling for weeks. As Abby Ruth pushed the stroller past, Sera dropped the gun into the blanket folds.

The three of them filed out the front door just in time to see police cars swarm all over the parking lot. Abby Ruth veered sharply toward her truck but wasn't able to make a clean getaway.

Teague cut them off and forced them to walk parallel to him for several steps. In a low tone, he said, "I don't know what the hell happened here, but I can promise you we will talk about it later."

Abby Ruth smiled to herself, because she'd expect nothing less.

LATER THAT AFTERNOON, Sera was still a bit frazzled from all the excitement at the mausoleum and the run-in with Teague outside. But oh, the relief at having Abby Ruth's guns back was like having someone take an elephant out of your backpack.

And Marcus's sweet request for another date had re-centered her as well as yoga ever did. She and Marcus drove around Summer Shoals, finally stopping at a little shop called A Charmed Life.

Sera meandered through the store, a warren of rooms holding specialty items that would've been right at home in a big-city boutique catering to high-maintenance women. Along the top of display cases, glittery black wrought iron swooped in a curlicue, giving the store an elegant look. A half-empty wall of cubbies held expensive handbags. It appeared the Hollywood folks had found A Charmed Life.

"This is the cutest shop. You must be Brandi Brittain." Sera extended her hand to the adorable young woman with pixie-cut hair and big green eyes. "I've heard so many nice things about you and your selection of gifts."

Brandi flashed a smile and a curious glance toward Marcus, who was settling in on a lovely settee. "Is that Marcus Johannesson?" she whispered. Sera smiled and the girl mouthed *Oh. My. God.*

Inside the display case, a three-stranded ribbon bracelet caught Sera's eye.

"I can personalize those," Brandi said. "And stamp charms while you wait. Are you buying something for you or maybe your daughter?"

"Hardly." From across the room, Marcus laughed. "More like grannies."

Sera flashed him a watch-it-buster look. "You mean the best friends ever."

"Fine," Marcus laughed. "Hot, sexy, smart, kick-butt grannies."

"I like what I'm hearing," Brandi said. "How many do you need?"

"Five." She couldn't leave Jenny out. She might not be a granny, but boy she was one of them.

Brandi showed Sera the different charms and helped her match them to the colored bracelets for each of her friends. Then she disappeared into the back and returned carrying the beautiful pieces of jewelry.

"They're perfect." Sera turned to Marcus, who was already walking her way to take a look.

"Very pretty." He draped the ribbon around her wrist and latched the lobster claw through the shiny metal ring.

"I think the girls will love them."

"You really love those women," Marcus said, his tone musing. "And Summer Shoals. You're alive here. At first I resented that, but after being here for a while, I understand. There's something grounded and real about this little town."

"Totally different from Los Angeles." She

hurried to add, "Not that LA isn't great too."

"But it isn't your place anymore."

"Marcus, I—"

"After you finish up here, I want to show you something," he said.

Sera paid for the bracelets and thanked Brandi before following Marcus outside. He took her hand and strolled down the sidewalk toward a bench in front of the old cotton gin.

"What are we—"

"Stay here." He dashed back to the car and popped the trunk. When he returned and perched on the other end of the bench, he was holding one of the guitars she'd found. Shame about her earlier suspicions swarmed over Sera. How in the world could she have ever believed he would do something like take Abby Ruth's guns?

Sera's heart sped up—both out of anticipation and dread. Marcus was a horrible musician. And a worse singer.

Then he started to strum, a light, almost Caribbean melody. It was simple but beautiful. Maybe he would just play—

He opened his mouth and sang. And she recognized the tune immediately. "I'm Yours" by Jason Mraz. The lyrics—about freedom, the shortness of time, and love—hit Sera as though they'd been written especially for her. And her husband's voice was true and beautiful as he crooned to her.

By the time he wrapped up the final "I'm yours," Sera's chest was tight and tears spilled down her cheeks. He was hers and she was his.

They always had been. They just needed to find their way back to each other.

"You're not the only one who has made mistakes, Sera. I finally understand what you were talking about when you said you felt like a bracelet," he said. "I guess since you were from California, I thought LA always felt like home to you the way it did for me. But now, seeing you here in Georgia, you're different. Happy."

"It's not—"

"Let me get this out." He turned toward her, brought their joined hands toward his face, and pressed a kiss to her knuckles. "Please."

Something about his affection felt different today. Easy instead of full of tension and expectation. "Okay."

"Hollywood's been my world for as long as I can remember, but that doesn't mean it has to be yours. These days, plenty of married couples live and work in different cities. What if I told you I still plan to make movies but I don't expect you to share that dream? That I want you to build your own dream."

Sera's tummy turned like a carnival ride. "Are you telling me you really do want a divorce?"

"No, I'm saying I think we can make this work. You'll live here in Summer Shoals, and I'll come stay with you—be *your* bracelet—between projects. And I'll be very, very picky about the ones that I take on."

All the heaviness that had been living inside her for the past few years began to lift. "You would do that?"

"That you have to ask kills me, but I understand because it's always been about me, about my work."

She threw her arms around his neck and pulled him close. "You've given me such a gift."

He looked down at her, a sheepish grin on his face. "Now, I know you want to make your own way, but would you be willing to accept one more gift?"

"I don't need anything."

"I found a beautiful old farmhouse and started to buy that for you, but then I realized that would be silly because you love Summer

Haven. But I wanted you to have something of your very own here." He tugged her toward the old cotton gin. "How would you feel about being the new owner of the Gypsy Cotton Gallery?"

"I would feel like the luckiest woman in the world." She went on tiptoes to give him a heartfelt kiss. "I love you, Marcus."

"I love you, Serendipity Johnson."

$\mathcal{W}$ith the small striped bag from A Charmed Life in hand, Sera walked into Lil's hospital room, relieved to see her sitting up in bed. Her color still wasn't good, but it was a huge improvement over when she'd been admitted.

Maggie was perched on the bed next to Lil, and Sera could picture those two gals fifty years ago sharing popcorn and romance novels back at William and Mary. Their friendship ran deep. Abby Ruth stood straight and tall, one boot crossed over the other, flipping through the channels on the television, probably in search of a ball game.

"Sera," Lil's voice didn't sound quite steady yet. "I'm glad you're here."

Jenny walked in behind Sera with a

cardboard box full of drink cups. "Me too. Teague is beside himself over that gun baby outing."

"Great. Probably lecture time the next time we have dinner at your place," Abby Ruth mumbled. "Chicken mull and a lecture is not like dinner and a movie, just sayin'."

Lil sighed. "Yes, well, I put us in jeopardy. I'm so sorry. I thought I could be part of your special team, but all I did was get myself nearly killed. I don't fit in. I promise I won't interfere again."

Maggie patted her arm. "Don't say that. You are one of us. All of us—we're a team."

Sera walked over to the hospital bed and pulled the rolling table closer so that Jenny could put the box of drinks on it. "I was thinking exactly the same thing," Sera said. "In fact, I picked up something special for us today."

She lifted the bag by the silky handles, then emptied the contents on the table.

With all five of them around the table, she pushed the Tiffany blue tissue paper to Lil, the red to Maggie, a turquoise bandana paisley patterned paper to Abby Ruth, white with silver stars toward Jenny, then took the pink and white striped paper for herself. Each bag matched the color of the bracelets inside. "I chose each of these out for a special reason." She gestured for them to pick the gifts up. "Come on. All at the same time." She slipped hers out of the tissue paper and held it up by the delicate ribbon.

An appreciative gasp came from Maggie. "Typewriter keys with our monograms on them."

Abby Ruth turned hers over in her hand. "What's the *G* for?"

Sera laughed. "Okay, stick with me here. You need the context of this story. It seemed perfect in that moment." She told them Marcus' comments about the grannies. The hot, sexy, smart, kick-butt grannies.

"I love it," Abby Ruth said with a grin. "We're cool grannies."

"We will always be there for each other. This bracelet symbolizes our unity," Sera explained. "If we're ever separated, as long as we wear these bracelets we can count on one another to get us through...even the toughest times," she said, glancing to first Lil then Abby Ruth.

Lil lifted her bracelet from the pretty tissue. Her blue eyes glistened as she read the quote punched around the bottom of each monogram, "She believed she could, so she did." She held out her wrist and had Maggie clasp it into place next to her hospital bracelet. Then she helped Maggie with hers while Abby Ruth and Jenny did the same. Finally, Lil motioned for Sera to hand hers over, and she secured it around her wrist with hands that shook slightly. Then she held on and reached for Maggie's hand too, nodding for everyone to do the same until they were joined in a circle. "Girls, in all my days, I have never had more special friends or shared a more special moment."

ALTHOUGH ABBY RUTH wasn't normally much of a jewelry gal, Sera's gift had touched her heart. Yes, she'd been angry and hurt that her friends had hidden their investigation from her, but now she could clearly see they'd only been guilty of protecting her.

In the hospital hallway, she let the light catch her bracelet's metal charms.

"Admiring your wrist?"

Abby Ruth turned to find Jenny standing there, a weary smile on her face.

"You have to admit Sera knows her stuff when it comes to baubles."

Jenny twisted her arm, her own charms making a pleasant chiming ping. "It was sweet of her to include me, especially since I'm not..."

"Not what?"

"Not one of you."

A pain far worse than she'd endured after surgery gouged Abby Ruth, and she slumped back against the hallway wall. She rubbed her hairline, no doubt making her grays stand out like the lights outside that strip club. Then she took Jenny's hand and pulled her closer. "If by 'not one of you,' you mean not of a mature age, then you're right. But Jenny, you will always, always be one of me. In fact, for a long time, you were the only bright thing in my world."

"Besides seeing naked men in locker rooms, you mean?"

"Well, that's a completely different situation." Abby Ruth wrapped an arm around her daughter's waist, and Jenny rested her head against Abby Ruth's shoulder. "I'm sorry if I've ever made you feel left out. That wasn't my intention when I stayed in Georgia."

"It's not Lil or Maggie or Sera that I resent sometimes."

"It's me."

"No, it's—"

"I'm sorry I tried to deal with this cancer diagnosis by myself."

Jenny's body went limp next to hers. "Mom, I—"

"But somewhere in my mind, I thought it would be better all-around if no one was burdened with all this."

"The crazy part of your mind."

She huffed a laugh. "Which is pretty much all of it." Still, she stared at the opposite wall when she said to her daughter, "Even though the outlook was good, I was scared spitless when I found out. And for some reason, I figured the less I talked about it, the fewer people who knew, the less real it was. Because if no one else found out, the cancer wasn't actually real, was it?"

"You're never scared."

"Pu-lease. Sugar, you're a mother yourself. And scared is the friggin' definition of the word *mother*. Tell me you don't have that tiny alarm bell going off inside you every time Grayson walks out the door."

"That's different. He's just a little boy."

"Jenny, no matter how old you get, you will always be my little girl. And I will always want to protect you. It's—"

"—just what mothers do." Jenny lifted her

head. "I'm sorry I pushed you about the treatment. You were right, it's your decision."

Dr. Dempsey's recommendations for the radiation had been right. Her prognosis was excellent, but why tempt fate? She should do it even though it would probably further change the way her breast looked. Hell, it wasn't as if she'd ever been Dolly Parton. What did it matter if her itty-bitty titties were even itty-bittier?

But tiny tits would allow her to continue solving cases with her friends.

"I've made my decision. You don't have to worry about me changing my mind because I will finish every last one of those radiation treatments. Dr. Dempsey says there's no reason I won't be around for a good long time. But maybe you and Teague might want to get going on that baby. I want to be buying cap guns and slingshots before too long."

"You already stock up on those for Grayson."

"Oh, but I have a feeling this next one is gonna be a girl, and she might have a hankering for weapons as flashy as Jessie Wyatt's gauntlets."

"I can't believe you're not still frothing at the mouth about your own guns disappearing."

"When it comes down to it, they're all just hunks of metal. Completely replaceable. But the people in my life? I couldn't replace a one of them, especially Grayson, Teague, or you."

"Mom?"

"Yeah?"

"What about Red Jensen? Do you have any plans for him?"

Jenny's questions set Abby Ruth's heart to jumping at what had to be an unhealthy rate, so she forced a casual note into her voice. She wasn't quite ready to tackle Jenny's curiosity about Red or Red's sudden move to Summer Shoals. "Why do you ask?"

"Because he's handsome and his eyes sparkle when he looks at you. Something about him feels special."

Oh, he was special in so many ways. "Let's just say that a part of my past might become even more important in the future."

FINALLY FEELING like her personal life was back on track, Sera walked into the parlor where Abby Ruth, Maggie and Lil were playing a hand of crazy eights. "I have some news."

Abby Ruth folded her cards into one nice

neat stack in front of her, and Maggie fanned herself with hers. Lil fondled the charm on the bracelet Sera had given her. "What's going on?"

Sera climbed into the fourth chair and sat cross-legged, her whole insides as tight as Tupperware bowl that had already been burped. "I've decided I'm going to LA with Marcus."

The air seemed to evacuate the room.

Lil reached for her hand. "Honey, he's a good man."

"I know. He's been so patient while I tried to deal with my dad's death and my midlife confusion."

"When we lose a parent," Maggie said, "or a spouse like Lil and I have, it can turn your world topsy-turvy. Marcus loves you, and I know you'll be happy together."

Abby Ruth crossed her long lean legs. "I'm going to miss you."

"Thank you, Abby Ruth. You know all of you are like family to me." She sucked in a long slow breath. "Lil, I'd like to keep my van here, if that's okay with you."

"Of course, dear, but don't you want it with you?"

"Actually I do." She broke out into a smile.

"And it will be, because I'm coming back to Summer Shoals to live. If you'll have me."

"What?" Lil leaped to her feet. "But I thought you just said..."

"Marcus and I have finally figured it out. I'll live in Georgia, and when he's between projects, he'll come here. With this creative lifestyle, Marcus and I might end up happier than we've ever been."

"That's perfect," Abby Ruth agreed.

"And if you're open to it, I'd like to live here at Summer Haven," Sera said. "But Lil, I want to pay rent."

"Don't be silly." Lil shook her head adamantly. "I will not take your money."

"But there are so many things that need to be done around here. Marcus thinks it's a good idea too. After all, he'd be staying here when he's in town. We want to ease the financial concerns here at Summer Haven. He's truly smitten with this place, Lil. Don't be surprised if he sends me back with a contract for that movie shoot."

Lil clapped her hands. "I'd love that, but I have some other ideas to ease the financial constraints around here too," she said with a smile.

"Oh Lord, when you get to thinking I

always get a little nervous," Abby Ruth said. "Teague warned me about you. It took me this long to figure out exactly what he meant."

A sly grin spread across Lil's face.

"Look what came today," Lil said, getting up from her seat at the head of the table. She crossed the room to the mahogany breakfront china cabinet. She opened one of the glazed glass pane doors and took out a deep burgundy box the size of a ream of legal paper. She carried it across the room as if she were one of the wise men bearing gifts, then set it down in the center of the table. "New beginnings."

The girls exchanged glances and waited. That eyebrow of Abby Ruth's was dancing around on her forehead the way it did when she got suspicious.

Lil nodded toward Sera. "You gave me the idea with our bracelets. You do the honors."

Sera blinked, and then leaned forward and carefully lifted the top of the box. She peeled the top piece of heavy linen stationery from the stack, then passed a sheet to Maggie and Abby Ruth. A logo bearing a typewriter key of the letter *G* with the word *team* in swirly embossed letters graced the top. Below that, a local PO box. Along one end of the box was a row of business cards printed with the same information.

"I'm not sure I understand," Sera said.

"If we're going to do this investigation stuff, we should do it right," Lil said. "And every respectable organization should have letterhead and business cards." She reached into her pocket and pulled out an iPhone, one of those big models. "And...we have a phone number, too." She waved the phone in a royal blue case with a black typewriter key logo on the back. The letter *G*.

"The G Team, huh?" Abby Ruth said. "*G* for Grannies. Hot, sexy, smart, kick-butt grannies."

"When in the world did you have all this made?" Maggie asked.

Lil ducked her head. "Does it make me sound opportunistic if I say the idea came to me right after Jessie's gauntlets disappeared? It became very clear to me that we'll never lack for cases to investigate."

"Amen, sister," Abby Ruth said. "Except next time, I hope our case doesn't involve any of my possessions."

Maggie, a grin on her face, held up the letterhead. "Lil, you know no one writes letters these days, right?"

Lil sniffed in that Southern belle way she had. "I aim to change that. If we expect to attract repeat clients, it's critical to send thank-you notes."

They each held out a hand, presenting their solidarity bracelets. "Here's to the newly created G Team," Sera said. "Looks like we have all the resources we need the next time we're under the gun."

ABBY RUTH WAS SO DARN RELIEVED to hear Sera wasn't abandoning their little Summer Haven commune that she didn't even put up a fuss when Jenny insisted on driving with her to Atlanta again.

Now she could admit that transferring her care from MD Anderson in Texas was the best decision she could've made. The medical care there was second to none, but the people here in Georgia, especially her friends, made all the difference.

Dr. Dempsey had reconfirmed today that early detection and surgery had left her in a good position. Sure, there'd be the radiation and more checkpoints, but for now things seemed to be going in her favor, and she felt as if she were walking ten feet off the ground as she left his office today.

Jenny kept pace with her. "Dr. Dempsey was totally flirting with you, and if I didn't know better, I'd think you were flirting back."

The surprise in Jenny's voice irked her. What? Did her daughter think she was too old to flirt? "Did you get a good look at him?"

"Yes, I saw him. But he's your doctor."

"He's single. And hot. A Falcons fan, but hey...can't hold that against a man born and raised in Atlanta. And he did have Dallas Cowboy blue eyes. I would catch that man's passes all day long." Except now she was much more interested in Red Jensen's...curve ball.

"Lord, Mom." Jenny's laughter indicated she was doing a mental eye roll. "I think there's some kind of rule against doctor-patient fraternization."

"Don't be a prude. You've got Teague. Maggie has Bruce. Sera has her hot Hollywood hunk Marcus. Why can't I have some fun? And besides, you heard him. I won't be in his care much longer. A little zip zap on the old boobage and I'll be good as new."

"I bet they add that testimonial to their next hospital brochure: 'The finest zip zap boobage treatment in the Southeast. Satisfaction guaranteed!'"

"You can be a real smart aleck, you know that?"

Jenny pulled her in for a hard hug. "I learned from the very best."

A shrieking hello came from down the hall, followed by a woman's voice. "There they are!" Sera, Lil, and Maggie came rushing toward Abby Ruth and Jenny.

What were they doing here?

Sera took Abby Ruth by the hand. "How'd it go?"

"Good news, things look shipshape. We've got a plan, and I'm doing the radiation. But you drove over a hundred miles. How did you know where we were?"

"It was on your calendar," Lil said.

"My calendar is in my room." Abby Ruth's face took on a suspicious cast. "You went in my room? Do I have to remind you what happened the last time y'all barged in on my space?"

"Hold on to your bootstraps," Lil said. "I was dusting the baseboards. I saw the note on the calendar when I was cleaning behind your bedside table."

"You can blame me," Maggie said. "We wanted to be here for you and it was my idea to surprise you."

"And the doctor thought the treatment would be the hardest thing for me to deal with. He's obviously never met y'all!"

"Thank goodness you're done," Sera said, pulling Abby Ruth along as she skipped down the corridor. "We only have four minutes to get over to the atrium. We have another surprise for you."

"I hope it's lunch." Abby Ruth let the group herd her down a long hallway where a group of people were congregating at the end.

"While we were waiting on you, I looked up the calendar of events. This place is loaded with amenities. It's like the Red Door Spa, except that insurance will pay for it. Well, and it's probably missing the cute massage therapists and monogrammed robes."

"What is this?" Abby Ruth asked. The space had to be a good fifty feet long and nearly as wide with a platform in the middle. "A picnic?"

Sera rose on her toes and spun, sending her ankle-length skirt into a parachute of filmy material around her toned legs. "Laughter therapy! Isn't it great?"

A rush of relief cruised through Abby Ruth. "I love comedy."

But then Dr. Dempsey and two other doctors leaped to the stage. When they leaned back, hands on their stomachs, and began to laugh, Abby Ruth's relaxed state returned to high alert.

From across the room, a cute blonde girl with a microphone headset announced, "Welcome first-timers! And helloooooo, Laughter Masters. Let's get this therapy going." She blew a kazoo, and people burst into hideous artificial laughter.

Fake as Hollis Dooley's teeth.

Shuffling back a step, Abby Ruth said, "What in blazes—"

The rambunctious blonde sang out, "Place your hands on your cheeks. Open your mouth wide. Now laugh until you feel the vibration in your fingers. Oh, yeah. HA. HAHA. HAHAHAHA. HA. HA. HAHA."

"Was that to the tune of 'Itsy Bitsy Spider'? Oh, hell no." Abby Ruth turned to make a speedy exit.

But Sera swept an arm out and caught her by the denim jacket. "Come on. Give it a try. Please?"

Maggie was getting right into it, leaning back and belly laughing. Lil was so tickled by Maggie that tears were streaming down her cheeks. Her face as pink as a piglet, Maggie seemed to be taking joy in Lil's uncontrollable response, and that got Jenny going too.

"Please?" Sera pleaded. "He, he, he with me, Abby Ruth. Just once."

Abby Ruth rolled her eyes and was about to walk away when Dr. Dempsey jumped down off the stage and jogged toward her. "Ms. Cady, glad to see you stayed for this."

Dr. McHottie took her hands and placed them on his flat stomach. Abby Ruth couldn't help herself and let her fingers do a little walking. She'd been wrong about his abs being flat, because under her nimble fingers she could feel the ridges of his—one, two, three, four, five, six, whew!—eight-pack.

Which meant she was very much in his personal space, and her fingers tingled with each puff of his laughter. She couldn't help but chuckle, and at that moment, she dropped all her defenses and let him spin her in a circle as they both laughed.

Five minutes later, a bell rang and the room fell into a soft titter of giggles and conversation.

"Great first time. Wish you'd come sooner. This will make those treatments go so much smoother. Sounds crazy, but I'm telling you if you come to the laughter therapy session, it'll help. Maybe we'll bump into each other outside my office. Have a cup of coffee." Dr. Dempsey patted her shoulder and walked away, pulling a stethoscope out of his coat pocket and placing it around his neck. Too bad his white coat was keeping her from seeing if his tush was as tight as his middle.

"Now, that wasn't so bad, was it?" Sera asked.

"There's definitely something to be said for what just happened here." And they could laugh all they wanted, but a man like Dr. Dempsey could heal anything that ailed her.

"You're the only woman...I know..." Maggie gulped in air, but her words were still breathy. "...who would pick up a guy in a hospital?"

"That's not a guy. He's my doctor." But although Dr. Dempsey was a handsome and charming devil, and she'd let Jenny believe she was interested, the man from her past was still first place in her thoughts these days.

"Seriously? You're the luckiest woman here!"

"I'm probably also the only woman in this room lucky enough to have friends who care so much that they would drive over a hundred miles to subject themselves to jester therapy." She spread her arms and pulled her friends into a group hug, something Abby Ruth Cady never thought she'd do.

But then, life had a way of changing you when you least expected it.

CHAPTER 26

Three weeks later, a woman wearing a bright pink suit walked down the hall of the mausoleum to the Myrtle alcove, took a seat on the marble bench next to the statue of Michael and crossed her legs, her hands in her lap.

She glanced down the long corridor. A man in a baseball cap and khakis stood near a niche at the far end. In the other direction, two men tinkered with the front of a crypt as if resealing the contents into place. It looked just like any other day at the mausoleum.

Lillian pushed the chestnut-colored wig back from her cheek and placed a finger to her ear.

"Everyone is in place. Relax, Miss Lillian. You're an old pro at this by now."

Pride swelled in her chest. Once Bad Charlie had spilled all the details about the gunrunning to save his own hide, Lil had stepped in to play the role of Rosemary Myrtle to help bring down the whole operation. Come to find out, Rosemary's deceased husband had left her in a bit of a financial pickle, having cancelled his life insurance without his wife's knowledge. So to keep up her big Victorian and all that staff after his death, Rosemary had committed some dark deeds.

Although Lil understood how keeping up family appearances could get out of hand and spur questionable behavior, what Rosemary had done was different. Both in scope and impact.

Guns in the wrong hands...not a victimless crime.

Add to that the fact that Rosemary had not only taken Lil as a fool, but also nearly taken her life? Lil would never be tricked like that again.

Fortunately, the queen pin was already behind bars, but now Lil was helping dust up the rest of the vermin.

A familiar voice echoed through her earpiece. "No reason this won't go down exactly as it has the past few weeks."

She moistened her lips and crossed her right leg over left, the signal that she could hear them.

Each week, it had been the same drill. She played the part of Rosemary and accepted the gun shipments, luring all the baddies right into the ATF's crosshairs. And each week, they'd successfully taken down one more tentacle of the gun ring.

Today she was waiting for a pickup from the bad guys who were distributing guns up the East Coast. All the incoming gun handlers, mostly operating out of Florida, had been arrested.

Only one crypt of weapons remained.

One last gunrunning team to take down.

What they had no way of knowing was the guns in this crypt had no firing pins. Completely harmless, unlike the ones Rosemary had been moving.

The undercover agent who was dressed like the security guard left his post for the scheduled daily break. Cars in the parking lot were cleared except for Rosemary's. The facility maintenance pickup truck and van were parked as usual at the loading dock's far end near the emergency exit.

The man at the end of the hall turned his

baseball cap around, the sign the pickup was about to go down.

Lil hands dampened but not because she was afraid for her life. Although she couldn't see the ATF agents, she knew plenty of law enforcement professionals were around. Even one in the ceiling, just in case. And they were trained in tactics she probably didn't want to know too much about.

Like clockwork, a double-honk came from the loading dock. Then, the triple-beep of the back door alarm, signaling someone had entered the code and was now in the building. Heavy footsteps headed her way, through the loading dock and into the hallway.

Lil dipped her head slightly to conceal her face under the thin layer of netting on her hat. But with her size and the reddish wig she wore, none of these criminals should be suspicious.

Rosemary herself had admitted this was a well-oiled operation that had been in place for years. With consistency and familiarity, people became less careful.

Three of them this time. Last week there'd been four. Three men and a young blonde woman who didn't serve any purpose except an ego boost.

A stubby bald man not much taller than herself led the way, flanked by two strapping young men. One with dark hair, the other as bald as the man in the lead but twice his height.

She rose to her feet, pivoted and pushed on the front of the crypt at the lower left. The granite wiggled, making a scraping noise. Stubby nodded in her direction and then motioned the two younger men toward the crypt. They pulled the remaining rosette clip and removed the front with ease, setting it aside. The older bald man leaned inside and grasped the coffin's handle. Then both men heaved the wooden coffin out and set it to the floor. When they lifted the lid, twenty automatic weapons lay nestled in a layer of bubble wrap.

The guy moved the guns, counting them off out loud. "All here," said the dark-haired boy.

Stubby pulled an envelope from his coat pocket and slid it into the narrow opening below the pedestal where Michael stood watch.

Lil shook the gun seller's hand then turned and stepped out of the way behind a pillar.

No sooner did that envelope settle to the bottom of the hollow form than ten men swarmed the small team of three to take them into custody.

She stood with her back to what was happening, out of harm's way, as she'd been taught, until she heard in her earpiece, "You're done for the day, Miss Lillian."

She smiled, knowing that although she couldn't see the man whose voice echoed in her ear, he had full eyes on her.

"Another fine job. That's the last of them."

She wiggled her fingers in a wave. And with that, the entire Myrtle gunrunning pipeline had been dissolved. And now Lil could admit, if only to herself, that Rosemary had spearheaded a brilliant but reprehensible operation. The woman had kept the incoming and outgoing shipments completely separate. No one seemed to know any other part of the ring because the groups dropping off and picking up the weapons came to the mausoleum on alternating weeks.

And Lil had help stopping every last transaction. She took comfort in the knowledge that she'd made a difference, had kept lives safer here in the Southeast. No wonder the girls were so eager to continue investigating crimes. Justice was a powerful drug.

And with her experience on the inside, Lil

had a new appreciation for how smart and organized crime was. A gal had to be twice as sharp as the baddies to take them down.

She'd heard the contents of the Myrtle estate would go on the auction block later this month. Perhaps she'd pick up that china, because the teacup she'd coveted would be an excellent reality check if she ever again got too darned big for her britches.

THE END

of this adventure...
Abby Ruth

BOOKS IN THE SERIES

Book 1 - IN FOR A PENNY
Book 2 - FIT TO BE TIED
Book 3 - IN HIGH COTTON
Book 4 - UNDER THE GUN
Jenny & Teague Novella 1 - ALWAYS ON MY MIND
Jenny & Teague Novella 2 - COME A LITTLE
CLOSER

Wonder which granny you're the most like?
Take the free WHO'S YOUR GRANNY? Quiz at
www.TheGrannySeries.com
then let us know by giving us a quick
shout on Facebook or via email!

You can sign up for occasional updates about
special sales, tour dates and the next books in
The Granny Series
by signing up for the newsletter.

ABOUT THE AUTHORS

Kelsey Browning writes humorous Southern women's fiction with a sprinkling of mystery and sexy contemporary romance. Her single title romances garner reviews that call her writing funny, sassy, and full of sizzling chemistry. Originally from a Texas town smaller than the ones she writes about, Kelsey has also lived in the Middle East and Los Angeles, proving she's either adventurous or downright nuts. These days, she makes her home in northeast Georgia with her tech-savvy husband, her smart-talking son, a rescue dog from Qatar, and her (fingers crossed) future therapy pup. Find Kelsey online at KelseyBrowning.com.

USA Today bestselling author **Nancy Naigle** whips up small-town love stories with a dash of suspense and a whole lot of heart. She began her popular contemporary romance series, Adams Grove, while juggling a successful career in finance and life on a seventy-six-acre farm. She has gone on to produce collaborated works with other authors, including the Granny Series and the stand-alone novel Inkblot. Now happily retired, she devotes her time to writing, antiquing, and the occasional spa day with friends. A native of Virginia Beach, she currently calls North Carolina home. Join Nancy on Facebook and sign up for her newsletter at www.NancyNaigle.com.

ALSO BY KELSEY BROWNING

Never miss a new release! Just pop over to my website at www.KelseyBrowning.com to receive updates on new books and exclusive giveaways!

PROPHECY OF LOVE series
Sexy contemporary romance
A Love to Last
A Passion to Pursue

TEXAS NIGHTS SERIES
Sexy contemporary romance
Personal Assets
Running the Red Light
Problems in Paradise
Designed for Love

BY INVITATION Only series
Sexy contemporary romance
Amazed by You

STEELE RIDGE SERIES (coming October 2016)
Contemporary romantic suspense co-authored with Adrienne Giordano & Tracey Devlyn
Going Hard
Living Fast
Loving Deep

ALSO BY NANCY NAIGLE

N ever miss a new release! Just pop over to www.NancyNaigle.com and sign up for my newsletter to receive updates on new books and exclusive giveaways!

THE ADAMS GROVE SERIES
Book 1:: Sweet Tea and Secrets
Book 2:: Wedding Cake and Big Mistakes
Book 3:: Out of Focus
Book 4:: Pecan Pie and Deadly Lies
Book 5:: Mint Juleps and Justice
Book 6:: Barbecue and Bad News

BOOT CREEK SERIES
Book 1:: Life After Perfect
Book 2:: Every Yesterday (2016)

SINGLE TITLES
Sand Dollar Cove
Christmas Joy

inkBLOT – co-written with Phyllis Johnson

ACKNOWLEDGMENTS

Once again, we want to thank the amazing folks who help us bring the newly renamed G-Team books to you.

Big hugs and major high fives to our incredible editing team: Deb Nemeth, who always pushes us to give our readers the best possible book we can. And to Tom Justice, thanks for batting cleanup, because Nan's never met a comma she doesn't love. ;-)

They say a picture is worth a thousand words so we owe lots to our artistic team: Michelle Preast, who originally brought our vision of the grannies to life. These gals have served us well and become the real face of this series. And a big thank you to Keith Sarna, who continues to make these book covers a knockout!

As always, our bang-up technical advisors often save the day: Adam Firestone, we think of you fondly every time Abby Ruth fondles one of her antique Spanish firearms. Your knowledge was especially useful in this book! And a frosty Manteo-rita to Retired Cpt. Charlie Winslow for his quick response to all of our crazy questions, ones that would worry a lesser man.

To the Dangerous Darlings and Kelsey's Sass Kicker fan group: thank you for celebrating and supporting every book release. Big hugs from us and all the grannies.

And to those who help us daily behind the scenes: Miss Bettie, Tech Guy, and Smarty Boy - we couldn't give our fans the books they love without *your* love, often in the form of things like dog sitting stints, pans of King Ranch chicken, and fun trivia that turns into plot points!

AND TO ALL OF YOU READING THIS ~ THANK YOU!

Peace   *Love*   *Grannies*